The Surrender Gate

Also From Christopher Rice

Thrillers
A DENSITY OF SOULS
THE SNOW GARDEN
LIGHT BEFORE DAY
BLIND FALL
THE MOONLIT EARTH

Supernatural Thrillers
THE HEAVENS RISE
THE VINES

Paranormal Romance
THE FLAME: A Desire Exchange Novella
THE SURRENDER GATE: A Desire Exchange Novel

The Surrender Gate

A Desire Exchange Novel

By Christopher Rice

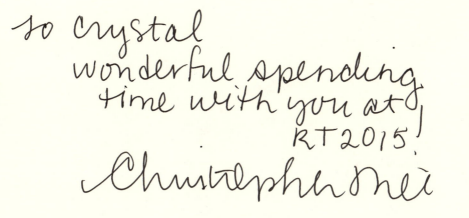

To Crystal
wonderful spending
time with you at
RT 2015!
Christopher Rice

EVIL EYE
CONCEPTS

The Surrender Gate
A Desire Exchange Novel
By Christopher Rice

Copyright 2015 Christopher Rice
ISBN: 978-1-940887-62-3

Published by Evil Eye Concepts, Incorporated

Acknowledgments From The Author

As with every book, there are too many thanks for one page, but I'll try.

M.J. Rose and Liz Berry, thank you for making Evil Eye Concepts such a great place to do business.

Jillian Stein, thank you for giving us such a great social media presence.

To the authors included in 1,001 DARK NIGHTS in both 2014 and 2015, thank you for working so hard to celebrate your colleagues.

And a mountain of thanks to Lexi Blake, whose gentle and generous guidance had made my transition into erotic romance a truly joyous experience. (And it would be remiss of me if I didn't give a shout out to the lovely ladies and gents of the Naughty Book Club on Facebook, who answer my queries about erotic romance in great and wonderful detail.)

Thanks to Kimberly Guidroz and Pam Jamison for their fine editorial eyes.

As always, I need to thank the people who make the day to day operations of my writing life possible. Everyone who works to make THE DINNER PARTY SHOW WITH CHRISTOPHER RICE & ERIC SHAW QUINN a reality each Sunday evening at 8 PM ET/ 5 PM PT at TheDinnerPartyShow.com, a list topped off by my best friend and co-host Eric Shaw Quinn.

And last, but certainly not least, a big thank you to those bloggers and romance readers who responded to THE FLAME with great enthusiasm. Thank you for taking a chance on a new novella from an author with no previous track record in erotic romance and for sharing your lovely responses with me and others. I hope this novel continues the universe of The Desire Exchange in a way that satisfies your every craving.

Sign up for the 1001 Dark Nights Newsletter
and be entered to win a Tiffany Lock necklace.

There's a contest every quarter!

Go to www.1001DarkNights.com to subscribe.

As a bonus, all subscribers will receive a free
1001 Dark Nights story
The First Night
by Lexi Blake & M.J. Rose

1

When the rain starts to fall, Emily Blaine is peering through one of the skylights in the pool house's roof, watching her best friend undress in front of a man old enough to be his father. She could care less about the weather's insensitive timing. She's too grateful to have made it this far inside the grounds of this palatial mansion without being detected.

Her journey here seems like a blur. First she hopped the wrought iron fence in front. Then she darted along corridors of shadow, snaking through the forest of banana trees and elephant ear plants that fill the Greek revival mansion's massive side yard. Then, after she watched Jonathan and his older companion disappear inside the pool house, she mounted the back staircase and hoisted herself onto the skylight-filled roof, all without setting off an alarm or finding herself in a security guard's furious embrace.

She has already watched Jonathan and the man he's come to visit share a half-hug, a brief peck on the cheek, and then a few minutes of conversation that appeared stilted, mindless. Perfunctory. If the older gentleman had focused his attention on anything other than Jonathan's tall, muscular body, their exchange could have been mistaken for an informal business meeting. But he didn't, not for a second. It was all just a prelude to this slow disrobing.

Because it is the end of summer in New Orleans, the drops that make it through the thick canopy of oak branches overhead are warm against her back. For now her view is perfect, but soon the skylights will start to fog, she's sure of it. Will the condensation be outside or inside? Or both? She has no idea. Either way, the drumbeat of raindrops on the sea of glass before her is loud enough that if she has to resort to wiping the panes with one bare hand, the patter will cover up any inadvertent squeak.

The pool is the size of most people's homes. In its soft, wavering light, Jonathan Claiborne's sculpted, hairless torso appears in between the folds of the baby-blue dress shirt he is unbuttoning with slow, cloying precision, the same shirt he wore to dinner with her only hours before, a dinner defined mostly by empty chitchat.

He'd spoke of the indecisive weather. She'd choked back suspicions he'd been working as a high-priced escort for months, while mentally listing the basic surveillance techniques she planned to use on him as soon as they'd paid the check and said their deceptively cheerful good-byes. She didn't have to follow him very far; just a short hop down St. Charles Avenue past Audubon Park, then a left into the blocks of gorgeous mansions that fill the bend in the Mississippi River.

Now, the smile Jonathan gives his older companion looks genuine. But smiles are Jonathan's strong suit and he deploys them all the time to great effect, along with charming comebacks, tenderness, and gentle affection, sometimes even with strangers and passersby.

At six-foot-three, he towers over most people, but he has the angelic facial features of a young boy. His Cuban mother gave him skin the color of sandalwood, but his Irish father studded it with sparkling blue eyes. Emily's oldest and dearest friend, the man who made high school endurable and adulthood enjoyable, is a study in delicious, physical contrasts, and over the years, she has watched many men (and a few misguided women) fall under his spell. But she's willing to bet this particular spell comes at a price and the man sitting in the cushioned, rattan chair has paid for it well.

Jonathan unbuttons his jeans and steps out of them, one leg after the other, hairless quads flexing, rock-hard ass filling his white briefs. But he's locked eyes with his companion, and he's chewing gently on his lower lip, as if this were the first time he's undressed himself in front of another man and it's giving him a naughty thrill.

You shouldn't be doing this, she tells herself. *This isn't about Arthur Benoit or his dying wish. This is about you. Your ego. After all you've confided in him over the years, Jonathan kept this a secret from you, and you're angry and you're hurt and—*

The hinges of the skylight she's resting both hands on let out a loud, brief squeak. For a second, she thinks it's her skin dragging against the glass. Her dark thoughts must have distracted her, causing her to lose her balance. But then, in a single, terrifying instant, every skylight in the roofline tilts at a forty-five degree angle. Suddenly, Emily is hurtling face-first through open air, the glittering blue rectangle below rushing up toward her with terrifying speed. She contorts herself at the last possible second and hits the water legs first.

When she surfaces, Jonathan gazes at her, gape-mouthed, wide-eyed. The expression makes him look both childish and foolish given that he's only wearing underwear. But the man sitting a few feet away shakes with laughter. In his right hand, there's a small remote that must have allowed him to open the skylights with the press of a button. He hits the button again and she hears the riot of squeaks as they rotate shut overhead.

There are two entrances to the pool house. A security guard the size of a linebacker appears through each one, right hands at their belts, hovering between holstered handguns and Tasers.

"*Emily!*" Jonathan hisses.

"So you know this girl?" the man asks.

Winded and treading water, Emily wonders what type of facial expression would make her look appropriately humble and self-effacing given that her lungs are on fire. Then she recognizes the man responsible for her fall.

His mane of black hair is gone, replaced by a polished, blemish-free cue ball. George Dugas is his name, and he built most of the condo complexes in the Warehouse District. Back when Emily and Jonathan were kids, the man was some kind of politician, a state senator or a congressional representative, she can't remember which. What she *can* remember are scores of articles detailing how he narrowly avoided a major corruption trial, and the rumors he'd done so by intimidating witnesses. Now her humiliation is edged with real fear.

"Sir?" one of the guards asks. He's a few inches from the edge of the pool, staring at Emily as if she were a trapped rat.

"One moment, Frank," Dugas says. "Girlfriend of yours, Michael?" In the shock of the moment, Jonathan seems to have forgotten what is apparently his alias. Further proof Dugas is a client, not just some secret lover. Not some random hookup.

"Sister?" Dugas adds, when it's clear no one's going to answer him.

"I should go," Emily says, feeling as dumb as she sounds.

"But you just landed," Dugas says.

One of the guards says, "Would you like us to question her, Mr. Dugas? We'd be happy to take her to the staff house so she's...out of your way here." *So you two can get back to whatever it is you were doing,* the guard wants to say.

"No. Thank you, Claude. But stay right there until I find out what publication this young lady writes for."

"She's not a reporter," Jonathan says as if he's been stung. His tone makes it clear a reporter is the worst possible thing Emily could be at this moment.

"Then what is she? Your wife?"

She's never seen such pain in Jonathan's eyes. Maybe once back in high school, after their friend Remy took his own life and they spent their nights drinking away grief with stolen bottles of Southern Comfort. But not since then. And she can't tell if he's embarrassed or frightened. One thing's for sure; she can't force him to lie for her, not after the way she's handled this. Sneaking around, breaking and entering. Falling out of ceilings.

"We discussed confidentiality, Michael," Dugas says. "I thought I was clear."

She raises her hands, walks slowly toward the shallow end of the pool. The water is bathtub warm but she is shivering. "He didn't tell me anything. I followed him here. I'm a friend of his. That's all."

"Why follow him *here*, young lady?"

"It wasn't... It wasn't personal. I just...I met him for dinner. I was going to follow him wherever he went."

"Because...?"

Because of the gifts, and the new BMW he shouldn't have been able to afford. Because he dropped back on his hours at the restaurant. And because of all those fancy health food supplements that started arriving in the mail, the ones that made his body even harder and more sculpted. But before Emily can wrap these facts in a polite lie, Jonathan breaks the silence.

"She's my friend, sir."

"*This?*"—Dugas makes a vague gesture to indicate Emily's plummet into the pool—"is not the behavior of a *friend*. This is the behavior of a girlfriend, a jealous wife."

"No, M—" Jonathan stops himself from mentioning the man's

real name. "She thought I was in trouble, that's all. It's my fault for not giving her a better—"

—idea that I was working as a prostitute. Escort. Companion. There might be real consequences for finishing this sentence in front of the guards, so Jonathan goes silent and Dugas laughs, a throaty, half-hearted sound that has more anger than amusement in it. "Trust me, darlin'. *Michael* can take very good care of himself. That's for sure. Your little aerialist routine on the other hand? That could use some work."

"I'm sorry for all this trouble, sir. I really am," Jonathan says. "Maybe if we could just reschedule then—"

"Oh, I don't think so," Dugas says, looking from Emily to Jonathan and back again. "That wouldn't be convenient for anyone now, would it? After all, this young woman…I'm sorry, what is your name, ma'am?"

When Emily and Jonathan both answer at exactly the same time, their eyes meet and they almost break out laughing before the gravity of their current predicament silences them once again. But still, the flash of warmth in Jonathan's sparkling eyes is a sudden comfort.

"Adorable. Well, considering Emily has worked quite hard to be here tonight, it would be unbearably rude of me to just send her away now, wouldn't it?"

Dugas rises out of his chair. His V-neck T-shirt hugs a trim frame, revealing a light patch of chest hair. His linen pants are lose and baggy. She tries to focus on his manicured feet in dark leather sandals instead of the prominent evidence that he is a well-endowed man who isn't wearing any underwear.

"Do you recognize me, young lady?"

Everything inside of her wants to say no. *No, I don't recognize you, Mr. Dugas, and I have absolutely no idea you're high profile and well known and would make an awesome blackmail victim.* But she's confident lying to him will have a worse result, and so she looks into his piercing eyes and nods.

"You do. *Good!* Then it should mean something to you when I say I didn't get where I am in life by misjudging people's motivations. Their *real* motivations. The ones they don't often admit to. What I'm trying to say, Emily, is that I only let you get this far for one reason. I'm just *dying* to know why you're *really* here."

Emily fights the urge to curse. Of course they *let* her get this far! A house this big, an owner this wealthy; she should have known she was being watched even if they hadn't let on.

"I told you," Jonathan says. "She was worried about me. That's all. Now may we go? *Please?*"

"Enough, *Michael*."

Jonathan's entire body goes tense, from the hard ridges of his obliques to his sculpted arms, which are both bent now as his hands slowly form matching fists. He is not braced for an impact; he's preparing a defensive strike on her behalf.

The guards bring their right hands to their holstered guns. Slowly, silently, but in almost perfect unison.

Even though he is outgunned and outmanned, and even though he is practically stark naked, Jonathan takes a single, threatening step toward his angry client. The older man's eyes light up at the promise of a confrontation weighted in his favor.

The guards take another step.

"*Stop!*" Emily cries, and miraculously, everything does. She can't have Jonathan getting hurt on her behalf, not after the way she's handled this. There were other ways she could have tried to get the truth out of him, more honest, more direct ways.

But Dugas is right. Her reasons for being here are...*complicated*.

"You're right. There's another reason I'm here. It's kind of a long story, but I'll tell it to you..."

"*If?*"

"If you send the guards away. And if you let Jonathan leave."

"I'm not going anywhere," Jonathan says. He's staring right at her and there's a trace of astonishment in his words, as if Emily is crazy to have suggested something as dangerous as being left alone with George Dugas.

"One out of two ain't bad," Dugas says. He dismisses the guards with a fluttering gesture, but the way he meets each of their looks in turn tells Emily they'll remain just outside the doors. "Come now, Little Miss Emily. Let's get you out of those wet clothes."

2

When Dugas allows Jonathan to step into the small changing room with her, Emily realizes there must be no easy escape, no unguarded back door for them to slip through. Despite his sudden good cheer, George Dugas is a captor, not a host, and she will do well to remember this, she's sure.

As Jonathan struggles to pry her rain slicker apart from her soaked blouse, they begin speaking in fierce whispers.

"I'm sorry," she offers.

"You could have just asked me."

"Would you have told me the truth?"

"Please! Like you would have stopped asking until I had. You're always persistent once you start on something, Em. It's getting you to start that's the problem."

"Really? *Now?* You're going to do a psych eval of me right now?"

"Just speaking my mind. That's all. I never said I was a psychologist."

"No. You're just a hooker."

Jonathan reaches behind her with both arms. It takes her a second to realize he's unclasping her bra. Her exposed nipples graze his bare chest, sending unexpected shivers of pleasure through her entire, freshly undressed body, then he draws the terrycloth robe up over her shoulders and fluffs its collar, their mouths inches apart suddenly. "The polite term is *escort*," he whispers.

"Oh, yeah? Why? *Courtesan* has too many syllables?"

They've been half-naked in front of each other before, but not in such close quarters, and not in this context, with Jonathan's statuesque body glistening and primed to deliver sexual gratification. Emily blames the evening's mélange of fear and shock for her sudden arousal—that, and the unexpected touch of his hard flesh against her breasts.

"So what were you going to do?" Jonathan asks. "Take pictures of us? Blackmail me into telling you the truth?"

"I would never *blackmail* you. Come on!"

"*Everything alright in there?*" The short concrete-floored corridor between the pool area and the changing rooms amplifies Dugas's voice, making them both jump.

"Yes!" Jonathan calls back. "We'll be out in a second."

"We could just run for it, right?" Emily whispers. "He's not really going to shoot us, is he?"

As she steps out of her wet panties, Jonathan's lips are pursed and he won't look her in the eye, the same expression he always uses to avoid answering a direct question. *Sure*, she thinks. *I should have just come right out and asked you. You would have told me everything.*

"Jonathan…"

"Yes."

"How dangerous *is* this guy?"

There's fear in his eyes, and whatever he sees in her expression, it makes him brush several strands of soaked hair away from her forehead.

"Let's not find out, okay?" he says, and before she can answer he's guiding her out of the changing room by one hand.

"Comfy?" Dugas asks.

They are all sitting in chairs that match the one Dugas has taken to like a king on his throne; large, rattan frames, plush cushions covered in painterly illustrations of jungle foliage. In a city that shimmers with heat for most of the year, Emily is curious to know why Dugas would want an indoor pool. Maybe his assignations with Jonathan are the least of what he gets up to within these walls, walls so white they almost mask the various wood detailing; crown moldings overhead, carved Doric columns running the pool's length.

Emily has seen photographs of turn-of-the-century gymnasiums that look similar to her current surroundings. But the glittering tile mosaic above the deep end screams, *I'm rich, just in case the mansion didn't clue you in!* His trident glistening in a powerful fist studded with jeweled rings, the great god Poseidon rises from frothing, turquoise waves. It takes her a minute to realize Poseidon's face has been modeled after Dugas. *Lord*, she almost whispers.

"Can I get you something to drink?" their host asks politely.

"No, thank you," Emily and Jonathan answer at the same time.

"What a pair you two make," he says, grinning. "How long have you been friends?"

"Since...forever," Jonathan answers.

Emily tries not to laugh. He looks comical now, sitting poised and upright in only his tight white briefs—*My God, I knew he was big down there. But that bulge is*—She silences her thoughts by clasping her palms between her knees and driving her knees together hard enough to send a little painful shiver up both arms.

"High school? Grade school?"

"Well, we attended—"

"Actually, Jonathan, I'd prefer it if Emily answered the questions from here on out." Jonathan starts to apologize before he realizes the man has used his real name for the first time. "Come now," Dugas continues when he sees their expressions. "A man with my resources? You didn't think I'd do my homework? *You* wanted me as a regular client. *I* needed to make sure you could be trusted."

"How much homework did you do?" Emily asks.

"Why do you ask?" Dugas says.

"Because maybe you already know who I am too."

Dugas smiles. In their brief absence, one of the guards—or possibly some servant she hasn't seen yet—brought him a mint julep in a tall, round glass. After a careful sip, he says, "And if I do, and I'm asking you anyway, what does that imply?"

"You're trying to find out if I'm a liar."

"Clever girl. *Very* clever girl you have here, Jonathan."

"She's *not* my girlf—"

Dugas silences him with a raised finger. "To answer *your* question, *Miss Blaine*—" He allows just the briefest pause to let his knowledge of her full name ripple through the vast room. "—I had Jonathan followed for several weeks after our first meeting. It was the only way to ensure he wasn't in the employ of one of my rivals."

"I see," Emily whispers.

"So yes, I know full well that your name is Emily Blaine and that you both work for a charming little restaurant in the Quarter called Perry's. You manage the front of the house, whereas Jonathan is the most sought after…*waiter*. I also know that when you prefer a nice meal for yourselves, you eat at Tableau on Jackson Square. Of course, every now and then Jonathan drags you Uptown for a meal at Gulfstream. But it takes some convincing. You just can't see the point in eating seafood from a chain restaurant when you've both spent your entire lives living in what is arguably one of the great seafood capitals of the world." To Jonathan, Dugas says, "I happen to agree with her on this point, by the way."

"Followed us?" Emily says. "It sounds like you had us bugged."

"My men can linger rather closely, but I do not *bug* anyone. I'm not the NSA. Now rest assured, Miss Blaine, I had no ill intentions with the information I gathered. I was simply protecting myself."

"From what?" Emily asks.

"From those who would judge a man of my stature for enjoying the sight of youth and beauty in action."

As these words leave the older man's lips, his eyes return to Jonathan's bare torso. Emily is suddenly aflame with a curiosity that feels like arousal. She wants to believe it's some protective instinct, this sudden hunger to know every detail of what Jonathan and this man have done together. Would the information prove useful? Would it help her to negotiate some escape for them both?

Does George Dugas like to watch and nothing more? Is the same true for all of Jonathan's clients?

She shifts in her seat, her robe brushing against her nipples. Her best friend freed her breasts as if it were a task as ordinary as closing a window on a cold night. In response, she'd peeled off her soaked underwear, but that had been more of a reflex. But why did Jonathan want her naked under the terrycloth?

What had Dugas just said? *I like to watch youth and beauty in action…*

He is not an unattractive man, their captor. It would take a pool house ten times larger to contain his ego, that's for sure. But his patient, focused gaze has scanned her chest too many times since she sat down for her to believe he's exclusively homosexual. Still, he's made no leering, lecherous comments about what her robe barely conceals. Her breasts are large, but so are other parts of her, parts that make her fiercely insecure when she studies them in a mirror.

Maybe Jonathan just thought she'd make a more convincing case if she showed Dugas a little flesh. Or *maybe—*

"I also know"—Dugas is looking her in the eye—"your late father left the N.O.P.D. to become security director for one of the richest men in New Orleans. A man whose vast holdings make this place look like...how do you say it? A humble *abode*?"

"Arthur Benoit."

"Yes. How is Arthur? Don't know him very well, but we've had a few dealings over the years. He seems like a kind man."

"He is. He's a *very* kind man..." She is seized by a painful, overwhelming vision of the man in question, pale and wasting, shrouded in expensive, silken sheets that do nothing to protect him from the chills deep in his bones, bones that seem closer to the skin on each visit. Arthur Benoit. The man who rescued their family from bankruptcy after her dad was driven out of the N.O.P.D; the man who became her surrogate father after her own dad was fatally sideswiped by a drunk driver a few years before. "He's dying," Emily whispers.

"Oh, Em," Jonathan says softly.

"I'm sorry to hear this," Dugas says, and she believes him. "How long does he have?"

"Weeks, a month. They're not sure. So you didn't know this part?"

"No. Just that you met with him at his home earlier this week." Dugas seems ashamed to admit this now. "It was after you met Jonathan for coffee so I just had them..." He flutters the fingers on one hand, as if the very revelations of the surveillance he'd used to frighten them just minutes earlier were now entirely irrelevant. He's embarrassed, she realizes.

"I see," Emily says. "So I guess you also don't know he's leaving me his entire fortune?"

3

Both men are startled into silence by Emily's revelation. Jonathan stares at her slack-jawed. After a while, he manages to whisper her first name as if it were a prayer.

"My," Dugas says. "That is *quite* a turn of events for a policeman's daughter. I take it you've seen the will. That you're confident this isn't some deathbed delirium that's filled you with false hope."

"Lawyers were present. Papers were signed."

"Well, then... Sounds official."

"And he's got no family left so I'm not sure who would contest it."

"There's no one at all? I find that hard to believe."

Arthur's rasping words return to her. *I'm a man who has discovered some things too late, Emily. Far too late. Help me make amends while I still can.*

"Well...there's one, apparently."

"Who?" Jonathan asks, so startled by the chain of revelations he's forgotten his client's demand he stay silent.

"Arthur has a son who ran away from home years ago, when he was nineteen," Emily says. "His name is Ryan. Ryan Benoit. Arthur's written him a letter and he wants me to find him and give it to him."

"As a condition of leaving you his fortune?" Dugas asks.

"It's not a condition. It's a request. And given that he's about to change my life forever, I'd say it's the very least I can do."

There is more bite in her tone than she'd intended, but Dugas seems more aroused by it than offended. "I see. Have you read this letter?" he asks.

"I have not. And I will not."

"Well…that *is* impressive. Certainly more self-control than you exhibited this evening. So you have no idea why Ryan ran away, but you're expected to somehow find him and bring him back?"

"I'm expected to give him the letter. The letter is supposed to bring him back. At least that's what Arthur's hoping for."

"And Arthur has made no attempt to find his son before now?"

"No…I mean, yes. He has but…"

"But *what?*" Jonathan asks.

"Ryan ran away so long ago that every few years, Arthur has an age progression done on computer. Then he hires a private detective to go look for him. A few years ago, one of the detectives turned up what looked like a real lead. But at the time, Arthur didn't want to pursue it. Now that he's dying, he's had a change of heart."

"And the lead was?" Dugas asks.

"The P.I. said a man matching Ryan's general description was involved with some sort of…secret *organization* called The Desire Exchange." Emily looks at Jonathan to gauge his reaction to these words. He's nowhere near as startled as she'd hoped he'd be. "I've only heard that name one other time and it was from you. You just sort of mentioned it in passing so I thought if—"

"You thought what?" Jonathan asks sharply. "That I was a member of a secret sex cult?"

"I just thought you might know more about it than you were letting on. But you wouldn't tell me unless—"

"—unless you caught me with a client and *embarrassed* it out of me?"

"Children," Dugas says. "Please."

"Emily. *Come on!* Some secret organization that helps millionaires live out their deepest sexual fantasies? It was somebody's idea of a joke. I thought it was funny. That's why I told you. It's not real, for Christ's sake."

"It is not a joke," George Dugas says quietly. His finality silences them both.

The man seems incapacitated all of a sudden. By shock? Memories? Emily can't tell. If she hadn't looked to Jonathan so quickly when she said those three shiver-inducing words, she might have picked up on the older man's reaction before now.

"And it's *very* real," Dugas whispers.

He rises to his feet, takes his drink in hand and strolls to the edge of the pool, as if it's wavering blue surface were a window onto the past. "The latest age progression. Describe it to me."

"He was about six feet tall when he ran away, so he should be around that now. Dirty blond—"

"Leave out the things he could have easily changed," Dugas says.

"Okay…bright eyes that have a kind of slant to them that looks almost Eastern European. I guess they'd make him look kind of angry. Or amused, I'm not sure. Anyway, his facial features, they're all proportional is what I'm trying to say. Especially his nose. He doesn't have one of those big Roman noses that can dominate a guy's face. Everything about him is more…classic. All-American."

"Any birthmarks?" Dugas asks.

"Yes. A small strawberry-colored one right above his left collarbone."

This concise description causes Dugas to straighten and suck in a deep breath, as if a wave of pleasure is coursing through his entire body.

"Oh my," Dugas whispers. Then he takes a quick sip of his drink. "Oh, my my *my*."

Jonathan breaks the silence. "Mr. Dugas, are you a…*member* of The Desire Exchange?"

"The Desire Exchange doesn't have members. It's not a club. It's an *experience*."

"An experience you've had, apparently," Emily says.

The older man drains the last of his cocktail with several long swallows. The mint sprig catches on the remaining ice cubes as he drinks. Whatever it is, George Dugas has trouble remembering The Desire Exchange without the balm of whiskey and powdered sugar to soothe the hot fires of his lust.

"Have you *seen* Ryan Benoit?" Emily asks.

"How about I give you the chance to see him for yourself?" Dugas says. "For a price, of course. *Several* prices."

When Dugas starts for Emily's chair, Jonathan straightens, watching the man's every move.

"There's the price of admission, of course. That you will pay directly to The Exchange. After I've given you a reference. And make no mistake, you *must* have a reference. The admission…well, I'm sure

Arthur Benoit will cover that for you. But he'll also need to give you some sort of fake identity, something that will make you appear to be in line with their usual clientele. Do you think he's up to it?"

Dugas is standing behind her chair now. Jonathan watches the man with the intensity of a cat watching a bird through a window. Emily studies Jonathan's facial expression with the same focus.

"Arthur would do anything to get Ryan that letter," Emily says. "Short of...*hurting* people."

"No," Dugas whispers, hands coming to rest on her shoulders. "Of course not. Pain is not on the menu."

"And the price for your reference?" she asks.

Gently, he pulls open the flaps of her robe, exposing her breasts to the humid air. Her eyes flutter shut against her will as she braces for the feel of the man's hands on her flesh. But the feeling doesn't come. He continues to tug on the robe instead until the loose knot in the tie comes undone. Suddenly her thighs are exposed, and then her sex.

Jonathan gazes into her eyes, trying to read her every emotion, ready to spring into action as soon as she gives him the word, she's sure of it. But her head is swimming and there is heat traveling the length of her body. Rather than feeling violated, being gradually exposed this way makes her feel included in a delicious secret.

"The Desire Exchange isn't just about *your* fantasy," Dugas continues. "It's about surrendering to the fantasies of others as well. To do that, you have to let go. Of labels. Of limits. Of fears."

"I'm still waiting to hear your price, Mr. Dugas."

The older man chuckles. "As if you'd ever say no, Miss Blaine. You'd be risking your incredible inheritance if you did."

"I'm risking my incredible inheritance by agreeing to find the only rightful heir. Some of us are motivated by other things than money, *sir*."

"Yes," Dugas says. With one final tug he separates the flaps of the robe and draws it down over her back, rendering her fully nude and exposed. "Desire."

Jonathan is on the edge of his seat, nostrils flaring, rock-hard pecs rising and falling with his deep breaths. The head of his olive-skinned cock has emerged from the waistband of his briefs, glistening with his arousal. She tells herself it's just Dugas acting the part of the masculine aggressor that has Jonathan engorged. It can't be *her*, for Christ's sake. How many times has he seen her breasts before now?

But she's right and she's wrong at the same time. It's not just her. And it's not just George Dugas. It's all of it. All three of them, the setting, the hint of danger, and the act of pure will that brought her here. It's this sudden swirl of desire they've been swept up by, and Emily realizes it's about to render comforting labels irrelevant.

"Nobody does anything for just one reason," Dugas whispers in her ear. "You can pretend you climbed onto my roof because you were after information that will help you find this Ryan Benoit. But you'd be lying. You'd be lying if you didn't also admit you wanted to see the expression on your best friend's face while he was in the throes of passion with a strange man."

She is not a prude. Her life has had its fair share of satisfying sex, but never sexual adventure. She knows what it feels like to be desired, mostly by men who found her nature mothering and her ample curves delicious. But no man has ever placed her on display as if she were a work of art, certainly not a man as rich and powerful as George Dugas. And just as he refrained from making leering comments about her body, he refrains from poking her or tweaking her as if she were a piece of meat. Rather, he has unveiled her, making her feel as if there were a source of energy emanating from her that can alter the room.

Dugas runs three fingers on each hand very lightly down her bare shoulders. Despite the humidity, gooseflesh spreads outward from his twin touch and she feels herself moistening.

"Why is it so difficult to give pleasure to the people we care for the most?" Dugas asks. "This is the type of question you'll have to answer if you visit The Desire Exchange. And you'll have to answer it with your entire body, not just your smart mouth."

Dugas withdraws, walks around the back of her chair and takes a seat in his chair. His expression is fixed and serious now.

When the silence between them becomes too much to bear, Jonathan says, "So your price is…the two of us, together?"

"With each other," Dugas says in a gentle whisper.

"And you'll give me the reference I need to get to Ryan?" Emily asks.

"I'll give you the reference you need to get to The Exchange. Ryan will be your responsibility."

"Emily…" Jonathan says softly. He's gazing into her eyes. "Is this what you want?"

She's not sure what he's referring to exactly—the reference Dugas has just offered or the chance to make love to her closest friend. For the time being, they are one and the same, and so the question seems irrelevant, the real consequences of what they're about to do as distant as a foreign country she might never get the chance to visit. Staring into Jonathan's eyes, Emily says, "Deal."

Jonathan swallows. Even as he sinks to his knees before the rattan chair she's sitting in, his hands coming to rest gently on her bare knees, he stares into her eyes as if he's afraid she might change her mind at any moment and whatever he sees there will be the giveaway. For a few seconds, they just stare at each other, as if she were a queen on his throne and he, a knight about to humble himself before her over some terrible failure of courage. Her heart races, as fast as it did when she found herself hurtling through the open skylight moments before.

Then, suddenly, his lips are against hers, the impact of his hard body rocking the chair back on its hind legs for a few seconds. The arc of pleasure that courses through her entire body is electrifying because its chief current is the white-hot thrill of the forbidden—it's *Jonathan!* Her first schoolgirl crush! Her best friend!

How many times had she listened to him describe his various sexual conquests, feeling a strange blend of arousal and jealousy? How many times had she felt the same way listening to his few boyfriends describe the magic he could make in the bedroom? And now she gets to have a taste for herself. And it feels like magic. His kisses are hungry, insistent, and he's taken both of her nipples in between his thumb and forefinger and he's pulling on them gently while rolling them back and forth at the same time, with just enough pressure to drive her wild. Because he knows what drives her wild. She's told him hundreds of times over the years in casual conversation. *Girl talk*, they used to jokingly call it. And he's remembering all the details now. He must be. And the result is anything but *girl talk*.

One hand works her right nipple; the other seizes her mound, the heel of his palm pressing against her opening while he dazzles her clit with three dancing fingers. In her ear, he whispers, "I'll take care of this, angel."

Angel! To hear his cherished nickname for her in this context makes her juices flow. His fingers work faster with this fresh assistance. He's trying to comfort her, she knows. Trying to put her at ease with their strange witness and the coercion that's brought them to this point. But she doesn't want to be comfortable. She wants some of what he's given countless men, and who knows how many clients.

"You better," she whispers back.

The genuine lust in her voice startles him. His lips leave hers, but his fingers work harder on her clit. He's staring into her eyes, and she watches the change overtake him. Watches the act fall away at the sound of the unbridled passion in her tone. Watches him lick his full lips and dive for her glistening sex. Her cry sounds pained, but the feel of Jonathan's tongue invading her folds is pure bliss. *God, he's good at this.* Are there women among his secret clients? This thought makes her even hotter.

He's gently sawing three fingers in and out of her, a slow and steady rhythm that works counterpoint to the mad, insistent flicker of his tongue back and forth over her nub. Every now and then he takes a break by licking his way up her inner thighs with long strokes. But it's all a constant, unbroken dance between his mouth and her sex. Not for a second does his mouth leave some part of her flesh. She'd seen his tongue a thousand times, of course, when he was taking a big bite of food or licking his lips in mock hunger. She's always known how long and thick it was. But the prospect she might one day feel it against her tender opening seemed as possible as sprouting wings and taking to the air.

"Jonathan..." she groans.

"Do you like that, angel?"

"More..."

He goes back to work. Her eyes drift open. She expects to find Dugas pleasuring himself a few feet away. But the man is sitting upright and fully clothed, looking thunderstruck, riveted, drained of all sarcasm and arrogance. The sense of power she feels at the sight of him is overwhelming. It appears as if his entire, vast world—the mansion, the glittering swimming pool, and the guards—has receded from his view. The only thing that exists for George Dugas now is the spectacle of her and Jonathan indulging a long suppressed passion.

"Stand up," Emily says. There's a small kernel of fear at the center of her desire, a fear that when Jonathan follows her order, she'll see a limp noodle resting inside his briefs and realize this was all a show for his client.

But somehow, while eating her out and probing her with his skillful fingers, Jonathan managed to pull off his briefs, so when he gets to his feet, he brings a thick, glistening column of flesh inches from her face.

Jonathan stares down at his own cock with an open-mouthed

look of wonder. Then he gives her the same look, as if her unbridled desire has shocked and sidelined him, while rendering him fully engorged and full of unexpected hunger for her.

Now it's her turn to remember the things he likes. She takes his balls in one hand and places the head of his cock in between her lips. Jonathan's always told her he can't stand it when guys try to deep throat his entire shaft, that he'd much rather have the head of his cock worked in tandem with the steady strokes of a powerful hand. And even his not-so-close friends knew how much he loved having his balls played with. So Emily combines all three, while Jonathan gently twines his fingers through her hair. She can tell he doesn't want to cup the back of her skull in both hands. He's probably not fucking her mouth the way he's used to fucking some dumb trick he picked up at a bar.

"Emily," he whispers. The soft insistence in his voice only turns her on more, makes her as wet as if his fingers and tongue were still working her over down there. She's always been afraid to admit how turned on she is by Jonathan's combination of boyish sweetness and hard-bodied perfection. And now she's got the feel and taste of him to add to this mixture.

She draws the head of his cock from her lips with a wet pop, and then slides down in the chair, spreading her thighs.

Jonathan sinks to his knees in front of her, while reaching behind him to pull a condom from the pocket of his rumpled jeans.

Once he's sheathed, he takes her ankles in both hands. His muscles ripple and tense as he finds the perfect aim against her wet, throbbing pussy. He locks eyes with her as he presses into her. With men he must be used to more resistance because his eyes widen when he slides into her with ease. Suddenly he's beaming with excitement and pride, as if they've found the last piece of a puzzle.

The sudden, delirious sense that Jonathan is hers—for now, entirely and completely *hers*—fills her with as much force and speed as his hard cock. As his thrusts gain a steady tempo, she brings her hands to his pecs, his nipples, down his abs, clamping her legs around his waist, driving him further into her until their sweat-slick bodies are sliding together, and he's whispering in her ear, "I never knew you were such a dirty girl, Emily Blaine."

"Yes you did."

Their bodies may be on display, but these whispered words belong just to them.

She's never been fucked with this amount of skill and coordination before. There's the pure thrill of it being Jonathan. Then there's the undeniable skill Jonathan has acquired over years of being, by his own description, a sex demon. His cock is doing the least of it. It's the flow and motion of the rest of his body, the energy he pushes behind it, and of course, the hand he's returned to her hard, throbbing nub.

It feels as if he's pushing her past the delirium. She's lost all control of the words coming out of her mouth.

"Fuck me like you fuck your clients, Jonathan."

"Really? Is that what you want, angel?"

"Fuck me like you fuck all those men," she whispers.

"Yeah?"

"And women? Are there women?"

"No," he says, breathless. He's pulled back some so he can look into her eyes, and so his right hand can have better access to her mound. "No other women. Only you."

When the orgasm hits her, she screams with as much surprise as bliss. She was so busy focusing on his words and staring into his eyes she almost didn't feel it coming. In a single fluid motion, Jonathan pulls out, bends down and brings his mouth to her clit. She shudders and rocks, one hand clutching the back of his head, jamming his mouth harder against her throbbing, searing sex. As the last waves of pleasure course through her, she feels a different motion and when she opens her eyes, she sees Jonathan pull the condom from his engorged cock. He's fisting himself now, brow creased, lips parted, working toward a veritable eruption. Politely, demurely even, he turns to one side.

She's not having that at all.

"On me, baby," she says.

There's that look of surprise again.

"I said *on* me," she repeats, firmer this time.

Chewing on his bottom lip, Jonathan gets to his feet, stroking his cock. The he erupts. His mouth flies open. Strangled groans rip from his throat. Emily remembers what Dugas said only moments earlier, about wanting to see the expression on Jonathan's face when he was in the throes of passion with a stranger. And he was right. Only the stranger had to watch this time, and the one in the throes of passion with Jonathan was her.

Her breasts, her stomach, her inner thighs—they're all splattered with his seed. And just when it feels like desire is about to retreat, leaving behind the sticky, cooling reality of their situation, Jonathan sinks to his knees and begins licking his eruption from her skin. Slowly, dutifully. Gently passing the tip of his tongue over her sensitive, aching folds as he moves back and forth between her thighs. Then up her stomach. He takes his time licking her breasts clean, making sure to pass over and briefly suckle each nipple as he does so.

Then they're eye to eye and Jonathan is smiling at her expectantly. A little dollop of his cum rests in the corner of his mouth, and before she can think twice about it, she scoops it up in one fingernail and places it in between her lips. The sweet taste surprises her.

"Pineapple," Jonathan whispers. "It's my secret."

"I *gave* you that secret," she whispers back.

And suddenly they're both laughing.

Then she's rising into the air. He's picked her up in both powerful arms. Before she realizes where he's taking her, the pool's warm water has risen around them both. She clamps her legs around his waist to keep from floating free of his hard body.

Perhaps he really does want to hold her this tenderly, this close. Or maybe he just wants some distance between them and their one-man audience.

Does it matter? He's still holding her. That's all she cares about for now. That, and the fact that George Dugas has started to applaud.

4

As a fresh storm pummels the French Quarter, Emily lies in her best friend's arms, his breath making gooseflesh on the back of her neck. They've snuggled like this before countless times, but never after rutting like porn stars for the secret delight of a voyeuristic millionaire. Where Jonathan has draped his arm across her chest and hooked one of her legs with his, there is heat just under her skin that feels new and fresh, fueled by a part of her that's been covered over until now.

His cozy, two-room apartment is one of many inside an old French Quarter mansion just a few blocks from the restaurant where they both work. At her request, he's opened the door to the second floor walkway outside his bedroom. This way they can listen to the rain slap the banana trees and rattle the building's old, sagging gutters. This way Emily can fool herself into believing the storm's song will eventually drown out her nagging worries George Dugas won't make good on his promise.

She's always loved the way a good storm in the Quarter softens the raucous echo of the drunken revelers, filters out the odors of booze and sweat, and purifies the fertile scents of sweet olive and night jasmine. Tonight there's also the gentle sound of Billie Holiday's voice drifting in from the apartment next door. Jonathan's neighbor is a D.J. at a karaoke bar. On more than one occasion, he'd told her classic jazz and the blues are his only effective tools for emptying his head of the rock anthems he's forced to play incessantly every night at work.

She's been quiet for a while now, ever since it became clear Jonathan knew nothing about The Desire Exchange beyond vague rumor. And she's tired of speculating about what *The Exchange*, as Dugas called it, either is or isn't.

Probably just a bunch of Eyes Wide Shut *nonsense*, Jonathan has proclaimed more than once. *Bunch of rich old dudes in masks and robes, playing with each other in some big warehouse out in the swamp.* She's inclined to believe him.

And that leaves them with other matters to discuss.

"Do any of them hurt you?" she asks.

"Do any of *who* hurt me?"

"Your clients, silly."

"There aren't that many. Low volume, high price point. That's my business model."

"That's also not an answer."

"No. None of them hurt me. And I don't hurt them. That's not what I offer."

"What do you offer?"

"Whatever they want...within reason. Most of them are like Dugas. They want to watch me jerk off, or watch me with someone else, like their boyfriend or their husband. Some of them want to talk. Others...they just want the usual."

"And what's the usual?"

"Mostly they want me on top, but every now and then..."

"What if you're not attracted to them?"

"I carry a pill with me just in case."

"Valium?"

"No," he says, laughing. "More like a performance enhancement drug."

"I see. The *other* V."

"I've never had to use it. You train yourself, Em."

"Train yourself how?"

"There's usually a part of each of them...sometimes it's a body part, sometimes it's just the way they say a certain word. Sometimes they remind you of someone. But there's usually *something* you can latch on to. Something your desire can reach out and *hold*. Focus on that and the rest is easy."

"I see. So being a hooker has taught you to see the inner beauty in everyone?" She manages to make it through the entire question before she bursts out laughing.

"*Em!* I'm serious," he says, giving her a light slap on the shoulder.

"And you're always safe?"

"Well, yeah…" He pushes himself up on one elbow and turns her gently so he can stare into her eyes. "If you consider making love to your best friend *safe.*"

"Making love? Is that what we were doing? I thought we were just putting on a show."

"You tell me, *angel.*"

His nickname for her hasn't just been changed, it's been forever charged. From here on out, whenever he calls her angel, she'll see his strong jaw lathered in her juices, the starry-eyed expression on his face when he saw how hard she'd made him.

"*You*, mister," she says, cupping his chin in one hand, "have done some of that stuff before. I want names."

"Oh, God." He grimaces and makes a show of trying to turn his chin from her grip, but it's no use. "Please don't make me, Em."

"Oh, now you *have* to tell!"

"Lacey Colter," he mutters out of one side of his mouth.

"What? No! Lacey was, like, the *worst* person in our high school."

"She got me drunk!" Jonathan whines.

"Lord, so you're like the opposite of most men. Three beers and suddenly you're in bed with a girl."

"I didn't need any beers to go to bed with you," he whispers.

"So it wasn't just for show?"

He rolls onto her carefully, reaches up and presses her wrists into the pillows, grinding his erection against the inside of her thigh. "If it was all for show, I wouldn't have been able to finish. We guys can't fake it the way you girls can."

"Yeah, I know. We girls would be a lot less sticky if you could."

"Emily Blaine, you are being very inappropriate," he says, beaming. "And I like it."

"Whatever. You're just all sexed up from the…scene."

"The scene? What do you mean?"

"You know, the forbiddenness of it all."

"Forbiddenness isn't a word, English major."

"Actually, it is. But thanks, Closeted Frat Boy Major. Whatever. You know what I mean. Getting caught. Dugas ordering you to have sex with me. The *scene*. That's what did it."

"Dugas didn't order me to have sex with you. *You* did when you accepted his offer."

"Fine. But it's the *scene* that got you going, is what I'm saying—"

"Em, I'm not going to give you a prize every time you say the word *scene*, so you can stop already."

"Nice evasion there but I'm not one of your clients, *Michael*."

"Damn straight. If you were just one of my clients, I wouldn't bother to do this." He licks his way up the nape of her neck. "Or this," he adds, gripping one hand over her mound. There's so much heat coming from his palm she can feel it through her jeans.

"Or you'd just charge extra," she whispers.

When he feels her eyes on him, he stops his ministrations. His sigh is that of a teenager who's been caught making a beeline for the front door ten minutes after curfew.

"Uh oh," he groans. "It's the *face*."

"I just…I mean, it was good. Don't get me wrong. It was like *great* good. But…come on, Jonathan. Let's not pretend I'm going to be enough for you in this department, okay? There are certain pieces of equipment I just don't have."

"Or we could stop pretending like we know what's actually happening and just sort of…go with it."

"Just go with it? Since when are you such a Buddhist?"

"Since when do I go down on my best friend?"

"*Jonathan!*"

"Hey, listen. If you want to make this a one-time thing, that's fine. But personally," he returns his hands to her mound, rubbing it forcefully and steadily with the heel of his hand. "I think there's a lot more research we should do before we make a final decision."

"Yeah, well, what if I just blew the door off and now you're going to be eating pussy all over town?"

"Gross! Don't use that word!"

"Wait, *seriously*? My hooker best friend, who just plowed me in front of a stranger, is going to get all bent out of shape about what I call my poo-nanny."

"That's worse!"

"My penis washing machine, you mean."

"Emily! Stop it!"

When he rears up and away from her, she goes for his tickle spots. He curls into a fetal position, trying, and failing, to shield himself from her two-handed attack. "My bearded clam!" she cries.

"Gross!"

"See. If you can't handle all the words for a vagina, how are you gonna handle vaginas? Plural!"

After a brief tussle, he grabs both her wrists, forcing her back into a seated position like his own.

"I don't want anyone else's vagina." He's started the retort with a smile, but then the seriousness of his proclamation settles over them both. The mirth vanishes from his expression. They're suddenly silent, save for their breaths, which are as deep and heavy as if they were in the midst of sex itself and not just talking about it. "Just yours," he adds in a whisper.

"But you're not going to stop wanting other men," she finally says because it would be more painful not to.

"I don't know," he whispers. "I mean, it's not like I planned this."

"Neither did I."

"But we both wanted it. So what does that mean? I mean...how long have we wanted to do this and *not* acted on it?"

Through the open doorway, she can see the spot where the gutter sends off a small jet of spray down into the courtyard below. But the reality fades before a vision, a speculation, really of what The Desire Exchange might be. How did Jonathan put it? Rich old farts having some kind of orgy inside a barn, while Ryan Benoit...does *what* exactly? Takes turns on each of them? Passes out cocktails in a waiter's outfit?

"I don't know. And honestly, I don't have time to figure it out. I've got a lot of work ahead of me already."

"Yeah, inheriting a fortune really takes a lot out of a girl."

"You know that's not what I mean. I'm talking about Ryan Benoit."

"You're talking about The Desire Exchange."

"Right now, they're the same thing."

"Maybe. Either way, you're not going alone."

"What do you mean?"

"I mean whatever The Desire Exchange is, I'm going with you."

"Jonathan, the price of admission is *literally* a million a person. You have that kind of cash lying around?"

"Arthur does. He's leaving it all to you anyway. And it'll improve your chances of finding his son without being...*violated* by a bunch of rich old men."

"And women, possibly. Dugas didn't say how many there'd be of each."

"Yeah, and I wouldn't count on him to say much. That's not his style. He'll want you to suffer through it by yourself and then he'll want to hear all the details."

"It can't be *that* dangerous, Jonathan. If George Dugas came back in one piece—"

"George Dugas is a millionaire real estate developer with a history of criminal activity *and* a knack for destroying people who get in his way. *Emily Blaine* is a restaurant manager with an English degree who tries to see the best in people even when they're stealing from the register."

"Wow. I actually thought I was kind of jaded."

"You are. But you're not a sociopath. And George Dugas is most definitely a sociopath."

"Alright, well, maybe he's lying to us about the whole thing then?"

"He's not."

"How can you be so sure?"

"What does he gain from lying about it?"

"He got to watch us go at it."

"There are other ways he could have pulled that off. No, Em. I think he really liked you. As much as a man like him can *like* anyone. My point is, whatever The Exchange is, he wants *you* to go through what he went through. And that makes me nervous. And that's why you're not going alone."

Or you're jealous, she thinks. She wonders if he's reading her mind. Just then he does what he always does when he's angry. He crosses his arms over his chest and pouts, which always looks a little silly and endearing given what a big guy he is.

Lightning flashes outside, strobing his biceps, his chest, his cute little pursed lips. Then they're back in the shrouded intimacy of the dimly lit room. *My hero,* she thinks, but saying it aloud would feel unbearably cheesy. *My jealous and suddenly protective hero.*

"Fine," she whispers.

"It's been a long night," he says quietly.

"Yeah. I should go." She's halfway to her car keys when Jonathan wraps his fingers around her wrist. Anticipating her move, he crossed the room in a flash.

"No, you shouldn't," he whispers into her ear.

"Jonathan—"

"What's the matter? You sleep over all the time."

"Before…"

"Before what?"

He lifts the wrist he's just grabbed up to one side, as if they're about to start a slow waltz around his bedroom. He smells like vanilla body wash and the last hint of whatever musky cologne he spritzed himself with before visiting George Dugas. It's not his usual fragrance, something he's reserved just for his clients. Or just for Dugas. Does he have a different scent for every customer? Will he have a scent that's just for her?

"Before I…" The words leave her as she's barraged by fresh memories of their lovemaking.

"Before you knew what my tongue felt like inside you?" he asks, and when she doesn't answer, he pulls her closer to him. "So you're afraid we won't get any sleep? Is that it?"

"Or I value our friendship and I don't want to ruin it."

"Oh, I won't ruin it. Especially now that I know how good it can taste."

"*Jonathan*," she groans.

Drawing them together, he releases his grip on her wrist, drags his fingertips down the inside of her forearm, and opens his mouth against her neck. Now there's real fear riding the throb of passion, and it forces words from her mouth before she can measure them.

"You like being wanted, J Man. You always have. At the bar, you never go home with the hottest guy. You go home with the ones who make you feel like a stud." Rigid, he pulls his mouth from her neck. But it's not enough to stop her. "Don't fool yourself into thinking you can be someone you're not just because…"

"Because you want me inside you again?" The way he's said it makes it sound like an accusation. And all at once it feels as if they've just left the embrace of a comforting dream and now they're walking on a cold, hard floor, rubbing sleep from their eyes.

"I'm tired," she says. "I just… Let me get some rest and then we can—"

"You think too much, Emily Blaine. You think too much and you have too many names for things."

When he turns his broad, naked back to her, she feels as if he's given her a light slap.

"I'll call you in the morning," she mutters. Then she's on the stairs outside, shoving her keys and wallet into her back pocket, half expecting Jonathan to pursue her down the rickety wooden steps. But he doesn't come after her, and the full implication of Jonathan's parting words hit her once she's outside.

Surrounded by rain-slicked parked cars and townhouses, Emily freezes like a lost tourist trying to get her bearings back. Her keys are in hand, but she can't bring herself to take another step toward her Camry. She couldn't care less she's getting soaked for the fourth time that night.

What did Jonathan mean? Would they have tasted each other's flesh before now if she weren't such a *thinker*? If she wasn't so busy coming up with *words* for things? Could the insane bliss she'd experienced earlier that night have been hers to enjoy years before if she hadn't been so caught up with labels and categories? Well, it's not like it was her fault, for Pete's sake! Jonathan was the one who came exploding out of the closet like a giant gay hurricane when they were just sixteen. Labels, T-shirts, bumper sticker, blowjobs and all.

Why is it so difficult to give pleasure to the people we care for the most? Dugas's question echoes in her crowded mind. It's the only real detail the man gave her about The Desire Exchange, his assertion that if she surrendered to the *experience* of it, she'd be forced to answer questions just like this one.

Well, she's got a damn good opportunity to answer it right now.

Before she can ponder what she's about to do, Emily is back inside Jonathan's courtyard and mounting the steps to his apartment as quietly as she can. The front door glides open as soon as she places her hand on the knob. He left it unlocked, for *her*. He sits up in bed, the comforter sliding down his smooth, sculpted torso, his expression unreadable in the dark.

He doesn't move, just watches her through the shadows as she peels off her wet jeans and then her panties. When she climbs up onto him and straddles his chest, all without pausing to remove her wet shirt, he sinks back into the pillows.

"I lied," she whispers. "I'm not tired."

Then she's straddling his face and when she drives her sex against his mouth, his lips part and his tongue goes to work instantly. She grabs the headboard with both hands and he grips the back of her thighs with both of his. All the anger and frustration and confusion turns to grinding hot lust as she rides the indisputable power of her best friend's skillful tongue.

Whatever happens tomorrow, or the next day, whatever secrets await them at The Desire Exchange, it's her turn to have a taste of Jonathan Claiborne. No aliases, no hourly rate, no strange bargains. She's been a witness to his smoldering sexuality for too long. It's her turn to feel his fingers and his tongue.

She grabs the back of his head in one hand, the headboard in the other, and drives his flickering tongue against her clit as the second orgasm of the night lightnings through her from toes to skull.

When she collapses onto the tousled comforter next to him, he spoons into her. Once she's caught her breath, he starts to peel her wet shirt from her skin. She lifts her arms over her head so he can slide it off the rest of the way, and then they're both naked and curled against each other, listening to the rain.

"*Now* will you sleep here?" he asks.

"I think I just gave you my answer."

He laughs gently and nuzzles his mouth into her neck.

The music from next door has stopped. Now there's just the rain, Jonathan's hard and confident embrace, and the wet traces of desire they've left to dry across each other's bodies.

5

"My God, Emily," Arthur Benoit whispers. "What have I've gotten you into?"

The man has uttered some variation of this question at least ten times since Emily started recounting a highly edited and distinctly G-rated version of her meeting with George Dugas. Each time, Emily allowed for a polite pause before continuing, but now she has reached the end of her story (and her bizarre request) and the silence inside Magnolia Gate's vast master bedroom feels electric.

Jonathan sits quietly in one corner, eyeing their palatial surroundings with a bright new awareness in his eyes. Someday soon, all of this will belong to Emily. From the portrait paintings of long dead, plantation-owning Benoits, to the grand four-poster bed, its columns carved into replicas of cornstalks, its large wood-framed canopy full of tufted burgundy fabric. The thought of inheriting just the contents of this bedroom feels so overwhelming, she can't allow her eyes to wander to the soaring window and its view of the expansive gardens outside, lest she collapse from the shock of it all.

"Jonathan..." Arthur whispers, one frail hand extended in the man's direction. Like a dutiful suitor, Jonathan pops out of his chair and approaches the bed. He's dressed the part of her reliable, stalwart best friend; a sober pair of pressed khakis and a mint green Ralph Lauren button-up—none of his usual flash and glam. No Prada, no Gucci, no patent leather. "You have agreed to this?"

"Going with her, you mean? I've insisted on it."

"You've insisted that Arthur *pay* for you, which isn't exactly the same—"

"I'll pay," Arthur answers. "I'll pay for all of it. Even though we have no real idea what this even is…I mean, an *experience*? Is that what Dugas said?"

"Yes," Jonathan says before Emily can. "Honestly, sir, whatever it is, I don't think it'll be all that impressive. Probably just—"

"Impressive?" Arthur cuts him off. "Some sort of secret…*sex* cult fails to impress you, does it?"

When Emily gives Jonathan a threatening look, he bows his head, knowing he earned it. They agreed to let Emily do the talking for just this reason. Arthur Benoit's been presented with enough new information for one day; Jonathan doesn't need to flash his credentials as a sex worker.

"So you'll both need fake identities," Arthur says. Now that they're discussing business, he tries to straighten himself amidst his cocoon of pillows. The giant headphones he was using when they first entered the bedroom slide off his blanket-covered lap, still emitting soft tinkles of flutes and violin. But just these limited movements trigger a massive coughing fit. It's so severe Emily reaches out and grips his shoulder gently, feeling his bones etched under her touch.

Arthur tries to give them a sheepish, embarrassed smile. When he speaks again, his voice is thin as a reed. "If Ry— If my son is involved in the administration of this…*group*, then we must take every precaution to make sure you all can't be traced back to me. The only lead we've managed to turn up in years has been this one and it's very circumstantial. Whatever identity he's been maintaining, it's entirely off the grid, I can assure you. If he runs—" *I'll probably die before we can find him again*, Arthur doesn't say, but the thought knifes through all three of them at once. "—So whatever this process is, I don't want you applying as some sort of couple. We'll give you different identities. And they won't…they won't be based here. Close, but outside New Orleans."

It's only been twenty-four hours since they made love for the first time; the thought of being separated from Jonathan makes her feel frightened and helpless suddenly. Jonathan starts to speak, then stops.

Is he feeling something similar? She's willing to bet his insistence that he accompany her is more than a protective instinct. Maybe he views The Desire Exchange as a chance to—how did he put it the night before?— do more research into this new aspect of their relationship. But if they're separated…?

"I'm sorry," Arthur says, studying their reaction as best he can through the haze of his medications. "I don't have much time, and I can't risk this falling apart."

"Mr. Benoit—" Jonathan begins, but the older man raises his hand to silence him.

"Please, Jonathan. Call me by my first name. If it were truly a comfort to be seen as an authority figure while staring death in the face, I would welcome it. But it is not. It is not a comfort at all."

"Arthur," Emily says quietly. "It isn't just the background check that we have to pass. Dugas says there will be a test of some sort."

"Lord, and he's given no more information than this?" Arthur asks.

"I'm afraid not," Emily says quietly. "Maybe we could get him to meet with us."

"Oh, that'll never work," Jonathan mutters.

"No," Arthur says, and for a second Emily's not sure whom the man is disagreeing with. "Dugas—I've had run-ins with him over the years. And we've no idea how deeply embedded he is with this organization. I can't risk having him squeal on us. I could always find a way to threaten him, but no…it's too risky."

When he sees Emily's worried expression, Arthur offers her a gentle smile.

"Dearest Emily," he says. "You don't need to manage my expectations, darling. I know you'll do your best. Both of you." His smile seems to take all of his strength. But then, he surprises her by reaching out and gripping each of their hands in turn. "But please, do it quickly. As quickly as you can. There is only so much that can be made right with a simple letter. And there is so much I need to make right with my son."

They're both speechless as Arthur reaches for a file folder on the nightstand. Handing it to her will force him to contort his precarious position in bed, so Emily reaches for it as soon as she realizes what he's trying to do.

"I figured it would be helpful for you to know as much as you could about Ryan before you meet. If he refuses to take the letter, perhaps there's something in there you can…use. Don't threaten him, of course. But if you can appeal to…I don't know….his better nature then perhaps…"

"Of course," Emily whispers.

6

After fifteen minutes of watching Emily study old photographs of Ryan Benoit, Jonathan thrusts his hand across the table and makes a sound like he just swallowed a mouthful of dry lettuce. The contents of Arthur's file are spread across the wooden table between them. The two of them look like house hunters perusing real estate listings they've printed off the Internet.

At first it bothered her, the way Jonathan dumped out the trappings of Prince Benoit's former life right out in the open, before she realized Ryan's old report cards, academic files, and e-mails home from summer camp wouldn't mean a thing to any of the strangers crowding the coffee shop on Magazine Street. True, some of the other patrons might have noticed Ryan Benoit was a stunningly handsome nineteen-year-old, but that's not the reason Emily's trying to keep the pictures to herself.

As she relents, sliding the stack of glossy photographs carefully into Jonathan's open hand, Emily finds herself studying every tic in her best friend's facial expression. He leafs through the images; she studies his eyes, the set of his mouth, even the steadiness of his fingers as they slip and slide across the photo paper. The night before, Jonathan was desperate to convince her they should add a sexual component to their relationship. Will he still react in the usual manner when confronted with a gorgeous male specimen like young Ryan Benoit?

"Golly," Jonathan whispers.

Not quite the same, Emily thinks. More like a toned-down version of his usual exclamations of lust, which typically include such gems as *Day-uhm*, *Da-dee*, and *gurl*, to name a few. But there's no doubt about it. Her best friend, the one who devoured her from head to toe just the night before, still blushes and loses his breath at the sight of male perfection.

"I'm calling this one *Come Sail Away*," Jonathan says with a smile. He's holding up a glossy eight-by-ten of nineteen-year-old Ryan, shirtless on the deck of a sailboat beneath a dome of blue sky. There's a slight curl to his dirty blond hair, and dark sunglasses offset his generous, easy smile. The first hints of muscle give light definition to his sun-kissed torso, almost like a pencil-sketch of a man in the making inside of his otherwise perfect frame. But it's the finely etched jawline, the button nose, and the broad shoulders that make him model perfect.

And Jonathan is just as aroused by all of it as she is.

"Indeed," Emily says.

"*Indeed?* Oh, come on, Em. I never said I wasn't attracted to men anymore."

"You never said you were attracted to women either."

"Nope. Just you," he adds. His devilish smirk sends a spike of fear through her.

So this whole thing is a joke now?

Maybe, maybe not, she tells herself.

But one thing is clear: she's doing exactly what she promised herself she wouldn't do before she drifted off to sleep in his arms the night before—lassoing her heart to his every turn of phrase like some simpering teenager.

Now she realizes she watched him so closely as he studied Ryan's photograph because she was protecting herself, looking for evidence that the old rules still applied. Because that's what she always does when she feels vulnerable and afraid. Looks for the rules, opens the handbook. *Any* handbook, it doesn't matter, as long as people who appear to be more put together than she feels wrote it. Although, she'd be hard-pressed to come up with a rule book that included a FAQ on *What To Expect When You Unexpectedly Sleep With Your Gay Best Friend...Twice.*

"Let's focus," Emily says.

"On what? The fact that we don't know what The Desire

Exchange actually is? Or the fact that we don't know if Ryan Benoit really works there? Or we could spend a few hours obsessing on the fact that we don't know which cities Arthur's going to relocate us to or what identities he's going to give us? Take your pick."

"You're free to back out at any time. You know that, right?'

"I'm not complaining, Em. I'm just saying. Kinda feels like we're more in a *wait and see* mode right now, rather than an *Emily makes a bunch of to-do lists* mode."

"I love it when you use air quotes. It makes you seem so sophisticated."

"So now we're in an *Emily gets really sarcastic 'cause she's freaked out about not having to fake her orgasms* mode. Why don't—"

"Alright, that's *enough*, Snarky Snarkerson!"

"Snarky *what*?"

"Whatever. Look, I'm very touched that you want to go along with me, but let's not start pretending this little trip needs to be tailored to meet your needs, alright? The mission here is very simple—"

"Yes! Of course it is! Assume fake identities so we can infiltrate a secret sex club about which we know next to nothing and which costs literally a million dollars to gain access to, oh and, also in the course of that, somehow slip a dying man's letter to one of their employees who may or may not work there and who may or may not look like one of the *ten* computer generated photographs we have of him. You're right. I mean, really. I can't think of anything that simple. I mean, not since Kleenex was invented has there—"

She hits the side of his face with the file folder with a loud enough whack for several jittery coffee drinkers nearby to jump and shoot them baffled looks. By then, Emily has retracted her makeshift weapon and all they see is Jonathan rubbing his left cheek and chin, wearing the pouty expression of a chastised ten-year-old.

"Ow."

"What do you want me to say, Jonathan? Do you have any idea how weird this is for me?"

"If you'd like me to stop giving you orgasms, I'll be happy—"

"Or," she says in a harsh whisper. "You could stop acting like giving me an orgasm entitles you to a Nobel Peace Prize. I know you haven't been in the lady pond for a while but they're not exactly that hard to come by if you have a showerhead and an imagination, okay? How does that sound?"

"Like you need another one."

"Maybe for five minutes, you could stop talking or thinking about sex."

"Sure thing, girl who's going to infiltrate a sex club so she can—"

This time she just picks up the file folder instead of hitting him with it. Jonathan goes silent, lips pursed, cheeks puffing as if the words he wants to keep speaking are a literal pressure inside of his mouth.

"He's leaving me *everything*, Jonathan. Everything. That house. Everything in it. His holdings, his companies."

"You say that like it's a bad thing."

"Because I don't deserve it. Sure, he and my dad were close. But my dad was just his employee and he's been gone for two years. Which means I have no idea why Arthur would pick me for this."

"Because you're an amazing person?" Jonathan asks.

"You say that like it's a question."

"Sorry. You're an amazing person!"

"I'm not, but thank you."

"I don't know," he mutters. "I think you're pretty great."

"I appreciate that, but it's not the point."

"Okay... So what's the point?"

"The point is I have to do something for Arthur to...*justify* all of this or else I can't...I can't even make sense of any of it."

"What about that thing you said to Dugas?" Jonathan asks.

"Lord. *Which* thing?"

"What if you find Ryan and they make up and Arthur changes his mind and leaves everything to him?"

"Honestly, at this point, I'd feel better about that."

"*Emily*, you can't be serious! Come on!"

"It's just...it's too much. I don't..."

"Well, if my having sex with you screws with your head so badly that you're going to give up an enormous fortune, I promise to stop immediately."

"I'm going to start carrying a stun gun whenever I'm with you. I swear to God."

"Not my fetish, but thanks."

"It's not mine either."

"Alright, so why not just go to Arthur now and say all this to him? Ask him to take you out of his will... Oh, my God. I need to lie down."

"I've thought about it."

"But instead you agreed to find his son."

"Yes," she answers.

"Okay… Why?"

"Because if Ryan doesn't agree to come back, the least I can do is tell Arthur that he's alive. That he's okay."

"And that'll make you feel better about inheriting his money. Which you apparently don't even want."

"Something like that," she says.

But she's dizzy, and Jonathan's right. Her obsessive belief that she's unworthy of Arthur's fortune has tied her in knots. And the memory of Jonathan's powerful grip on her hips isn't helping her focus.

"Just say what you're thinking, Jonathan. But just, please. Try to say it without making me want to throw you into traffic."

"Also not my fetish," he says.

"Jonathan…"

"You *want* to go, Emily."

"Well, of course, I want to go. I mean, I just got through—"

"No, no, no," Jonathan barks. "I saw your face when Dugas was describing it. You want to know what it is. It's an *experience* and you want to have it. And that's okay. You're allowed, Em. You're allowed to have fantasies and you're allowed to act them out. I know you don't like talking about him, but ever since Charles—"

"Oh, please. *Charles?* Really? We have to drag Charles into this?"

"I'm not *dragging* Charles anywhere. I wouldn't slow down for the guy if I saw him in a crosswalk."

"Alright, come on," Emily mutters. "He wasn't *that* bad. It's not like he cheated on me or something."

"No. He just spent months trying to get you to open up about your fantasies and when you finally did he slammed the door in your face and walked out on you. I can't think of anything worse to do to your partner."

"Jonathan, we'd been dating for less than six months. We weren't *partners.*"

"He was your boyfriend and he punished you for being honest. And Christ, it's not like you flipped out when he told you he got off on some kind of weird Girl Scout role-play with—"

"Alright, alright. I was there. I don't need to relive that part."

"But…what? You go and tell him you fantasize about hospitals and doctors and...what? He just walks out on you?"

Because it wasn't about hospitals or doctors, Emily doesn't say. *I told him about that night on the dance floor with you and that hot dancer you were dating, that night when you both pinned me in between your hard bodies and I wanted the dance to go on for hours after the music stopped, wanted you both to probe and taste and grip and pinch.* But she says none of this to Jonathan. And oddly enough, now that they've actually slept together, now that one half of the fantasy has essentially come true, the omission feels less like a betrayal than it used to.

"Don't run over Charles in a crosswalk. He's not worth it."

"Emily, you don't need permission to live out your fantasies."

"Don't run over Charles in a crosswalk. He's not—"

"Yeah. I got it the first time. I promise. But don't dismiss—"

"I'm not dismissing you, Jonathan, but...."

"But what?"

"Isn't the best part of a fantasy the fact that you don't *have* to live it out?" Emily asks. "Isn't that what makes it a fantasy?"

"I don't know," Jonathan says. Then, in his best impersonation of George Dugas's drawl, he bends forward and says, "Maybe that's one of the questions you'll be forced to answer at *The Desire Exchange.*"

With a broad smile, she extends her hand, and after a few seconds of confusion, Jonathan realizes what she's asking for and returns the glossy photographs of a beautiful young man named Ryan Benoit to her eager grip.

* * * *

Bad idea, Emily thinks, *to let Jonathan drive.*

That morning, when he'd followed her home so she could shower and change clothes before they met with Arthur, she'd been exhausted, under-caffeinated, and grateful to have anyone chauffeur her to Magnolia Gate, let alone the man with whom she'd just spent a night of impossible passion. But she should have known the long ride back to her place would come right at the time when the afterglow would start to dim, leaving them with looming shadows of doubt and worry.

Her apartment is on the second floor of a purple duplex with screened-in front porches on both levels. When Jonathan slows the BMW in front of a driveway clogged by her downstairs neighbor's

SUV, she finds herself at a loss for words. A block away, Bayou St. John's flat, dark surface reflects the wavering halos of the streetlights that line its grassy banks.

"Want me to come up?" Jonathan asks. He sounds nervous, like they're concluding their third date and not their fifteenth year of being best friends.

"I think...I think I need a night to myself, you know, before everything gets crazy."

"*Gets* crazy?"

"Maybe five minutes without sarcasm?"

"Sorry." And he sounds like he means it. "Although, that was actually kinda sarcastic."

"I know. But it'll probably be easier for both of us to hit the mark, if we, you know, take a night off or something. What do you think?"

"Yeah. Okay."

Chastened, he grips the top of the steering wheel with both hands, his jaw working as if he were chewing a piece of gum. But he hates gum. He also hates introspection and limits and rules and anything that encourages him not to follow the dictates of his desire. She's often considered this a fault of his, a side effect of staying in the closet for most of high school, for feeling like the entire world had always told him *no* and for suspect reasons. But before she let him taste her from head to toe, none of this was a real problem. None of it seemed like a threat. Now there are parts of Jonathan—hard edges, hot appetites—that no longer feel contained and removed from the tenderest parts of her heart. And she knows if she's going to make good on her promise to herself, it's her responsibility to get out of the car. Now.

But there's a flutter in her chest, and she can't tell if it's fear, desire, or some new sensation that proves there's often very little difference between the two.

For the first time in twenty-four hours, Jonathan doesn't seem like he's wildly, inexplicably on fire for her. After the silence of their ride across town, he seems just as full of doubt as she is.

"Just say it," he finally whispers.

"What?"

"Whatever you're thinking, just say it. Don't edit. Don't censor. Don't..." He's staring into her eyes now and even though his handsome face is sliced by streetlight glow, there are new possibilities in that stare that would have seemed absurd just a few days before. "It's me, Em. It's *still* me. No matter what happens, it will always still be me."

"Fine...I think there's a switch you know how to turn off, Jonathan. You turn it off with your clients and last night you turned it off with me. And it doesn't make me special or not special. It just...It just means we did what we had to do in that moment. And I'd hate to think that..."

"Hate to think what?"

"I'd hate to think that the only way we could *be* together is if we kept sleeping together. Even if we didn't really want to."

"I don't sleep with people I don't want to sleep with."

"Except your clients."

"They're my clients *because* I choose to sleep with them, Em."

You chose to take their money and then *you chose to sleep with them,* she wants to say. But she knows this is an argument for another night. She knows that Jonathan's attitudes about sex have always been different from her own. He is far better than she is at using the other parts of his body to mend a broken heart. Although, she can't remember the last time his heart has been broken all that badly. Except for maybe Remy, but that was so long ago.

"Alright," she says. "Fine. But I'd hate to think we were just having sex with each other because we've destroyed our friendship."

"Emily, I don't—*what?* I mean, what does that even—"

"It means we keep screwing because we know there's nothing to go back to if we stop, Jonathan. That's what it *means*, okay?"

Why does he look like she's just slapped him? How can he seem so sidelined by this idea? Has he not paused to consider the very possibility himself? Is he truly that progressive, liberated, enlightened—whatever he's calling it this week?

"You really think we've *destroyed* our friendship?" She hates the injured tone in his voice. He sounds half his age suddenly and she feels like some cruel school marm, raining on everyone's parade with her talk of pesky things like probable outcomes and reality.

"I don't know," she says. Now she sounds like the whiny fifteen-year-old.

"So we make a decision that we stay friends, no matter what happens."

"Is it that easy?"

"It is for *me*."

So is being a hooker, she thinks. And then is enormously, epically relieved she didn't say it out loud, so relieved, it drains the sting from her tone when she finally responds, "Don't pin this on me, Jonathan."

"I'm not pinning it on you...I'm just...Maybe you could try something different."

"This is already pretty different, Jonathan."

"No, I mean. Maybe... Maybe it doesn't have to be a relationship as much as, I don't know, an *addition* to what we already have."

"An addition, but not a relationship."

"Right," Jonathan says.

"What does that mean, Jonathan?"

"No labels. No limits. No rules." If these words weren't cheesy enough, the cocky grin and wink he gives her once he's said them makes her feel like she's in a beer commercial.

"Oh, okay. So you still get to sleep with whoever you want and I'm just the token girl at the nonstop sex party that is your life."

The breath goes out of him. His lips sputter. Suddenly he's staring off into space as if she's presented him with some unsolvable math problem, and she's sitting there waiting for him to say something, *anything*, that could convince her the scenario she just described bears no relation to what he's trying, sort-of, to offer her.

"Well, it's not like you've got a bunch of marriage offers on the table," he says, then he sees the expression on her face and suddenly he's saying everything he can think of to stop her response. "Oh. Crap. No. I didn't... Aw, shit, Em—"

"So because nobody wants to marry me right now, I'm supposed to sort of, but not really have an open marriage with you?"

"I didn't mean it like that," he whines.

"How did you mean it?"

Just then, his cell phone rings. Instead of dismissing the call, he studies the screen, and in its harsh glare, she can see his fixed expression. A client, it has to be. Is he calculating a price?

In that instant, she has a mad urge to tell him he never has to turn another trick again. That she'll use her newfound fortune to rescue him from a life of depravity. But there's no evidence of some terrible debt in Jonathan's life he's been working to pay off. Just more cash and prizes, thanks to his extra income. Indeed, it doesn't look like Jonathan turned to escorting out of some kind of desperation. His new and not-so-secret life seems like the next step in a life of constant sexual exploration and adventure.

Can this be true? Or is she being blinded by what Jonathan wants her to see? It wouldn't be the first time, that's for sure. But none of that is relevant to her now.

Jonathan Claiborne has not asked to be rescued. Period. And until he does, she'd better not offer to do so with money she hasn't inherited yet.

"Client?" she asks.

He's about to lie; she can feel it. But instead he shoves the phone back in his pants pocket. "They'll wait."

"Well, don't let me keep you."

"Emily, if I've done anything to hurt our friendship, I'll reboot the last twenty-four hours right here, right now. I'm serious. Nothing's more important to me than that. But...you're wrong."

"About what?"

He reaches out and cups the side of her face tenderly in one hand. But there's a lightness to his touch, a hesitancy, and she can feel a gulf spreading between where they sit now and the things they did to each other the night before.

"I don't have a switch that I can turn off, Em. My switches are always on."

Emily reaches up and grips Jonathan's hand, gently guiding it away from her face, down to the space above the gearshift.

"I know. But mine aren't."

Another noise comes from Jonathan's phone. This time it's the text message tone, probably from the same person who just left him a voice mail.

"Your client awaits," Emily says.

"Maybe he'll let you watch," Jonathan says with a big goofy grin.

"Uh huh," she says, sliding out of the passenger seat and into the humid night air.

"Don't go falling through any more skylights, Emily Blaine. There might not be a swimming pool there to catch you next time."

"Goodnight, Michael," she says, thinking *So much for a sarcasm-free evening.*

When she looks back from her front walk, she sees him smiling at her through the driver's side window.

When they were teenagers and Jonathan first got his license, he made a practice of waiting until she was all the way inside her front door to pull off. But as the years wore on, and Emily started carrying pepper spray in her purse, Jonathan fell out of the habit, often driving away as soon as he saw her keys in her hand, and Emily didn't think much of it. But tonight, for the first time in years, he's waited patiently and like a gentleman to ensure she's well inside her apartment before he leaves.

He waited so long this time she's watching him through the small glass window in her front door when his shiny new BMW finally pulls off into the night.

Of course, she would see him again. How foolish of her to think otherwise. No, that's not the fear that's suddenly chased the breath from her lungs.

Emily is afraid the Jonathan Claiborne she spent the previous night with has, in an instant, become more fantasy than man, a spectral version of her best friend who just passed out of her life as quickly as his BMW left her neighborhood. She's sure he will be replaced by the old version again—goofy and friendly and cheerful, a little too confident in his looks—but she's not sure if that's a good thing, and she wonders how many solitary moments she will spend trying to resurrect the memory of his first hungry and forbidden kiss.

7

Emily dreams of Jonathan.

She stands at the edge of a swimming pool full of writhing human limbs while her best friend is passed from disembodied hand to disembodied hand, like some crowd-surfing kid at a rock concert. Only he's unconscious and nude, his body glistening with some translucence thicker than water.

And then someone's banging on her front door. Half-asleep, and half-convinced it's the real Jonathan, beaten and bloodied by some terrible client, Emily opens her front door, but whoever it is, he's pounding on the door at the base of the inside stairs that lead to her second floor apartment. Relieved that whoever it is hasn't broken into her duplex, she stumbles down the chilly steps, clutching the hem of her oversized T-shirt to the side of her waist.

The door's not open an inch before a tide of shadow rises before her and Emily thinks. *Is this my test? Already?* Then she's slammed against the sidewall of her building, a powerful arm clamped around her chest. In that moment, she's convinced George Dugas is a liar and a murderer and she's stupidly walked everyone she cares about into some giant deadly trap.

"You're dead, Emily Blaine," a male voice says in her ear. The voice is accent-less and psycho calm. "Reckless, trusting, and *dead.*"

She tries to scream. There's no hand covering her mouth, after all. That's when she realizes her captor has applied equal parts pressure to her chest and throat, turning her cry into a dry, breathless wheeze.

"Don't scream," he says. But how he says it is the way someone would say, *Don't touch that stove*. And he's let up the pressure on her throat.

Suddenly she's free. She rocks forward on her heels, thinking surely his other arm had her pinned somewhere. But he's walking up the dark stairs toward the apartment door she left standing open behind her, back to her, as bored with her now as he was intent to choke her just a few seconds before.

"Burglar alarm?"

"Who the fu—*hell* are you?"

"Drop as many F-bombs as you want, Miss Blaine. Whatever'll make you remember not to poke your head out of the front door at one in the morning like a chicken about to get—" He makes a swift, axe-falling motion with one flat hand.

Breathless and half-dressed, Emily is still standing outside the front door to her apartment, as if her name was no longer on the lease. The guy's all shadow, but he looks incredibly tall. He's also one flight of stairs above her now, staring down at her from the top step.

"Burglar alarm?" he asks again.

She's got a dozen furious remarks cycling through her head, but she's too frightened and breathless to manage anything other than a shake of her head.

"We'll have one installed tomorrow," he says. Then he turns and vanishes into the shadows.

Emily expects to find the guy sitting at her kitchen table, feet propped on the table, beer open beside him. But there's no such cockiness on display when she steps back inside her apartment. Instead, the tall stranger is checking the windows, throwing the old, paint-flecked locks, opening each one a few inches to test the smoothness of its glide.

"Did Arthur send you?" she finally says, hating the stammer in her voice.

"He's Mr. Benoit to me, but yeah. I'm your shadow now. *His* words."

"There was a better way to do this, you know. You didn't have to—"

In what seems like one motion, he hits the switch on the nearest lamp and turns to face her. She's not sure what's sidelined her more:

his hard-edged intensity or the fact that he's a Nordic god in form-fitting black jeans and a hooded sweater. His face is all hard ridges and angles except for his generous, full-lipped mouth, which makes him look like he's either about to snarl at her or kiss her, she can't tell which. And she can't tell which one she'd like more.

"You scared?" he barks.

"What?"

"Right now. Are you scared? Shaking? Can't decide if you want to run screaming from the room or break my frickin' nose?"

"*Yes.*"

"Good. Then you'll remember this moment for the rest of your life, and you'll never throw open your door for a stranger at one in the morning again. *Ever.*"

Having delivered this unforgiving pronouncement, and with no regard for whatever reaction might be written on her face, the guy returns to the task of checking her windows. She's tempted to comment that if he's going to be her shadow, he might want to consider not pacing her apartment loud enough to wake her downstairs neighbors, but she's pretty sure the joke won't go over well.

"Own any weapons?" he asks from the kitchen. "Knives, guns."

"Kitchen knives and pepper spray. That's it."

"Good. If you're not well trained on them, an assailant will just use them against you."

"You know, it's not that dangerous, what we're doing. It's not like—"

"It's not my job to know what you're doing or what you're involved in."

"Well, if you're going to be my *shadow*, it's going to be kind of hard *not* to know, isn't it?"

When she enters the kitchen, he's frozen in front of her sink. But he's staring over one shoulder in her direction. His startled expression suggests he's not used to being spoken to in this way by a woman half his size, a woman shifting nervously from one foot to another, wearing only a baggy night shirt and no bra, a woman who is, despite her best efforts, gazing at the hard swells of his chest underneath his black T-shirt, wondering if he's the kind of man for whom anger is just a hop, skip, and a jump away from arousal.

"It's not like I'm going to watch you in the shower, Emily Blaine."

His voice gets hoarse when it gets quiet, and even though it only lasts a second, the time it takes his eyes to sweep her body leaves trails of gooseflesh up the front of her half-exposed thighs. She feels a sudden, strange stab of guilt, as if these lustful thoughts about her intruder amount to cheating on Jonathan.

She reminds herself that Jonathan is her best friend, and that his last offer wasn't anything close to what she'd call a real relationship.

Also, he's gay.

Then she reminds herself the man before her is a colossal jerk and all she really wants to do is go back to sleep. (Provided she can manage to have a less disturbing dream this time.)

"So you're, like, from a private security company or something?" she asks.

"I've worked for Arthur for three years."

"Well, I haven't seen you."

"That's because it wasn't my job for you to see me."

"But now it is?" she asks.

He turns the knob on the backdoor and the door opens in his light grip.

"Woops."

"You didn't mean to leave this unlocked?"

"Downstairs one's probably still locked."

"Still. This is Mid City, not Chateau Estates."

"Yeah, well, technically I'm still a restaurant manager, not a spy."

"We're talking about intruders, not assassins."

"I get it."

"You *don't* get it. You have a smart mouth that makes people think you get it. It might even make *you* think you get it. But it won't mean squat when you're in a dangerous situation."

"And what do you rely on? Shock and awe?" *And lips, and that jawline, and those biceps and that…brawn.* That's the word that keeps strobing through her head. It's rare that she meets a man who truly personifies it, but that's what this guy has. *Brawn.* She slaps herself, silently, on the inside, without lifting a hand, and tells herself she's just sexualizing the guy to distract herself from her fear, from the loss of control she felt when he threw her up against the wall outside.

Bullcrap. She's sexualizing the guy because he's sexy.

"You're getting a burglar alarm tomorrow," he says.

"Can't wait."

"Your attitude will be your responsibility."

"Good, then I assume you'll stop having such a big opinion about it."

Even in the kitchen's harsh overhead light, his face looks sculpted by a master. And his eyes are blue, with lots of white that give them a focused, slightly wild gleam.

"Whatever you're doing, Miss Blaine, *you* may not think it's dangerous, but Arthur Benoit does. That's why he assigned me to you."

"I see that."

"I'm just saying, he's not a stupid man. And he's scared. Maybe you should be too."

It feels like the first honest moment they've had together, and the way the man's eyes suddenly cut from her feet, to the front door, to the far wall, suggest he doesn't have honest moments with strange women often. But given how many times she's probably driven past him while he watched her from one of the guardhouses at Magnolia Gate, can he really consider her a stranger?

"What about Jonathan?" she asks.

"He's got a shadow too."

"Well, I hope the shadow's a bottom," she whispers.

"Huh?"

"Nothing," she says with a smile.

But he looks nervous and insecure suddenly, maybe because he just failed the test she put to him. She didn't say who Jonathan actually was, didn't mention they were working together—if that's what you could call it—and he gave her the information quickly, without pause. *Maybe you've been as thrown off guard by me as I've been by you, Mister...*

"Marcus," he says suddenly, as if he's been reading her mind. "Marcus Dylan."

"Emily Blaine."

"I know."

She cracks up suddenly. Marcus responds with the closest version of a smile she's probably going to get out of him for a while—one cocked eyebrow and a tense spot in the corner of his mouth. "What's so funny?"

"Nothing, just the thought of my gay friend being tailed by some hot mercenary type. I'm sure Jonathan's devastated."

"Yeah, well, who says the other guy's hot?"

Now he's the one smiling. Because she just called him hot

without intending to. And now she's blushing all over and she feels like pulling the hem of her nightshirt down and folding her shoulders in toward each other, but instead she watches Marcus Dylan wet his lips with the tip of his tongue and scan her from head to toe. He takes a deep breath and she hopes it's because the sight of her ample curves has filled his head with thoughts he's trying to suppress.

"Besides," Marcus finally says. "I saw you two earlier. He sure looked like more than your *gay* friend."

"Huh. How long have you been tailing me?"

"Since Benoit called me in this afternoon. Picked you guys up at that coffee house on Magazine. Where he also looked like a lot more than your *gay* friend."

"Well," she manages, her cheeks aflame, "he probably looks super gay to whoever's tailing him now. That's all I'm saying."

"Uh huh. Well, just so you know, we're not a messenger service."

"What does *that* mean, Prince Charming?"

"I mean I won't be using my colleague to tell you what Jonathan's up to, and whether or not he's, you know, acting...*gay.*"

"Right, 'cause you're too busy letting me know that Jonathan's also being *shadowed* and your colleague is the one doing it."

The last time Emily was this satisfied by the shocked expression on someone's face it was when a drunken customer found himself being ejected from the restaurant for reaching out and smacking her on the butt every time she passed near his table.

"If you don't want to be so easily distracted, Marcus, maybe you should try frightening women when they have more clothes on."

He's closing the distance between them suddenly. Her heart skips a beat, but in a frightening, *is this an aneurysm and do I have all of my affairs in order?* kind of way. When he takes her right hand in his, his touch feels both hurried and clinical. Then he's sliding a plain gold ring, almost like an engagement band, onto her ring finger. "It's heat activated. You make a fist three times in a row, ten seconds each, and I'll be here in thirty seconds."

"What if I have to take it off?"

"You *don't* have to take it off. It's waterproof."

"What's the range?"

"The northern hemisphere."

"Seriously?"

"The range is what I need it to be. You *don't* take it off, Emily Blaine. Got it?"

Apparently, Marcus Dylan is distracted again, but he's staring into her eyes with what looks like an angry, disciplinary glare. The only problem is he's forgotten to release her hand, and together, their entwined fingers have started drifting out to one side, as if they're about to start waltzing. He lets her hand go and takes a step back.

"If it's heat activated, why isn't it going off right now?" she asks.

"It's activated by a temperature differential. Hence, the fist. Three times."

"Okay."

He's headed for the door. He's in a hurry now, nervously trying to put distance between them. Or maybe this is all just part of his *float like a butterfly, sting like a soldier of fortune* approach to busting in and out of apartments in the middle of the night?

"Goodnight, Marcus."

"Uh huh."

He's halfway down the steps when she calls out to him.

"The alarm. What time should I be ready?"

"I'll text you."

"Okay. Just give me enough time to get dressed, that's all."

The shadows on the stairs are too deep to see his expression, but from the angle of his head she can tell there's a few seconds of hesitation before he heads off into the night. Then she remembers he's not going very far at all and wonders if it's possible to feel both safe and violated at the same time. Possible or not, it sounds like something Jonathan's clients might pay top dollar for.

8

Emily can't pull up to Arthur Benoit's grand mansion without seeing her father striding down the front walk, his stiff security guard pose cracking under his excitement at seeing his only daughter. But with each visit, the memory gets dimmer and she has to work harder to recreate his half-smile, his bright-eyed gaze, and the way he'd throw the front gate open with one stubby but powerful arm, never once taking his eyes off his daughter until she was safely in his embrace.

Those were the days when all the guards at Magnolia Gate were handpicked by her dad, most of them former N.O.P. D. officers like him. They were good men, for the most part, all of them happy to have a cushy alternative to the culture of lousy pay and rampant corruption that defined the police department where they all met.

But now the guards who watch over Arthur and his estate are mostly icy, ex-Navy SEAL types, like her new shadow, Marcus Dylan. And when they see her familiar green Camry, they nod without smiling, probably because they know she's more than just a visitor. In a few weeks or a few months—no one really knows—this short, smart-mouthed young woman, a restaurant manager with an English degree that makes her vaguely employable—will become their boss. Perhaps the idea seems as absurd to them as it does to her.

She wouldn't know. The guards barely say a word to her. Or to anyone, for that matter.

Now that she's under the watchful eyes of his colleagues, Marcus has slowed the black Lincoln Navigator in which he followed her across town.

The half-circle of a street used to be lined with five massive residences before Arthur bought them up one by one. Of the old houses, only two are left, both perfectly restored, two-story Greek Revivals, with blue and yellow pastel paint jobs that make them look like brassier, younger sisters to the antebellum palace that is the main house. In any other neighborhood, these two smaller houses would be considered mansions, but here on Chatham Circle, they are dwarfed by the grandeur of Magnolia Gate.

Within each one, in rooms cosseted by lush custom draperies and Oriental carpets, Arthur Benoit's legal team and financial advisors work side-by-side, conducting with the disarming gentility of a bygone era business more suited to the offices of a downtown skyscraper. On any given day, Arthur's staff is more likely to send her a handwritten note than a text message.

High above Magnolia Gate's long, flat roof, the interlocking oak branches entwine so harmoniously they always seem as if they've been positioned just so by a giant hand moments before Emily's arrival. At various times throughout the day, the great trees have the same filtering effect as a stained glass window, and the swirls of pollen and brief rains of blossoms appear electrified by the shafts of golden light.

The front porch is a vast arcade lined with fat Doric columns. Its ceiling is painted sky blue, an old device for tricking insects out of nesting there. Enormous ferns spill from hanging brass planters, and there's enough wicker furniture to fill several living rooms in the Jefferson Parish neighborhood where Emily grew up.

Emily tries to take it all in without thinking *mine, mine, mine* over and over again like one of the seagulls from *Finding Nemo*. Because she suspects, even after she inherits it, none of this will ever feel like it truly belongs to her. It will always feel like she's living in a museum of Arthur Benoit's life. And maybe that's not such a bad thing. Maybe seeing things that way will help keep the infinite potential of Arthur's vast fortune from going to her head.

She is expecting to meet privately with Larissa Danneel, one of Arthur's most trusted attorneys, so she's shocked to see Arthur waiting for her in the dining room, alone, his wheelchair pushed to the far head of the twelve-person dining table. Through the wall of French doors, concrete steps lead down to a vast, flagstone patio terminating in a rectangular swimming pool with a dark, stone-colored bottom. The view is lovely but the light streaming through the glass falls harshly upon Arthur's bloodshot eyes and blotchy, pale skin.

When she kisses him on the cheek, he manages a weak smile, then he pushes a fat brown envelope across the table toward her with one talon-like hand.

Her new identity.

When she tears it open, a passport and driver's license slide to the hardwood, followed by a clatter of credit cards. She sits and flips through them slowly, as if they were each endowed with a particular heat. Their authenticity is astonishing.

"Lily Conran," she says.

"You are the owner of several paper mills throughout the Gulf South and even though they're barely profitable, you've invested wisely over the years. Wisely enough to own a beautiful house right on the beach in Destin. Which is where you'll be living when Mr. Dugas makes his reference." Arthur lifts a larger manila envelope from his lap to the table. "Here are the details you'll need to play the part convincingly."

"You own the paper mills?"

"In a manner of speaking. They'll be sold as soon as this business is over."

"And the house in Destin?"

"A friend's rental. Not much of a connection to me. On paper, anyway."

"Do I own the paper mills or does Lily?"

"Lily."

"Who doesn't technically exist."

"That's correct."

"Is *any* of this legal?"

"Not a whit."

She nods.

"Getting cold feet?" he asks.

She wants to tell him that her cold feet have nothing to do with The Desire Exchange, and everything to do with their sparkling, palatial surroundings. But first she checks the doorways and her view of the adjacent hall; they're all empty. No sign of the ever-present team of housekeepers, or the nurses who have joined their ranks in recent months. Arthur has cleared the house for this secret meeting, which in his current state entails some risk.

"At least I'll have protection," she finally manages.

"So you've met Marcus?"

"Indeed. He's a charmer."

"Yes, well, charm school is not where they teach you how to blast your way into a terrorist hideout."

"So he's seen combat?"

"He's seen a great many things he's not at liberty to discuss. As I imagine you will too. Soon. Nowhere near as violent, of course...I hope."

"Marcus seems to bring a touch of violence wherever he goes, so..."

"So I'm sensing your first meeting didn't go so well."

"He's very direct. I'll say that much for him."

"So are you, Emily. So was your father. That's why I valued his advice."

"I'm not sure Dad would have known which paper mills to buy and sell."

I'm not sure how he would have felt about me infiltrating a sex club to find your long-lost son either, so let's not tell any Ouija boards, okay?

"No, but he knew which men had character and which men had only the illusion of it. And at times, he was willing to point out when I had...*lapsed* into the latter category, if you will."

Even for a man who has become something close to her surrogate father, this is a startling admission, and Emily can't help but wonder if it's the result of whatever medications he's been given that day. His eyes have wandered to the empty head chair at the opposite end of the long table. "I'm sorry you and Marcus aren't getting on," he says, but he sounds distracted. His words have returned to the present but his tone and his gaze can't quite make the trip. "But I think you'll find some common ground...at some point..."

"Common ground?" she asks.

"I think you'll get along eventually is what I'm trying to say," he says quickly, adjusting the blanket across his lap.

"Did you pick him yourself?"

"Oh, no. He picked you."

"What does *that* mean?"

"It means he was overheard making some...*choice* comments about you after one of your visits."

"*Choice?*"

"Suggestive."

Don't blush, she orders herself, but she feels a surge of both desire and relief to know she wasn't imagining the sexual tension in her apartment last night. The last thing she wants to be is that woman who goes around trying to convince everyone that the whole world is just dying to sleep with her. People only buy it if you're Angelina Jolie, and she's not Angelina Jolie.

"And so you thought it would be a good idea for him to be my security guard?" she asks.

"You know, Emily, personally I don't buy into all that nonsense about emotional detachment being the key to success. Sometimes we do our best work when we're trying to protect something we really care about."

"I'm not sure I'd call suggestive comments—"

"Oh, come now. You know what I mean."

"I certainly know why he felt the need to bust in on me when I was in my underwear and give me a lesson in personal security."

"Did you mind?"

I could have done without the windpipe action, she thinks.

"Where's Jonathan?" she asks.

"I had Larissa meet with him at his apartment and give him his...*documents* there."

"I see..."

"What? What do you *see*, Emily?" The sight of a wry smile on Arthur's wasting face is such a welcome sight it brings a smile to Emily's face as well.

"God, you're good. No wonder you're so rich."

"I beg your pardon?" he asks, playing coy.

"When we were here yesterday, you could tell. You could tell that something happened between us."

"The energy between you two was...*different*, that's for sure."

"I see..."

"So something has indeed *happened* between you two, has it?"

"It's a...moment, that's all. We'll get past it."

"But things are essentially alright between you two, aren't they?"

"Of course. There's no reason not to let him go with me if that's what you're—"

"No, no, of course not," he says so quickly that she knows it was exactly what he was asking. "But...let's just say I'm not very confident in Jonathan's ability to ensure your safety. Emotionally, perhaps. But not physically. That's why I've involved Marcus."

"And because he made suggestive comments about me in the

guardhouse."

"Let's call them admiring comments. How does that sound?"

"Like a reach, but I'll go with it. For now."

Arthur's smile fades. He rests his clasped hands against his dry lips while he studies her. The intensity of his gaze lights hairs on the back of her neck. "Your father was always concerned about your relationship with Jonathan, you know? He feared you two *hid out* in one another. That's how he put it."

"Yeah, well, Dad had a learning curve when it came to the gays."

"Perhaps, but these concerns were more recent than that."

"He never said anything to me."

"I know. But still…he was afraid the two of you didn't quite extend yourself as far out into the world as you should have because you always knew you'd have each other."

"Our friendship's a crutch. Is that what you're saying?"

"It's what your father said. And I'd hate to see you brought down by a moment of confusion, Emily. Jonathan's. Or yours." Arthur's words are hard to swallow. She's heard some version of them for most of her adult life, but usually from her girlfriends after they've had one too many. Not from a man of Arthur's stature and maturity and intimate knowledge of her background.

"So Marcus is supposed to *unconfuse* me, is that it?"

Arthur spreads his hands in a gesture of supplication and gives her his best wide smile. She can't help but laugh.

"I thought perhaps they could bring us a bite to eat," he says quickly, studying the empty table in front of him as if expecting a bowl of gumbo to suddenly appear before him. "Then, perhaps you could stay a while and we could take a walk around the grounds. Have some tea. I know you love tea. And—" But just listing these activities seems to have exhausted Arthur past the point of being able to execute any of them. And Emily can see his sudden nervousness for what it is.

She reaches across the space between them, closes her hand over his. "You'll be here when I come back with your son, Arthur. You'll be here and you'll be up and around and you'll have the chance to say everything you need to say to him. I promise."

His eyes are moist and he brings his left hand down to rest atop the one she's placed across his right one. "I've never been a man who's had to rely on people's promises until now," he whispers.

9

When Emily hears the siren above the shower's rush, she assumes police cars are speeding past her duplex in the direction of the bayou. Then there's a terrible crash in the kitchen, followed by the unmistakable sounds of a scuffle.

She does the math instantly. Forty-eight hours of answering Jonathan's voice mails with dismissive texts plus a brand new burglar alarm divided by one soldier of fortune who claims his only job is to watch her everywhere but the shower equals the current chaos outside her bathroom door.

I'm so not rushing for this, she thinks. But she towels herself off in half the time she usually takes, if only because neither one of the Ultimate Fighters in the kitchen has decided it's a good idea to kill the screaming alarm. Her towel tucked across the top of her breasts, she flips her still damp hair behind both bare shoulders and throws open the bathroom door with the stiff upper lip she's seen on celebrities appearing in court on a DUI charge.

By the time she enters the kitchen, Marcus has Jonathan pinned to the linoleum with one hand around his wrist and a knee against his lower back.

"How 'bout I put out some oil so you boys can make this a real fight?" she shouts over the alarm, and then thinks, *Wow. That idea sounds a lot hotter than I—Turn off the alarm, Emily.*

When the siren dies, she turns to face her dueling suitors.

Jonathan is pulling a Linda Blair in his attempt to get an eyeful of the tower of aggression and muscle bearing down on him.

Through gritted teeth, Marcus says, "Didn't feel like telling him about the alarm, huh?"

"And you didn't recognize him?" Emily asks.

"I recognize him now," Marcus says.

"How come yours is hot?" Jonathan whines. "Mine's not hot."

Marcus shakes his head and gets to his feet. Emily studies the man's face for the slightest hint of homophobic disgust. But there isn't any. He looks bored and detached, as if Jonathan is just a noisy child running in between tables at a fancy restaurant and she's the negligent mother who set him free.

Then Marcus looks at her. Finally she sees a flicker of anticipation and desire that confirms what Arthur revealed to her during their last meeting.

It's about time, she thinks. Marcus resisted even polite attempts at conversation when she approached him outside Perry's yesterday morning after she gave her two weeks' notice. Same deal outside the drug store that afternoon. Never once looking her in the eye, probably to avoid giving her the look he's giving her now.

"Actually, I'm fine, thanks for asking," Jonathan says sharply, sitting up now. "No bruises or anything."

"Relax," Emily says. "It's nothing your clients haven't done to you ten times over."

"Emily! Not in front of the *boy*."

Marcus says, "The code is 5542. Don't give it to any of your clients."

"Where's *your* guy?" Emily asks Jonathan.

"Dupuy? He's outside. Enjoying the hell out of this, I'm sure. He's got a sick sense of humor. You should see some of the videos on his phone."

"Sounds like you two are getting along better than…" Emily loses her nerve before she can complete the comment.

"Better than what?" Marcus asks quietly.

Jonathan gives up on the idea of either of them helping him to his feet. He enlists the side of the kitchen table in the task instead.

"Note to file, Rambo," Jonathan begins. "If y—"

"*Rambo?*" Marcus snaps. "When was the last time you went to the movies? 1983?"

"I like this guy, Emily," Jonathan says with a bright smile. "Do you like this guy? What do you say? How 'bout we both...*like* this guy?"

Before a quiver of desire can finish its dance up her spine, before she too vividly recalls the feel of Jonathan and his flavor of the month pressing their hard bodies against her on that long ago, but oft remembered, night on the dance floor, Emily clears her throat and focuses her attention on the target of Jonathan's—unwanted, she assumes—antics.

Marcus smiles. "You're not my type," he says.

"Oh, yeah. Why's that?" Jonathan asks.

"Too much balls."

Well, at least somebody's *sexuality is easy to figure out right now*, she thinks.

Jonathan laughs louder than he would if someone who didn't look like Thor's hotter younger brother had made the same joke. When he sees Emily's glare, his cackles come to an abrupt halt. "So what name did they give you?" he asks her.

"I'm not sure we should be discussing everything—"

"Oh, come on. Just tell me so I can be mad. Mine *sucks*."

"Lily Conran."

"*Lily Conran?*" Jonathan wails. "I'm *Leonard Miller*. You sound like you should be buying diamonds in South Africa and I sound like some douche who should be selling crap watches at the Esplanade Mall."

"Are you drunk?"

"A little, yeah."

"Apparently you had a note for our files," she says.

"Yeah, so this little test The Exchange is going to spring on us? It's gonna be a surprise, in every sense of the word. As in it might involve dark shadows that don't know about burglar alarms. What I'm saying is the thing probably won't go so well if you're on a hair trigger, Rambo. So I don't know. Maybe less Red Bull or something? Unless you want us to fail or get shot or both. I'm going out on a limb here and guessing that sex cults aren't that interested in people with fresh bullet holes, even if they do have tons of cash on them."

"Wait," Emily says. "You *spoke* to Dugas about this? When?"

"Last night."

"And you didn't tell anyone?"

"Uhm, I *was* going to tell you, if you'd bothered to return my calls with anything besides emoticons you haven't used on me since high school." Jonathan pops open the refrigerator door and helps himself to a Corona. "And one more thing. Handbells!"

"*Handbells?*" Emily asks.

"Yeah. Apparently that's the signal. That the test is about to begin."

"Handbells," Emily says again. The last time she ever saw a handbell was when she was dragged to her aunt's fancy Episcopal church as a little girl. Her memory of white-gloved rich kids waving polished brass handbells through the air in front of them doesn't quite fit with her depraved imaginings of what The Desire Exchange might turn out to be.

"Oh, and also, since, you know, everything's out in the open now, I have a strict escort-client privilege policy. Unless you're in the room with us. And last night, you were *not* in the room with us, Emily Blaine." Before she can ask him not to, he punches the cap off the beer bottle using the side of the counter and the side of one fist. "You were probably in *this* room. With *this* guy."

"Marcus, if you could excuse—"

"Or maybe *that* room," Jonathan says, gesturing toward her bedroom door with the beer bottle.

"Marcus, could you please give us a moment alone so I can beat Jonathan to death with my shoes."

"You're not wearing shoes," Marcus says quietly. His eyes tally everything else she's not wearing as he brushes past her and heads for the front door.

Once they're alone, Emily pulls the bottle from Jonathan's hand and takes a long slug.

"Cut it out," she says quietly.

"Cut what out?"

"You're being weird. And kind of a jerk." She's said it as quietly and as casually as she can. But it stung him—that much is clear. And when she gives him back his beer, he tugs it from her grip with just a touch more force than necessary.

"You're my best friend," he says, "and for forty-eight hours you've been treating me like a mistake. How's that for weird?"

"I'm sorry," she whispers.

"Are you?"

"Am I your best friend?"

"Of course you are."

"And that's all?"

"Why aren't you a lawyer? I swear to God—"

"I'm just saying, 'cause the other night you wanted more. You were offering more. I mean, I think you were. When I tried to interpret your offer, you didn't like what I said. So if I'm wrong, tell me now. Make your offer."

"I can't offer you something I don't have a name for," Jonathan whispers.

"Come on, you have a name for it! It's what you do for a living now."

"They're *not* the same thing and you know it."

He brushes past her, pulls a chair out from the table, and throws himself into it with enough force to suggest what he'd rather be doing is slamming the back door several times in a row, maybe tossing his beer bottle down the back steps. But that's not Jonathan Claiborne's style and never has been. But neither is bearing his heart. Now that he's about to do it, she's more frightened than when she fell face-first through the skylight and landed in the middle of his secret assignation.

Does she really know him as well as she thinks she does? If there's a different Jonathan hiding under the clever one-liners and sexual bravado, will he surprise her as much as the one who made love to her the other night?

It takes all of her self-control, but Emily forces herself to join him at the tiny kitchen table, forces herself to watch him as he traces one finger around the lip of the beer bottle and gazes at the wall as if it's collapsed and given way to an expanse of dark memory.

"With me," Emily finally says. "Did it feel different than being with a guy?"

"Of course it did."

"Better? Worse?"

"Different. Different from everyone. For the first time in my life, I had good sex with someone I actually cared about. You can't blame me for being a little messed up, okay?"

Emily's entire body warms, a stronger heat than the one she felt when George Dugas casually unveiled her naked body. "Come on," she whispers, because a whisper is the best she can do. "You know that's not true."

"Isn't it?" he asks.

"Remy..." she says, and it's all she has to say. The memory of Jonathan's first true love fills the space between them—perpetually smiling, cherubic Remy, with his infectious laugh and his wicked sense of humor.

"We were just kids, Emily," Jonathan mutters, but he pulls hard on his Corona, swallowing so much beer at once his next breath sounds like a startled gasp.

To bring up Remy in this context feels as risky as everything else the two of them have done to their friendship over the past few days. She can't even mention the guy's name without remembering the suicide note he left for Jonathan at his bedside. *Can't. Sorry. Love you, always—R.*

"I've never seen you look at anyone the way you used to look at him," she says.

"We were *kids*," he says again. This time, there's a quaver in his voice.

"Teenagers, not kids. And what matters is you were too young to talk yourselves out of how you really felt about each other."

"So you think the way I felt about Remy back then is proof that I'm gay? Always and forever?"

"I know you're gay. I don't need proof."

"Gosh. Was I *that* terrible?"

She's tempted to play along, to match him joke for joke and steer them back to calmer waters. But there's a moment here, she's sure of it. A chance to speak a truth she's never voiced to him before, and if the frenzy of pleasure they gave each other has made that possible, then maybe this whole episode in their lives, in their friendship, will be worth something more than confused longing.

"You didn't kill Remy by loving him, Jonathan. Your love has never killed anyone and it never will. Give yourself permission to love people you actually care about. You deserve it."

He blinks rapidly enough to stop the threat of tears, but there's a catch in his voice when he speaks again. "People like you?" he asks.

"No. Men with Remy's laugh, with his eyes. Men who hang on your every word the way he used to. Me? I'd just be this comfortable little corner you'd come back to again and again after you lived out your sexual fantasies with more men who don't matter to you as much as Remy did. As much as he could have if he hadn't..."

"Are you giving up on me, Emily Blaine?"

There's no holding back the tears now. It's fitting, she thinks, or a cruel irony that when Jonathan Claiborne cries, he looks fourteen again.

Emily gets to her feet and pads barefoot across the linoleum. She wraps her arms around him as best she can without letting her towel fall to the floor. When she feels no resistance from him, when his giant, muscular body melts backward into her embrace, some tension inside of her releases.

"I'd walk through fire for you, Jonathan Claiborne. Even if it was only to get you a beer."

She can't tell if he's shaking with laughter or sobs or a mixture of both. After a while she lets him go, and he spins around in the chair to face her, eyes bloodshot and moist, but a huge smile screwed onto his face, and one pinky extended.

"Friends till the end?" he asks brightly.

"Friends till the end," she says, then wraps her pinky around his. "With our clothes *on*."

"Deal," he says, but he looks away from her quickly and pushes himself to his feet. "But don't expect me to drop my clients anytime soon. I'm makin' a *fortune*, girlfriend!"

Before she has time to react, he's sprung into her bathroom. The door is closed and the faucet is running before she can point out to him that she's actually the one who isn't dressed.

So far they have passed the test she has set up for them both, but that fact doesn't make sleep any easier. Emily is wide awake, watching the rise and fall of Jonathan's back in bed next to her, trying not to recall the feel of its hard ridges beneath her grasping sweaty, palms.

The boxers and T-shirts they're both wearing don't match exactly, but they're pretty close. And in the glow of the bedside clock, Jonathan's profile is a play of shadows and pale green shapes.

The desire is still there, of course, awake and stirring like a nervous cat at the foot of the bed. But in time it will settle, she's sure. Maybe after another night or two like this, another night of lying next to him, fully clothed, their bodies inches apart but not touching, the memory of their insane and reckless coupling losing its glisten and luster and dangerous invitation with each passing, sleepless hour.

She should be grateful they're able to return to this chaste and secure place that calls to mind the sleepovers of their teenage and early college years. But a part of her that's caught between fear and longing expects Jonathan to roll over at any moment, bring his mouth to her neck and his fingers to her sex, and his whispers to her heart.

Lucky, she tells herself. She can feel her lips move against the pillow. She hopes she hasn't whispered the words aloud. *What we did was stupid, dangerous, and we're here together in this bed and we're still okay. And that makes us lucky, any way you look at it.*

There's a buzz and a flash of light next to her, a new text message. From an unfamiliar number. The messages just prior to it, a curt back and forth between her and Marcus about scheduling the burglar alarm install two days before.

he spending the night?

Emily responds:

yes...but not like that.

none of my biz, comes the response. **just don't want him surprising me again.**

or vice versa, she writes back.

Where is Marcus? Is he parked outside? Across the street? Perched inside the back door?

true

So now he's chatting with me, she thinks. The guy who could barely look her in the eye a few hours before is now sharing casual observations with her via text message.

thank you, she writes.

for what?

Good question, she thinks.

for keeping me safe.

A second ticks by, then another, then another, and she figures he will simply ignore this moment of kindness.

no thanks necessary

Oh, you charmer, Marcus Dylan. I bet that line worked on all the Al-Qaeda girls.

do you ever get to sleep? She writes back.

not big on sleep.

I see...

do you?

no. but maybe you'll tell me.

maybe...maybe not.

why not?

I don't want you to sleep as badly as I do.

yikes.

yeah, kinda.

Her finger hovers above her phone's screen, but she's got no clue what to write next, just a burning urge to say something, anything, that will make Marcus invite her to his late-night post, wherever that might be. But that feels like she'd be cheating at this test she's set up for the the two of them, her and Jonathan. And God knows, she hates it when men use her as a distraction; she imagines Marcus would feel the same way.

Just then, there's a stirring beside her. Jonathan's arm slides across her chest like a giant, drowsy snake, forcing her to set the phone down gently on the nightstand. She rolls over onto one side, allowing Jonathan to spoon against her back. But the phone's screen still glows, Marcus's last message staring out at her. It's not a question, but it feels unanswered. She reaches for the phone with one arm, doing her best not to wake Jonathan, doing her best not to monitor every stirring, real or imagined, in his groin.

goodnight marcus dylan, she types, slowly, cautiously, with one finger on the hand she's gripping the side of the phone with.

A few seconds later comes his response.

sweet dreams emily blaine

10

It feels final and she doesn't want it to.

If Emily hadn't hopped out of the car, the two of them wouldn't have ended up standing on the curb together like lovers reluctant to part, the taxis and airport shuttles a steady, bleating river beside them while she fumbled for the best good-bye. But whatever they needed to say to each other, she didn't want to say it in front of Marcus. So here they are; she in her jeans and polo, and Jonathan in his brand new sage-colored poplin suit and navy blue tie.

Given that he's only an hour flight away from his temporary home, he's decided to get into character early by dressing the part of Leonard Miller, dapper trust fund baby and only son of a nonexistent widow who has been living in the south of France for a decade. Emily's got about five hours in the car with Marcus before she reaches Lily Conran's beach house. Six, if you add the stop off in Pensacola to pick up the brand new car Arthur just had registered to the nonexistent paper mill heiress.

"So if we pass our little tests," Emily asks, "what happens then?"

"I don't know. We regroup? Come back here? Or maybe stay in our fake lives for a while so we don't arouse suspicion. I figure we'll get our instructions once we pass...*if* we pass. Anyway, Dugas says we should be fine."

"You told him the plan?"

"Well, it's really *his* plan, Em. Remember? He's the one who suggested fake identities. Something in keeping with their usual clientele. Wasn't that how he put it?"

"Something like that, yeah."

"Once we're settled, Dugas meets with them to see if we've been approved."

"And then how long do we have to wait for our test?"

"Dugas says they'll show up on our doorstep within forty-eight hours."

Travel time, she thinks, hoping this won't be the last time she can channel her father's investigative skills. *Forty-eight hours is plenty of time to plan a last-minute trip, provided you're in North America.*

"Are we're sure it's our doorstep they show up on?"

"They come at night. When we're alone. So..." He cuts his eyes toward the idling Navigator a few feet away. "...Make sure you're alone. For those forty-eight hours at least."

Just beside the sliding doors to the terminal, Jonathan's shadow, a stubby Iraq war vet named Frank Dupuy, scans their surroundings with almost imperceptible jerks of his neck. He is the opposite of Marcus Dylan, a younger, stockier version of Cliff Clavin from *Cheers.* When Emily first saw the contrast between the two men, she almost burst out laughing. Not because she thought anyone's appearance should subject them to ridicule, but because everything about Frank Dupuy made it clear Arthur Benoit didn't want Jonathan sleeping with his new bodyguard. (Although, if Arthur's plan was to truly keep Jonathan and Emily from getting *confused* again, he should have tried a dual-track approach and set Jonathan up with a protector who looked like an Olympic gymnast.)

"Why am I scared?" she asks him.

"I don't know. Maybe Arthur's the one nerving us out here. What with the guards and the black cars..."

"This is his last shot to find his son, Jonathan. *He's* the one who's nerved out."

"The guards are a risk then. If these people get wind of them, they might bolt and then there's no shot of finding Ryan at all."

"What are you saying?"

"I'm saying Arthur's concern for your well-being might be working against Arthur here."

"And you think Arthur's got nothing to be afraid of?"

"I think people are more afraid of sex than they should be. Always have, always will."

"Got it."

"Look, Dugas wouldn't tell me anything about the test he went through. But he did say there's no pain, no torture. That's not the game these people play. It's not the game people *pay* them to play."

"So what is the game?"

"Pleasure and fantasy."

"Those are his words?"

"His words exactly."

"Okay."

"But also, Em... Come on. When have you ever not been scared of something?" These words would feel like an accusation coming from anyone besides Jonathan. But he's spoken them with the level intensity of someone who's known her almost her entire life, and the moment feels more intimate than the feel of him inside of her, or even the long hours of strained nocturnal proximity they shared the night before, side-by-side, fully clothed, as chaste as siblings forced to share a bed.

"I guess you're right," Emily says. "But if there's nothing to be afraid of, why are you going with me?"

"'Cause you have a tendency to freak out over things that aren't actually scary."

"I see. So you think I'm going to freak out?"

"I think you're stalling because you don't want me to get on the plane," he says with a broad smile.

"I think you're kinda right."

He takes both of her hands gently in his and gives her a lingering kiss on the cheek.

"See you on the other side, Miss Conran."

"Have a nice flight, *Leonard*."

Jonathan grimaces. Then he takes a few steps in the direction of the Navigator and gestures for Marcus to roll down the passenger side window.

"Hey, Robocop!" he calls. "If anything happens to her, I'll hunt you down and choke you with a pink scarf."

"Sounds good," Marcus says, but he's already rolling the window back up.

To Emily he says, "Twenty-four hours and the guy's already losing his touch. Be sure to talk real slow in case he can't keep up."

But the Navigator's window is plunging again. "*RoboCop?*" Marcus shouts back. "Dude. Seriously. That's like from nineteen eighty-four."

"Nineteen eighty-seven, *dude*. And they remade it in twenty fourteen. Just saying!"

"Good-bye, Jonathan," Emily says. "Try not to seduce anyone until you're back on the ground."

"How else am I going to mend my broken heart?" he asks with one hand to the aforementioned injury and a pouty lower lip. It's a clownish expression and gesture, but there's a flicker of real hurt underneath it, and for a few seconds, the pit of Emily's stomach goes cold, separation anxiety swirled with a tangle of other dark predictions.

When they see each other again, will they be the same people? Are they underestimating these silly sounding tests The Desire Exchange will put them through?

The doors slide open behind him and Jonathan raises one long arm. At first she thinks this will be only her good-bye, but then he pitches forward in a dramatic bow that's half Broadway star, half maître d', before a thoroughly unamused Frank Dupuy takes him by one shoulder and steers him into the crowded terminal.

Emily steps back inside the Navigator. She's braced for some comment from her shadow. But Marcus is too busy fiddling with his phone.

"All set?" he asks.

"Yep."

"Good," he says, still swiping and tapping and pretty much ignoring her.

"Looking for some tunes?" she asks.

A car horn bleats behind them. Marcus shoots an angry look in the rearview mirror, sees it's an airport cop, and pulls away from the curb, his phone still in one hand. "A distracted driver is a dangerous driver," she says in the light, singsong voice of a television mom from the 1950s.

"On long drives like this, there's only really one kind of music that keeps me focused. I hope you don't mind."

"I guess not as long as it's not—" Before she can say the words *death metal*, a peal of strings comes pouring out of the stereo speakers, lush and surprisingly melodic. The chord changes that follow sound distinctly Asian. Marcus stares dead ahead as he steers them out of the tangle of airport traffic. Is this some stilted attempt to bare his soul, to prove he's not some big dumb lug?

Then the singing starts.

Emily lets out a startled cry, as if she'd been poked in the ribs. Her fingernails bite into the armrest, which she realizes she's suddenly holding onto as if for dear life. The woman's voice—she thinks it's a woman; it might not be human—is a piercing, warbling sound, like what she imagines a monkey might sound like if it were being murdered, slowly, or maybe nails on a chalkboard if the chalkboard had nerve endings and a mouth and was screaming out in protest. She's not familiar enough with Asian cultures to know what language it is, but it's definitely from that part of the world. Marcus closes his eyes for a second or two and then takes in a slow, deep breath, as if the shrieking, ear-piercing, jangling music coming from the speakers is feeding his soul, sustaining him even, as he steers the giant SUV onto the access road and toward the onramp to Interstate 10.

"What is this?" she asks. She's trying her best not to be a bitch, but it comes out sounding the way people in a dentist's chair ask *how much longer?*

"Cantonese opera," Marcus shouts back. "It's called *Sacrifice of a Princess.*"

"Oh. Okay."

"You like it?" he asks. "I think it's really *beaut—*"

And then he loses it. He snorts so loudly she can hear it over the shrieks coming from the stereo. He's doubled over laughing, his watering eyes still fixed on the road, but one fist coming up to make sure his eruption hasn't sent anything flying from his nostrils.

She kills the stereo with the flick of one hand. "I can't believe you!"

"What? You don't like it?" He's actually giggling now; boyish sounding things that make him grimace while his shoulders and upper back shake.

"Seriously?"

"Were you really going to let me listen to that all the way to Florida?" Just the mention of this prospect causes Marcus to lose it again.

"No, of course not, but I didn't want to sound like some racist who hates Japanese opera."

"Well, that's good, 'cause Cantonese is Chinese."

"Alright, you know what—"

"No. What? What do I need to know, Emily?"

"Never mind," she says. She turns her face to the window

because she figures if he can only see one blushing cheek, it will somehow diminish how badly he just duped her. And then she finds herself laughing in spite of herself.

"Hey," Marcus finally says, "I just wanted you to see that your gay friend isn't the only one with a sense of humor, alright?"

"Well, congratulations, Marcus. You've made that very clear."

* * * *

"Unbelievable," Marcus mutters.

Parked in the overgrown backyard of a modest brick house just off I-10's passage through Northwest Pensacola, a few yards from a drainage canal spackled with hovering insects, Emily's gleaming new car looks like a princess at a flea market.

Lily's new car, she reminds herself.

Marcus ordered her to stay outside while he obtained the keys and registration from their secret car broker. Whoever he is, the guy lives like a humble schoolteacher so she has no idea if he's in the habit of selling insanely expensive cars to people who don't technically exist, and that's fine with her.

"Argento Grey leather," Marcus begins, walking in a slow circle around the Aston Martin. "20 spoke silver wheels. Arizona Bronze exterior. And a convertible? Christ, almighty. I swear to God…" He's made each one of the car's specs sound like an accusation.

"Didn't figure you were much of a car person, Mister Dylan," Emily says.

"What made you figure that?"

"I don't know. You just seem more…practical. Jeeps, Hummers, tents. That kind of thing."

"Nothing practical about a Hummer. And besides, practical people can appreciate a work of art. And *this* car is a work of art."

"Can't argue with you there," she says quietly. She's running one finger along the car's driver's side like someone in a commercial. She wills herself to stop, but it's no use. The shiny gold paint exerts the same gravitational force on her fingers as a box of Wheat Thins in the pantry on a lonely Saturday night. "I like how the headlights go back as far as the tires. And it's like… The whole car looks like it's just got these energy waves in it. Like it's building up energy just sitting here… *Oh my God*. What's happening to me? I sound like some…car nerd. Is that what they're even called? Car nerds?"

"I think the term's gearhead. Or it used to be. When I was a gearhead."

"I am *not* a gearhead. I refuse to be a gearhead. Now Lily Conran? It looks like she's a gearhead for sure."

"Unbelievable," Marcus says again. He's crossed his arms over his broad chest, and he's shaking his head with parental disapproval.

"So I'm sensing some judgment around me and this car."

"Emily, giving you a car like this, well…it's like giving a Van Gogh to a five-year-old."

"*Excuse me?*"

"Do you even know how to drive this thing?"

"It's a *car*, Marcus. It doesn't go to the moon."

"It's an Aston Martin, Emily It's not just a car. Saying an Aston Martin is just a car is like—"

"*Don't!* Don't finish that sentence, Marcus. I have this image of you as something other than a douchebag, and I just want to hold on to it for as long as I possibly can."

"Oh, okay. Let's go back to talking about how the car has *energy waves* moving through it. Does it have a *chi* too?"

"Hey, soldier of fortune. If you're going to get this bent out of shape about a *car*, I'm not sure if you're up to the task of protecting me twenty-four, seven."

"I'm bent out of shape because this car is being given to someone who might not appreciate its full magnificence."

"That's a big word for a jarhead."

Eyes ablaze, arms falling from his chest to his side. "I am *not* a *jarhead.* I was a SEAL, not some bullet sponge with a bunch of bullshit sayings who goes running headfirst—"

"Watch it. My dad was a Marine. I know the drill. You think you're hot stuff 'cause you can tread water for a whole day. But you'd have to do it with ten pounds of gear on your back everywhere you—"

"Osama bin Laden is dead! You're welcome!"

"Was that you?"

"No. But I knew one of the—"

"What's his number? I'll send him a fruit basket."

"Emily, we need to talk about you and this car."

"Or we could talk about how condescending you're being right now. I mean, when was the last time you drove an Aston Martin?"

"Never," Marcus says in a lustful whisper.

"Well, start being nicer to me and maybe I'll let you."

"Don't play games with me, young lady. Not with this car."

"Fine. What kind of games should we play then?"

She wasn't planning it. She hadn't rehearsed it. It just slipped out. Their little back and forth had a hard edge to it; maybe that's what pried the comment loose and brought it to the surface in the form of a brazen come-on. He's studying her, sizing her up. It looks like he's forgotten about the car altogether, and now there's just her and his silent fantasies, which she can feel electrifying the stretch of driveway between them.

He's trained to kill with his bare hands, fully capable of taking her, restraining her, finding her soft spots. But for some reason, he's holding back. Surely, it's not professional consideration. Did Arthur not tell him this whole thing is basically a fix-up? Or is that her job? And should she do it now, here, in the dingy backyard of this anonymous little house they might never see again?

"I figured you'd be saving up your energy," he says. "You know, for your *test*."

Emily has never been slapped before. She can only imagine it would release the same combination of anger and bewildering sense of shame. There's remorse in his eyes, but if he's got an apology to offer, he's sitting on it. And as far as Emily's concerned, he's chosen to sit on it just a second too long.

"I see," she finally manages. "So you're only into virgins, is that it?"

"Emily, I—"

"You must be one too, right? Saving yourself for marriage?"

Brow furrowed, he's staring at the space between their feet. He's drained all emotion from his expression, but that fact seems more telling than anything that might be written on his facial features.

"Don't do stuff you don't want to do just to get his money," Marcus says, his words quiet and halting, like those of a frightened young man.

"Are you accusing me of—"

"I'm not accusing *you* of anything."

"You think Arthur's using me?"

"I think it's easy to convince a woman like you, a woman who's…different that—"

"Wait. *Different?* What?"

"A woman who brings a different set of gifts to the table is what

I'm saying. And it's—"

"Oh, right. Like fifteen extra pounds and a brain? That kind of different?"

"A woman who doesn't know what she has, alright? How's that? What I'm saying is it's sometimes easy to convince a woman who isn't the...*traditional* type that the only way people are going to like her is if she makes herself do all kinds of crazy, *freaky*... You know what? Forget it. Just forget it."

"Marcus!"

But he's already stalking down the driveway, and for a second or two, she's afraid he actually wandered off into the neighborhood. But then he returns, carrying the plastic Ziploc bag in which he's placed Lily Conran's brand new smartphone, passport, and the Louis Vuitton wallet that now holds her credit cards and fake ID. They're a few feet apart now, but he won't look her in the eye. And maybe it's a trick played by the security light above the garage door, but it almost looks like he's pouting.

Emily reaches into her purse, pulls out her own wallet and phone and trades them with her suddenly silent, suddenly stoic, and obviously embarrassed protector. Marcus's insult notwithstanding, she's been dreading this moment since they discussed it earlier that day. If all went according to plan, Jonathan has just conducted the same ritual with Frank Dupuy, which means they have no real way of contacting each other, or any friend or relative whose number they haven't memorized.

"Here's the map to the house," he says, pulling a folded piece of paper from his jacket pocket. "I'll follow you there. I'm set up across the beach road. Ten minutes away on foot, five if I run. You'll be on camera the whole time. The house is fully wired."

"Even the shower?"

"You've got your ring," he says. The slight hitch in his voice tells her the comment hit its target. "Apply pressure to it three times in a row if there's an emergency."

"You think 'cause I don't look like a swimsuit model that I'm...what? Desperate for validation?"

"That's not what I think of when I think of your body," Marcus whispers.

This admission has stilled him to his core. In another man, holding his current pose for this long would result in small muscle tremors, but the folded map doesn't shake where it rests in between the fingers of his extended hand.

"And no, I'm not saving myself for marriage," he says.

He places the keys to the Aston Martin in her hand, takes time molding her fingers closed over them. Then he walks off into the shadows, bound for the SUV he's been following her in for days now, with a Ziploc bag containing most of the proof that a woman named Emily Blaine still exists.

11

When he reaches the entrance to Hotel Monteleone, George Dugas pauses to watch his massive bodyguard open one of the front doors for him before the uniformed doorman has a chance to help. The doorman rolls his eyes, then catches George's look and gives him a quick, polite nod as they walk past. Maybe he's embarrassed to have shown his annoyance so obviously. Or maybe he recognizes George Dugas from his days of crushing political and business rivals in the public square. Either way, George feels a little sorry for the guy; if he were being forced to stand outside all night, sweating through his drawers in some heavy uniform, he'd want a mindless activity to keep him occupied too.

It's a busy, hot night in the Quarter. The block of Royal Street in front of the hotel is clogged with cars caught behind a clattering horse-drawn carriage full of tourists. From a short distance away, George can still hear the second-lining wedding party they sat behind in traffic for almost twenty minutes before he decided to hop out of his chauffeured Bentley and walk the rest of the way to the hotel with Melvin at his side.

The Monteleone's vast, marble-floored lobby is no quieter. Rowdy conventioneers process in and out of the Carousel Bar. Four drunken frat boys try holding each other up as they make their way to the elevators like exhausted contortionists performing their last act of the evening.

"I hate the French Quarter," Melvin growls under his breath.

"Nonsense. The Quarter's lovely. It's the *tourists* you hate."

"You aren't riding up with those fools, are you?" Melvin thumbs one giant paw in the direction of the frat boys who have just piled inside one of the elevators. As the doors start to close, one of them starts sliding down the wall. The hand he brings to his mouth at the last second does little to contain the spray.

"She's in the Faulkner Suite," Dugas answers. "Other side of the hotel. Thank God."

"And I don't like you going to see this woman alone."

"She's harmless."

"Harmless people aren't this damn secretive."

"It's called discretion, Melvin. In another era, it was considered the equivalent of class."

"In another era, you could have owned me for a couple hundred dollars."

"You're not my type."

"I'm going up with you. Only way to make sure you don't get barfed on."

"You're doing nothing of the kind. You're staying down here in the lobby where I will meet you when I'm done."

"You don't even know her name, do you?"

"I most certainly do. Melvin, for a second, you might want to consider that *I'm* the one trying to keep this woman a secret from *you.*"

George gives Melvin a three-fingered wave good-bye, then the elevator doors close inches from his nose, leaving him alone in a quiet cell with his thoughts.

Why does he feel the need to explain himself to Melvin? The man is his bodyguard, not his father. George's father has been dead for thirty years and the world is all the better for it. The clownish antics all throughout the Monteleone's shiny, elegant lobby were nothing compared to the changes his daddy would undergo after a few bottles of Dixie beer. Having his only son go from poor white trash to multimillionaire real estate developer by the age of thirty didn't give the old man any gratitude in his later years. George's father died like he lived, a mean drunk who thought the world owed him, no matter how many homes and cushy rehabs his son paid for on his behalf.

As for Lilliane, is she truly as harmless as he just let on?

George can't be sure. During his visit to The Desire Exchange, he witnessed many things that defied easy explanation, but he never felt threatened or in danger. Still, would the woman he's here to meet lose her cool if she found out George had a bodyguard standing sentry just outside the door to her hotel room? Probably not.

Based on his past interactions with her, she doesn't seem the type to lose her temper easily. Like him, she operates with the quiet confidence of someone with resources so vast they render raised voices or open threats too trivial to be relevant. Unlike him, she has the power to make elaborate, detailed fantasies reality. Sure, he's got enough cash on hand to realize plenty of dreams, but not as quickly or as effectively as Lilliane and her colleagues.

Still, parking Melvin outside the door to her suite isn't worth the risk. Screw Jonathan Claiborne and his confused little girlfriend, Miss Emily Blaine. George doesn't want to endanger his own chances of visiting The Desire Exchange again. Although, given the depth and power of what he experienced during his first visit, he's not sure that's possible. Or necessary.

Someday, I'm gonna find out what was in that punch they made us drink and I'm going to bottle it and make a fortune.

No sooner has this thought entered his head, then a voice that sounds surprisingly like his mother's says right back. *You'll do nothing of the kind, George Dugas. For once in your life, you'll do what your father never could. Be grateful!*

These sudden desires to do something other than enslave something—or someone!—he enjoys, is so unlike him, he wonders if Lilliane has cast an hypnotic, submissive spell down through the old walls of the historic hotel. But he's not quite sure he'd call the woman *magical.* A magician, for sure, but truly, deeply, *inherently* magic? To apply that label, you had to believe in magic in the first place.

If someone pressed him on the subject—and they never would given he'd never shared his experiences with anyone—George would insist that what happened to him at The Exchange was some sort of drug-fueled hallucination, possibly brought on by chemicals that would make the FDA mess their shorts. An amazingly coherent, sustained and overpowering hallucination, a hallucination that released him from old, bad ideas about who he truly was. But a hallucination, nonetheless.

The results were magical, that was for sure.

Maybe that's why he's more than a little nervous about seeing Lilliane again.

Because she'd done something most people who knew him would've thought impossible. She'd turned him into a halfway decent guy.

Let's not go that far, kid. Better, maybe. But decent?

He raises his hand to knock. Just then the door to the Faulkner Suite sweeps open over plush carpeting. Lilliane's hair is brushed out in a rich, mahogany halo. Her slinky black dress is a few shades darker than her skin. The hotel suite is a bright symphony of turquoise upholstery and powder blue carpet. She moves through it like a knife cutting wedding cake.

George blinks. He needs a moment to contain himself. He wasn't prepared for the shock of seeing her again. In his lifetime, he's only met a few black women as self-possessed as Lilliane, and they all hightailed it out of the South as soon as they found the right husband or academic scholarship.

But it's not Lilliane he's seeing. He's seeing what she turned into the last time they were together, when she slid both of her hands up his naked thighs, brought her lips gently to his, and whispered the mantra everyone at The Desire Exchange was so fond of, "Trust your fantasy."

Within seconds, they were no longer on the dais she had asked him to step up onto, naked as the day he was born. Suddenly they were inside the elevator George rode to his office every day. Only now it was just George and that beautiful young lawyer he often shared a ride with. The one he'd never spoken more than a few words to, the one he always looked away from quickly because the sight of his sparkling blue eyes and delicate jawline and full lips always made him...*frightened queasy sweaty nervous.* George was no stranger to bedding beautiful men and women. But only if he was paying them. Only if he was in control. This young man was different. And when Lilliane brought her lips away from his, she was *him.* She was the handsome, bright-eyed young lawyer. And she was unfastening her tie and bringing one veiny, muscled hand—a man's hand—to the side of George's cheek.

The elevator's walls seemed vaporous and thin, but George knew, on the same level you just know something in the middle of a dream, that he and the young man were trapped together in the elevator, finally. It was the very fantasy Lilliane had made him write out as part of his test and somehow now, her kiss, her touch, had made it a reality. But what he'd written during his test was just the beginning.

What came next was wholly unexpected, wholly unpredictable, wholly...*magic magic magic*, he wants to whisper.

Don't be an idiot, he'd told himself then. He says it to himself again now as he stands just inside the threshold to her suite, watching her pour him a scotch and soda without asking what he'd like to drink. *It was the punch. The punch they made you drink. It was drugged.*

But how could the drugs have been so powerful as to recreate the divinely musky smell of the young lawyer's cock? Or the devilish, oh-so-real glint in the young man's blue eyes after George tore his suit off and he rocked onto his back on the elevator floor, his sandy blond hair tousled, drawing his powerful, naked legs back so he could offer himself up to George in full—cock, balls, everything? And the words! The words he'd spoken next, they'd pulled down a dam inside of George's soul.

"Well, Mister Dugas, would you like to taste or would you like to watch?"

And without a moment's hesitation, George gave a response that changed the course of his life and made every dollar he'd given to The Desire Exchange seem worthwhile. "Both. But mostly...I want to watch."

Him? A *voyeur?* How could that be? On some level he'd always known, but he'd also doubted with a force that had made his knowledge useless. George Dugas was a master of the universe, a man who'd built entire neighborhoods, a man who had made and derailed careers, a man who had sampled almost every pleasure on offer among the world of consenting adults. And this was his greatest desire? To taste briefly, then set in motion and observe? It wasn't possible. But the proof was in his feeling of total rapture as he watched the prone young man stroke his cock, still slick from the brief ministrations of George's lips and tongue, until an expression of almost religious ecstasy transformed his fine, beautiful features and slender threads of cum shot from the tip. The proof was in the shuddering, hands-free orgasm that tore through George at the sight of the young lawyer's body bucking and tensing against the elevator's floor, his high, barking cries turning to rough growls.

The man rose to his knees, powerful chest heaving, cheeks flushed, his lips meeting George's gasping mouth. The next thing George felt was the gentle scrape of Lilliane's blood-red fingernails traveling down his bare thighs, circling the threads of his cum without disrupting them. The hallucination's components faded gently, the elevator's walls and floors, the heat radiating from the drained young lawyer, all of it replaced by Lilliane's confident, steady touch and the feelings of The Desire Exchange's other visitors watching him again from the nearby shadows.

"And now, Mister Dugas," she had whispered to him. "From this day forward, your true fantasies shall be your guide."

As George chokes back memories of this experience, Lilliane places a rock glass full of his favorite drink in his hand and gestures toward the nearby love seat.

There's a spread of pictures on the table next to her. They're Photoshop jobs created by Arthur Benoit's men. The originals were society photos taken of George and various other muckety-mucks at two different charity events earlier that year. Gone are the muckety-mucks. In one set, the one in which George sports a blood-red Hermès necktie, Jonathan Claiborne has been inserted next to him in each image, dressed in a black designer suit he doesn't own and probably couldn't afford even after a solid month of visits to George's pool house. The second set were taken at a swanky outdoor fundraiser for the Audubon Zoo. In each one, Emily Blaine holds a fleshy arm around his waist. Her white chenille sweater flatters her ample curves, but it's the red polka dot skirt that doesn't quite seem her style. It's amazing what can be done on computers these days.

But the smiling people who have been grafted onto old photographs of George are not Emily and Jonathan anymore, he reminds himself. Not here, at least. Not right now. They are Lily Conran and Leonard Miller, and in less than a few days they've been given complete fictional lives on paper.

George spent most of that afternoon getting familiar with their new identities. Not because he's all that interested in Arthur Benoit tracking down some estranged son he blew it with long before he got sick. There is, to George's mind, a distinct advantage to being the man behind the curtain of Emily Blaine's visit to The Desire Exchange. No doubt, she'll want to keep the secret after her financial situation dramatically improves. Who knows what respectable high-powered friends she might start running with after she inherits Benoit's money? And that might be exactly when Dugas might require a favor. Or three.

But there's another motive he doesn't feel quite as comfortable with, another surge of surprising altruism. Should this surprise him?

After all, he's the one who gave Emily Blaine—*Lily Lily Lily*—that grand lecture about how nobody ever acts on just one motive.

When you have an experience like he had at The Exchange, you can't help but want to share it with others.

"How are you, George?" Lilliane asks, snapping him back to the present.

"Eager."

"Too eager to have a seat apparently..."

She says it with a smile, but it has the force of a command. The next thing he knows, he's on the love seat, trying not to fidget.

"Eager?" Lilliane asks.

"For us to come to an arrangement."

"For your friends, you mean? Lily and...Leonard"

"I think they're prime candidates."

"Candidates?"

"For The Exchange," George adds.

"Yes. George, I'm aware we're discussing The Exchange. I'm just a bit taken aback by your language."

"I'm sorry... My language? What do you—"

"Well, you just sound so clinical. That's all. So businesslike. Did your visit with us not end with us specifically requesting that you refer your friends to us?"

"Provided they were single," he answers too quickly. Is his face red? He feels hot. "And rich enough to afford it."

She gives him another disarming smile. Then she studies him. The force of her gaze chills the pit of his stomach. Makes sense, he thinks. After all, the last time they were together, she pretty much stared right into his soul, didn't she?

No, kid. It was the punch. You saw a lot of crazy things because of the punch and she just whispered all the right words to trigger your lustful thoughts. Get a hold of yourself.

"And so are you not doing exactly what it is we asked you to do?" Lilliane asks him now.

Sorta. But with a twist.

"I am... It's just..."

"Just what, George?"

"The last time we were together was... It was powerful. And I wasn't prepared for how I'd feel when I saw you again and I just—"

Avoiding one truth has forced him to confess another, one far more personal and revealing. She makes a small, indulgent sound in her throat.

"Have you been intimate with either of them?" she asks.

"No."

"Good. That's good. It's complicated to send a lover to The Exchange."

"Why's that?" He knows full well why it is, but he wants to keep her talking so he has fewer chances of lying...badly.

"Chances are, they'll come back changed. That can be very damaging to a preexisting relationship. Were you not changed by your time with us, George?"

"I was..."

"I hope so."

"Do it again," he whispers. "Change me again, Lilliane."

All life seems to drain from her expression.

His cheeks flame.

The direct approach usually suits him in life, but these words slipped from him with a child's careless enthusiasm. And without meaning to, he's set her up. Could she alter the very air around them just by running her fingernails along his skin, just by bringing her lips to his? Could she unleash his fantasy without the aid of some silly punch that tasted like sugar water with a hint of Chloraseptic?

"Do you *need* to be changed again?" she asks quietly. But he can tell his question has thrown her. She straightens, running one hand briefly along the back of her neck as if to wipe away a stray drop of water. Or sweat.

Does she sweat? Was she sweating that night on the ship? Is she...

Are you human?

He's so relieved he didn't voice this question, he's able to get his composure back.

"Of course, if you wish to return," Lilliane says, "we could arrange it. And there would be a process, just like the last time. But I thought tonight we were here to discuss—"

"Lily," he cuts her off. "And Leonard. Yes, I'm sorry..."

"You called them prime candidates. Why?"

"They're both lost," he says. "They both believe they're in control of their lives. But what they want...what they *really* want, it runs counter to who they think they are. Isn't that what you do? You show people who they truly are?"

"We show them what they really *want*. There's a difference."

"Yes, of course. But you can't be who you are until you know what you want."

"Or who you want," she says. A shadow passes over her face. She stares down at the carpet by his feet, chews her lower lip absently before appearing to remember George is still seated across from her. "It's like we told all of you—"

"Trust your fantasy," George whispers.

"What you trust it to *do* is up to you. Some people live out their fantasy with us just once, and they're set free. Because that's all they needed. Their system is purged. Their heart begins anew when they leave us. But for others, the fantasy they behold, the fantasy they live out, it sets the course of their future. It doesn't release their heart, it guides their heart. Which one are you, George?"

"Let's just say I threw out all that bondage equipment that was taking up so much space in my attic. These days, all I need is a comfy chair and a good view."

Lilliane's rich laughter sounds satisfied. She rises to her feet and leafs through the photographs of Jonathan and Emily's alter egos.

"Your friends are very beautiful," she says. "And very young. Younger than most of the people we see."

"They're also very rich. I figured that mattered more."

"It does. Our operation is not cheap to run. I'll say that much."

"I saw. I'm sure whatever's in that punch alone costs a fortune."

Lilliane doesn't answer. She picks up the picture of George and Lily Conran at the zoo fundraiser.

"And they haven't met?" Lillian says. "These aren't the same events?"

"No. They're both in town often. They're regular social butterflies. But I have no evidence they know each other."

"That's important. Even if they're casual acquaintances. The shock of recognizing someone else inside of The Exchange can be…distracting. I don't know why, but it's easier for our guests to be vulnerable in front of strangers."

"Of course…"

When she turns to face him, she sets her drink down on the table, and there's something final about her rigid posture that causes George to straighten against the love seat.

"You may inform your friends we will call upon them sometime in the next forty-eight hours. Please give them no details of what awaits. I shouldn't have to explain why it's important they come to all of this…fresh."

"Fresh. Of course."

George stands. Lilliane smiles. Something about her penetrating, clear-eyed gaze makes his face get hot all over again.

"So I guess you're not going to do it again, are you?"

"I can't do it again, George. I don't have all my tools with me."

She wears a half-smile, but there's a tightness in her voice that sounds threatening. *She didn't say punch. She said tools. That could mean anything. It could mean she's lying.*

"Besides," she continues. "You've had your turn at the wheel. It's time to share the wealth."

She makes a show of gesturing for the door, with a broad toothy smile.

Dizzy, and half afraid he'll say something else terribly stupid if he doesn't leave, he hurries from the room, then stops and takes care to shut the door gently behind him.

He's headed back to the lobby in the elevator when he realizes Lilliane didn't shake his hand, either in greeting or farewell.

If she was all that eager to prove her very fingers didn't harbor special powers, a handshake was the least she could have done.

12

Emily is awakened from a deep and dreamless sleep by a sound like an elevator chime in an upscale office building. For a few seconds, she has no idea where she is. Then she feels the ocean wind moving across her bare legs. She's in her new beach house, *Lily Conran's* beach house, a modern glass and steel box tucked into a sea of sugar-white sand dunes.

The master suite is located at the back of the house on the second floor. But it opens onto the great room's two-story atrium. All Emily had to do to fill her new bedroom with hypnotic ocean breezes was pull back two giant taffeta curtains in the bedroom, then part the great room's soaring walls of glass with the touch of a button. The surrounding houses also sit on huge lots, but almost all of them are salmon and beige colored Tuscan villas. Not Lily Conran's. Arthur chose a house for her as shiny and sleek as her new Aston Martin.

The chime sounds a second time, but it's the third time she's heard it. Marcus tested it earlier that evening while giving her an orientation tour of the house and its many hidden cameras. She goes for the bedside phone before she remembers his instructions. Every inch of her surroundings are on camera and each camera records sound. She pulls a tiny beige earpiece from the nightstand drawer. It melded perfectly with the skin of her ear when she tried it on earlier, becoming almost invisible; it also allows her to hear his every word.

"Sounds like you're almost in," Marcus says quietly.

Through scores of cameras, he's watched her wake up, watched her blink back sleep, and watched her draw the sheet up over her chest to make sure she's fully covered, even though she's wearing a T-shirt and panties.

The surveillance trailer is parked on a construction site just down the road that's been abandoned since the lot's owner ran out of financing. She glimpsed it on the drive in, tucked behind the ghostly skeleton of the half-built mansion that might never be. And she's also got a view of it from one of the kitchen windows, which he showed her during the painfully awkward fifteen minutes it took to give her a tour of the house. It wasn't an effective orientation, given their every footfall on the vast marble floors seemed to echo with his regrettable warning in Pensacola when they picked up her new car.

"What do you mean?" she asks.

"Dugas called," Marcus says. "He met with his contact tonight. You've both been cleared for a test. They've given us a forty-eight hour window."

"So are we just supposed to sit here for forty-eight hours?"

"Dugas says they only come after dark, so I guess you're free to do whatever during daylight hours."

"It's dark now. Are they on their way?"

"That would be fast. Dugas just made contact."

"And he didn't say anything else about what this test is going to be?"

"Nope."

"So are you telling me to go back to sleep?"

"Are you being difficult because you're still pissed at me for what I said?"

"Kinda. Yeah."

"That's mature."

"Know what else isn't mature? Knocking a grown woman for having more than one sex partner in her lifetime."

"You got me there."

"Or for being chunkier than the swimsuit models you probably date."

"*Woah*, there, lady. Now wait just a—"

"Please. Don't start lecturing me on how they might be swimsuit models but they really want to work with animals and change the world."

"Don't put words in my mouth, Miss Blaine."

"Is that what I'm doing? Putting words in your mouth?"

"I've never once dated a girl who wants to work with animals. And I never called you *chunky*."

"I'm going back to sleep now, Marcus."

"So? I can still see and hear everything."

The edge leaves his tone on the word *everything*. She can hear the undisguised pleasure he's taking in this fact, imagines him intently staring at a night-vision image of her legs twined in these luxuriant silk sheets. He promised her he could move the camera angles away from the shower whenever she was in the bathroom. But did he keep his promise earlier when she showered? Did she want him to? Did she not maybe linger a little too long, spending too much time toweling off places that weren't exactly wet?

Besides, it's not like she'd asked him to move the camera lenses. He'd just volunteered that he *could*.

"I'm sorry," Marcus says.

"For?"

"For the fact you so totally and completely misinterpreted what I said."

"Goodnight, Marcus. It's a little late for mansplaining."

"And for not turning you around and taking you right over the hood of that Aston Martin to show you how wrong you were."

Her breath catches, but another Emily responds. "Charming," she whispers.

"Your hand seems to think so," he says.

He's right. The warmth she's been feeling against her thigh is coming from her own palm. Just the sound of his voice has charmed her fingers onto her thigh. And he can see it all. The parted taffeta drapes blowing in the breeze, the tangle of silk sheets sliding down across her white T-shirt, the rise and fall of her chest as she tries to get back the breath he just stole from her.

"It's not gonna be that easy," she says.

"What? What isn't going to be that easy, Miss Blaine?"

"Put a little distance between us and then you turn into Christian Grey, when there's no risk and you don't have to—"

"Don't have to what?"

"I want to hear what you said."

"When?"

"Arthur said he assigned you to me because you made some comments about me that got back to him. I want to hear them. The comments."

"They weren't comments," Marcus says.

"Then what were they?"

"Observations."

"About my weight?"

"About your eyes. You were coming down off the front porch of the main house one day and when the sunlight hit your eyes, they were so beautiful they looked like a painting."

"Well, now...that's kinda sweet."

"And then I said if I ever get inside that woman I'm going to do whatever it takes to make her look into my eyes the whole time. To make her feel like there's no one else except for me, and nothing else in the world except for what I'm doing to her body."

She hopes her sharp intake of breath is too soft for the microphones to pick up, but she doubts it. And besides, her silence is telling enough.

"Watch that hand, Emily."

"Is that how you said it? In exactly those words?"

"I said it in a way Scott could understand. He was the other guy on duty that day. He doesn't read books with big words. Just magazines with big guns."

"I see..."

"I see too," he says. "But I'd like to see more."

Before she can think twice about it, she draws the sheet back a few inches, exposing the crotch of her panties to the ocean breeze, revealing it to the darkened bedroom and its myriad of hidden but prying eyes. Revealing it to Marcus's tortured hunger for her, on which he seems to temporarily lose grip every few hours or so.

Me, I'm the reason he loses control. I'm the thing he wants but doesn't want to want...yet.

Fear sends gooseflesh up her thighs, fear of being exposed, fear of moving too fast, fear of giving too much of herself away too soon. But they're her thighs and her panties, goddammit, and for the time being, this is her bedroom, and she's technically alone, so what is there to be afraid of—

"Are the cameras recording?" she asks the darkness.

"Not unless I tell them to."

"Don't tell them to."

"Then show me more. Quid pro quo, you know."

"Never reference *Silence of the Lambs* when you're trying to get a woman naked."

"You have a real mouth on you, Miss Blaine. Do you know that?"

"I do. And that's why you keep talking to me."

"Or it's just my job."

"There are other jobs, with quieter people."

"Smart girl."

She tries to suppress a smile. Beneath the sheet, she works her arms out from her T-shirt, then slides the entire thing up and over her head before dropping it to the carpet. Just at the moment when Marcus probably believes she's about to expose her breasts to the open air, she rolls over onto her stomach.

Marcus growls.

"You want to see more, then I get to hear more," Emily says.

"More of what?" Marcus asks.

"I want to hear about the swimsuit models."

"I don't *date* swimsuit models."

"Fine. Who do you date?"

"I don't...*date*."

"Really?"

"Yeah. Roll over."

"If you think that's any kind of answer—"

"No, I think, *I want to hear about the swimsuit models* isn't any kind of question."

"Fine. Why don't you date?"

"So we're not dating?" he asks her.

"Answering another question with a question will result in an automatic bonnet and flannel nightgown."

His laughter sounds more relaxed than anything that's come out of his mouth since they first met.

"Seriously," she adds. "I'll turn it into an episode of *The Waltons* in here if you're not careful."

"The last girl I *dated* embezzled ten million dollars from her father and set me up to take the fall for it. Now turn over. I'm dying here."

"Seriously?"

"Yes, seriously turn over."

"Marcus..."

There's a long sigh from his end. "Yes. True story."

"Jesus..."

"Yeah. It was rough."

"Did you?"

"Take the fall for it?"

"Yeah."

"No."

"Good."

"But I did take the fall for sleeping with a client's daughter. Because that's who she was."

"Oh…"

"Yeah. Oh. So as a sidenote here, and even though I'm running the risk of never seeing the rest of that beautiful body by saying this, when you tell me Arthur Benoit set us up together because he overhead me make some comments about you in the guardhouse…well, let's just say it doesn't exactly ring true."

"Meaning?"

"Meaning he knows my history. That's all I'm saying."

"You mean he's counting on you to have a weakness for the daughters of super wealthy men?"

"Meaning he does things for his own advantage, and maybe without the highest regard of other people's…weaknesses. If you're about to inherit the keys to his kingdom, it's probably a good idea for you to remember that. Also, last time I checked, you're not his daughter."

"According to his new will, I might as well be. Back to your weakness for—"

"I don't have a weakness for the daughters of rich men, Emily. I have a weakness for smart, confident women who know exactly what they want and tell me how to give it to them. I'm just looking for someone who doesn't use her smarts to steal millions of dollars from her own family."

"And frame her boyfriend for the crime," Emily says.

"Apparently I wasn't really her boyfriend."

"You thought you were," Emily says carefully. His voice is ticking up a notch with each new response, and she realizes she's on sensitive, thin skin. "That's what matters. That's what makes it two crimes."

"Thank you," he whispers.

She's so caught off guard by his quiet words of gratitude, she doesn't know what else to say for a few minutes.

Emily laughs.

"What?" he asks.

"Smart, confident women who tell you what they want and how to give it to them. Is that really your style?"

"You think I'm lying?"

"I think that doesn't seem like your type. You seem...more controlling than that."

"Dominant, you mean?"

"Both."

"Yeah, well, once I find out what you want, I give it to you when I think you most need it. How's that for dominant, Emily Blaine?"

Making her the direct object of the sentence paints her inner thighs with gooseflesh, bathes the crotch of her panties with wet heat. Who knew grammar could be so sexy?

"Do I get to ask questions too?" Marcus asks.

"Not unless you're going to take something off."

"You wouldn't be able to see it if I did," he answers, but his desire for her has made his voice as tight as a drawstring.

"We could change that," she says.

There's a heavy silence suddenly. It reminds her of his words from earlier today, the jealousy that caused him to practically sneer with disapproval when he referenced her upcoming *test*. She's too flushed and aroused to go back to that raw, hurtful place. That means allowing him to indulge whatever resistance is keeping him from vaulting the sand dunes in between his trailer and Lily Conran's beach house. For now, at least.

"Fine," she says. "Ask me a question."

And just leave me here, alone, kissed by wind and aching with hunger for you, you bastard.

"You and Jonathan," he says. "How many times?"

"Twice."

One and a half, she thinks, given that the second time she simply rode Jonathan's forceful tongue and hungry lips.

"But he's gay," Marcus says.

"Yes."

"You still believe that? Even after you guys..."

"Yes."

"Why?"

"Jonathan is sexual before he's anything else. But who you want to have sex with is not what makes you gay. It's who you fall in love with. It's who you want to share the remote with."

"Are those his words?"

"No, they're mine. But they describe him. They describe the way he's been since I first met him."

"And you don't think you can change him?"

"That's more than one question. My turn. Is Jonathan the reason you won't come down that road, Marcus?"

"Nope."

"Why then?"

"I don't have time. The feeds are about to switch over so I can get some sleep. If I come down there now, we'll be putting on a live show for the night crew over at Magnolia Gate."

"Wait, *what?* I thought that happened at, like, four in the morning."

She rolls over onto one side and looks at the bedside clock for the first time.

"It's 4:20 a.m.!" Emily cries.

"Yep."

"You woke me up to tell me Dugas made contact...what? Like twenty minutes ago?"

"Something like that."

"You expect me to believe they called you at four in the morning to tell you this?"

"Not anymore. No."

"You are a bastard, Marcus Dylan!"

"It kind of turns me on when you call me that."

"Yeah, well I'm done turning you on tonight. You set this whole thing up so you'd have an excuse *not* to come to this house no matter what I took off."

"Restraint, remember?"

"Or fear."

"A healthy dose of fear is...you know, healthy."

"What you should be afraid of is me marching up that road and wailing on you."

"Hot! I love assertive women. Five minutes 'till the switch, Miss Blaine. Better put some clothes back on."

No click, no dial tone, no heavy breaths.

Several minutes pass without a response.

Is he really gone? She imagines him yanking whatever headset he might have been using off his head, then quickly straightening his bristly hair with one veiny, powerful hand. Or maybe he just put her on mute. The thought of him laughing while her lips move silently on the monitors inside his trailer makes her mad enough to hurl a pillow at the wall. But she stops herself. After all, it's not really her pillow. Or her wall.

Can she really blame him for holding back?

Wouldn't she feel the same way if their roles were reversed? She felt the same when Jonathan asked her to turn some labelless, limitless, undefined explosion of passion into a relationship he couldn't and wouldn't name.

Now? Really? She thinks. *Now is the moment I meet a strong, beautiful man willing to give me his all?*

It's Jonathan's voice she hears next, but he's not whispering her pet nickname in a fiercely naughty way. He's chastising her with that condescending tone that sometimes makes her want to pour a drink over his head. *Poor little Emily, with your new Aston Martin, and your fortune-to-be and your gorgeous, devoted Navy SEAL. I just don't know how you can stand it all...*

She knows what this is, this sudden blizzard of embarrassment and regret and self-obsessions. A counselor she saw once in college referred to it as a shame spiral. If she doesn't take action, doesn't at least swing her feet to the floor and pace the bedroom, one self-defeating critical thought will pile on the next, and she'll be tossing and turning and staring at the ceiling for hours, convinced that her entire life is about to fall apart as soon she utters a single word or takes a single misstep.

Have the feeds switched?

She's so lost in thought she forgot about the sudden countdown.

Leaning over the side of the bed, she collects her clothes off the carpet in one hand. Once she's barely dressed again, she hurries to the walk-in closet, which is half the size of her apartment and packed with designer beachwear, shiny cocktail dresses and ridiculously expensive blouses; the kind of second wardrobe that only a multimillionaire could afford to leave mostly unworn in her second home. Buried at the back of the closet is a row of silk robes. She ties one on; she thinks it's dark blue, but it's too dark for her to be sure it's not as black as her mood.

Halfway down the stairs, she realizes she's still got the earpiece in. But Marcus hasn't spoken to her through it, hasn't asked her where she's going at this late hour. Maybe he's already asleep. When she reaches the kitchen, its chrome and marble surfaces sparkling even in the pale moonlight, she yanks the earpiece out and leaves it on the marble counter. Then she hurries barefoot down the long wooden walkway over the dunes.

When her feet touch the sugary white sand on the other side, her heart starts to pound. She was so eager to punish Marcus in some small but meaningful way, she didn't stop to think that the cameras inside the house also made her feel safe and protected. Now, with the wind tossing her hair and rippling the silk robe against her flushed body, she feels vulnerable and exposed. On the western horizon, a condo high-rise blazes, but the rest of the sky is still dark and star-studded; the beach in front of her is desolate and blanketed with shadows.

Forty-eight hours. The clock is already ticking. She has no idea who these people really are, no idea what's in store for her, and yet, here she is, alone on an empty beach in the middle of the night in only a fluttering silk robe that barely comes down to her knees.

There's a row of wooden beach loungers out here somewhere; she spotted them before the sun went down, and she didn't see an attendant put them away. After a few minutes of stumbling through sand and shadow, her extended, grasping hand finds the edge of a lounger just before her chin does. The cushions have been removed, but she's able to adjust the back to a relatively comfortable angle.

Just a few minutes, she thinks. *I'm just going to sit here for a few minutes and listen to the wind and watch the waves and try to remember who I was before all of this started. Before Arthur told me about his will, before I followed Jonathan, before I ever heard those silly words, The Desire Exchange.*

But soon her eyes are closing and she's seeing a slow montage of seemingly random visuals, a sure sign that sleep is near. Some are snapshots from her day, like Marcus driving the Navigator with a stern expression and a two-handed grip or the master bedroom's taffeta curtains billowing in the breeze.

The others are memories. Jonathan at sixteen, waltzing her across the grassy area outside the cafeteria during lunch. Spinning her, dipping her, smiling so big his teeth gleam in the sparkling sunlight, singing some stupid love song to accompany their waltz, a song she can't remember now, his body already swelling with curvy muscles, some of which are visible under his one-size-too-small Polo shirt, the whole routine warming her heart even as it embarrasses her in front of the other kids who think the two of them could kinda, sorta be a couple but wasn't Jonathan, *you know*— And why is she seeing this again?

Is it because the whole thing seemed like a parody then, and it still seems like a parody now? Because swooning over a woman, even her, is not something Jonathan Claiborne has ever done in a real, authentic way. Because a relationship with her is not what Jonathan really wants, and the only reason he might have tricked himself into thinking so is because Jonathan Claiborne still doesn't know what it is he really wants.

She sees Marcus again, driving. That stern expression. That two-handed grip. And then the way he furtively bites his bottom lip whenever he glances in her direction. The hungry once-over he gives her when he's confident enough to take his eyes off the road, the quick, bashful smile when she catches him looking.

When sleep finally comes, it brings only darkness with it. When she feels a powerful hand against the back of her neck, she assumes it's a dream. Then the back of her head comes to rest against something soft, and she feels a soft blanket being drawn up over her body. Then, just at the moment when she's sure she's alone again, she feels two of his fingers stroke the side of her cheek, and in a whisper almost stolen by the wind, Marcus says, "Sweet dreams, Emily Blaine."

She pretends to be asleep. Not to punish him. She pretends to be asleep because she knows he wouldn't have touched her if he thought she was awake. So she keeps up the act, hoping that he'll touch her again, hoping that he might even grace her with a gentle, hesitant kiss. God knows a peck on the cheek is hardly the extent of what she craves from him in this moment. But it would still mean something. A gentle kiss from a man as strong and gorgeous and dominant as him would be as remarkable and special as a single red rose in the extended fist of a Nordic god.

But he doesn't kiss her.

Maybe it's for the best. Maybe she wouldn't have been able to respect his boundary if he had. Once his sand-squeaking footsteps recede entirely, sleep returns.

When she wakes a few hours later, the first light of dawn is casting wavering orange beams through the gentle, translucent blue surf just offshore, and Marcus Dylan is standing guard several yards away, watching the sunrise after watching over her all night.

13

"You need to sleep, Marcus," Emily says.

Her Aston Martin is several car-lengths ahead of his Navigator, and she's listening to him through the same earpiece that got him in to trouble with her the night before. *Night before? Try a couple of hours ago, dude. She's right. You need sleep.* She's also wearing the companion microphone transmitter, which is about the size of a thumbnail and buried in her bangs. The thing's got a range of about sixty miles, but the sound quality is so good she might as well be sitting next to him. Price tag for the microphone and earpiece together is in the low five figures; Arthur gave them four sets.

"Focus on your driving, not my sleep patterns," he says.

"*My* driving?"

"Yeah."

"Okay. So drive in two lanes like you're doing right now? Is that what you're saying?"

He corrects the Navigator with the frenzied speed of someone swatting at a bumblebee. At least he didn't curse.

When he tries to focus on the road, the Aston Martin gleams like a solar panel in the bright sun, and the glare, along with every other object that reflects sunlight along this pine-fringed highway, sends needles into his skull.

"Got it," Emily says. "Ixnay on the oo-lanestay."

"Pig Latin isn't going to get us to your breakfast meeting on time."

"Seriously, Marcus. Couldn't we have canceled this so you can get some rest? Why do I need to meet with a lawyer anyway? I'm not even real."

"If they're already watching you, they're going to wonder why you do nothing but sit at home alone all day trying on clothes you don't own. You need to do normal things."

"Lily Conran is a multimillionaire who owns property all over the world. Normal for her is airplane shopping."

"I see you've been reading her file. What does it say she likes for breakfast?"

"I'm gonna go out on a limb and say it's only born once a year in the Caspian Sea and it costs them a fortune to fly it to the U.S."

"Good. You're getting into character."

"For breakfast? This guy's a friend of Arthur's and he's in on the whole thing. Marcus, seriously. Stop deflecting."

"I'm not deflecting. I'm driving."

"I know. That's the problem. You should be slee—"

"Emily! Enough! For Christ's sake, I survived Basic Underwater Demolition Training. Not to mention three ops I couldn't tell you about unless I killed you first."

"After."

"What?"

"Unless you killed me *after.* Not before. If you killed me before you told me about it you'd just be killing me for no good reason. Just promise me you'll nap while I'm in the restaurant."

"No. And I'm not going to drink my Ensure or go for a mall walk either! Get off it already."

When she doesn't say anything back, the silence around him feels electric.

"I can handle a night without sleep. That's all I'm saying."

But can I handle you? he thinks. *Can I handle the way you don't take my shit, the way you're always two steps ahead of me, and how it makes me want to plant a vampire's kiss on that smooth, pale neck of yours while I slide deep inside you, cup those luscious, full breasts and own you own you own you own...*

"School bus!"

The sound of a bus horn rolling across him like thunder, Marcus swerves back into his lane. When the bus flies past him, he can't tell if the driver is flipping him the bird or just flipping out. And he doesn't really care. It's the letters painted on the side that grab his attention.

"We're cool," he mutters.

"That was *cool?*"

"Whatever. They're prisoners, not kids."

"Yeah, 'cause I was worried about *them*."

"You'd choose me over a busload of school kids? That's kinda sweet, Miss Blaine."

"More like I'd choose a school bus over a Lincoln Navigator at a monster truck rally."

"Monster truck rallies…you're into those?"

"Are you drunk?"

He certainly feels drunk. Because sure, he sailed through BUD/S, did things overseas he hasn't told anyone about and never will, but there was no Emily Blaine to deal with during any of those brutal, soul-churning moments.

Correction: there was no *resisting Emily Blaine* to deal with during any of those moments. He's spent most of his life being dragged past the edge of his physical limits, only to hop to his feet on the other side and dust himself off, with ten new pounds of muscle to show for the whole experience. But now, thanks to Emily, he feels like he wouldn't be able to hold his breath underwater for as long as he once could. He can't tell up from down anymore, can't tell how many strokes it would take to reach the surface or how many minutes to sink straight to the bottom.

The GPS tells him the entrance to the restaurant is a half-mile ahead.

"The Shore Club's up here," Marcus manages. "Turn right."

The restaurant is a one-story stucco building that sits in a woodsy corner of a massive condo development. Beyond the pines and palm trees, he can glimpse the sea of identical-looking villas stretching to the high-rises at the beach. But the shaded valet court, with its shiny necklace of freshly parked luxury cars, might as well be in Beverly Hills.

He pulls over just shy of the valet court's entrance, rolls to a stop until he's got a perfect view of the young valet springing into action at the sight of a car with a sticker price equal to most people's annual salary. For three years. Emily steps from behind the wheel, dressed the part of Lily Conran. (Or how Arthur told her Lily should dress. Marcus wonders if that info was already included in the "Lily file" Emily keeps on her iPad.) Straw hat and a flowing sundress, strappy, designer looking shoes with a low heel, topped off with an assortment of jewelry that was waiting for her in the master suite.

And then she's striding toward the Navigator, wooden heels clacking against the concrete, silver bracelets tinkling on both wrists. Even when it becomes clear she's headed straight for him, Marcus refuses to power down the window. He's trying to act the part of the conscientious bodyguard, but it just makes him feel like an obstinate jerk. But still, he doesn't move, not until she raps her knuckles against the tinted glass, and then they're staring into each other's eyes through the shimmering heat.

It's the closest they've been to each other since he brought her a blanket and pillow on the beach that morning. Only now she's awake and redolent with a floral perfume that has a dark, earthy edge to it, an edge that makes his neck tingle and his balls tense. And he must be delirious, must be on the verge of losing his mind, because the unreadable expression on her face seems to reduce each breath he takes to half-strength. He's terrified of what she's about to say.

You'll be my employee soon, so no more late-night chats about what you want to do to my body. Got it?

"Take a nap," she says.

"Seriously? Right here?"

"Yes, right here," she says. She reaches through the window and gives him a light tap on the tip of his nose. "You've got an hour so get to it." It's not the smoothest of gestures, but that's what he likes about it. He likes how she hesitated a little once her hand was through the window. As if her fingers couldn't decide whether to bop him on the tip of his nose like he was a loud-mouthed third-grader or claw his T-shirt from his body.

When she starts back toward the restaurant, Marcus watches each swing of her hips, imagines gripping them until her smooth flesh whitens under his fingers, imagines driving himself into her, her mouth becoming a silent O and her eyes slit as her body proves a weak, shuddering cage for the pleasure he's filling her with.

He's still imagining these things when she pauses in the front door of the restaurant and turns.

"*Nap, Marcus!*" she shouts, loud enough to frighten the valet. "*Now!*"

He powers the window up.

He doesn't take a nap.

Instead, he calls Frank Dupuy.

Three years before, Marcus joined Team Benoit as a full-time member of Arthur's travel detail. Back then he spent most of his time accompanying Arthur on business trips to Asia and Latin America. But when the man's cancer took hold two years later, travel detail meant somber stays at various experimental clinics around the world where the news was always the same; there are some things you can't buy your way out of and cancer is one of them. That whole time, Frank Dupuy worked property security, a senior member of the cultish group that made the guardhouse at Magnolia Gate their little fiefdom of late-night card games and arguments about the New Orleans Saints.

As a result of their different contrasting career paths, Frank and Marcus have spoken to each other more in the past few days then they have in the past few years.

"All's quiet here," Frank answers.

"Not why I'm calling," Marcus says.

"Everything alright?"

No, actually. I'm falling head over heels in...in... Don't finish that sentence, Dylan. Not until you've had a nap. Emily's orders!

"Where are you guys?" Marcus asks. "Can you put him on the phone?"

"Jo— Excuse me. You mean *Leonard?*"

"Yeah."

"Hmmmm. That doesn't really seem like the rules of play here, friend."

"They're not supposed to be talking to each other, Frank."

"I know, but how do I know you're not passing a message?"

"I'm gathering information that'll make things quieter on my end, okay?"

"No connections between the two of them until this whole thing's over. Benoit's orders. Remember?"

"I'm not *connecting* them, Frank."

"See if it's okay with Benoit and then I'll be okay."

"Dupuy. Seriously, man."

"Hey. Speaking of serious, do we have to watch the whole thing?"

"What thing?"

"The surveillance equipment they got in this townhouse. I swear to God, I've never seen anything like it. Guy clips his toenails and I have to put my fingers in my ears. So I'm just asking you...this test.

Are we going to have to watch the whole thing?"

"This feels like a question for Benoit," Marcus says.

"Yeah, well, maybe you can ask him when you're asking him if it's alright for you to talk to Mr. Miller here."

"What's the matter, Frank? Watching Jonathan in the shower making you doubt your sexuality there?"

"Yeah, no. I'm still a giant homosexual who loves dick, Marcus."

Marcus waits a beat for Dupuy to say he's kidding.

Dupuy doesn't say anything.

Because he isn't kidding.

"I didn't. I'm sorry…" Marcus tries.

"Why? I'm not. Dick is amazing."

"I'm a fan of mine."

"And the kid's got a nice one, I'll give you that."

Marcus grips the steering wheel hard enough to whiten his knuckles. If he tells Dupuy to knock it off with the compliments to Jonathan's anatomy, he'll sound like a homophobic jerk. Or worse, he'll reveal that listening to any description of Jonathan Claiborne's body will make him imagine it all tangled up in Emily's, resulting in flashes of jealousy as blinding as the sun.

"I've got motion control on the cameras here," Marcus manages. "Turn the lenses if there's something you don't want to see. That's all I'm saying."

"You think I'm gonna be able to look away once the crazy starts?"

"Suit yourself."

"Look, as far as I'm concerned," Marcus says, "the test is the creepiest part of this whole thing, so—"

"Wait, really? What do you think they're going to make them do?"

"They're not going to *make* them do a goddamn thing!" Marcus barks. "She'll do what she wants and that's it. If any of those weirdoes tries to force anything on her, I will fucking bowl with their skulls."

"Wow. That's dedication to the job, man. Gotta say, though. Not sure I'm that committed to my charge, if you get my drift."

"Jonathan's a six-foot-three tower of muscle. He can defend himself."

He also gets paid to have sex with strangers for a living, Marcus thinks.

"I don't doubt it. We've got our SIGs just in case, right? But honestly, you think there's any chance Prince Benoit's gonna show up to either of these tests?"

"Well, Jonathan has a copy of Arthur's letter too, just in case."

"Yeah, I know. I was just asking what you thought the chances were. 'Cause that would sure make our job easier. I don't want to find out how many more shopping bags I can fit on one arm here."

"Shopping? Seriously?"

"Yeah, apparently this little gig comes with a nice stipend for them. I haven't seen this much cash since I watched *Scarface*."

"Nobody gave me any cash for Emily."

"Lily Conran, you mean?"

"You sure he didn't bring it with him? Guy's got pretty loyal clients, from what I hear. One of them got us into this whole mess."

"Nope. There was an envelope in the townhouse with Leonard Miller's name on it. I know, 'cause he asked me about it."

"Yeah, well, maybe she found hers and didn't mention it."

"I doubt that."

"Really. Why? It's all gonna be hers soon enough."

"Shopping. He took you shopping. Weren't you in the Marines?"

"A sniper. I was a *sniper* in the Marines and now I'm standing outside of Christian Lowbootin holding his bags."

"*Lou bah taun*," Marcus corrects him.

"What?"

"The designer. It's Christian *Lou bah taun*."

"Seriously? *You're* correcting me on this, Special Ops?"

"Last girl I was with, she was into nice things."

Like the ten million she needed to steal from her dad, but not before setting me up for the crime. But I'm only talking about that at least once every forty-eight hours and you don't know me well enough yet, Dupuy.

"Put Jonathan on the phone," Marcus says.

"Yeah, we kinda covered that, Dylan."

"I'll deal with the fallout, but there's not going to be any because I'm not going to say anything to Arthur about it. Are you?"

"No, but *Leonard* might, if you shoot off your mouth. You get my drift?"

"I'm sorry. That's a *drift*? Felt more like...I don't know...dragon's breath. Right in my face."

"Are you drunk?"

"People are asking me that a lot today."

"Look, I wasn't one of those college douchebags who went around talking about how sexuality was *fluid*. I think women are great and so I spare them the sight of my limp dick by not getting naked with them."

"Did you just ask me if *I* was drunk?"

"Blind man could see there's something weird going on with her and the two of you, and I ain't getting in the middle of it."

"Weird? Really? *I'm* the weird one here?"

"You have a problem with the women you're supposed to protect, Marcus. Sorry to be all Chief Justice about it, but it's not a secret around these parts, and to be blunt, I love that son of a bitch we work for. Sure, he's kinda nuts and his ego's the size of Texas. But if he hadn't hired me when he did, I'd be on a barstool somewhere boring the shit out of people with my war stories and pretending not to drool over the busboy. You get me?"

"No."

"This might be the last job I do for Arthur and I'm not gonna let it get fucked up."

I really should have taken a nap.

"Jesus Christ," Dupuy says suddenly. "These shoes he's trying on. They're like two porcupines stuck in quicksilver. Am I having a stroke?"

"The letter…"

"What about the letter?"

"Did he read it?"

"No. The thing's sealed and it's got the old man's handwriting on the envelope so Ryan will know it's legit."

Same story as Emily's copy.

Maybe he *is* drunk. Because what he wants to do right then is drive back to the house, find the envelope, tear it open and use whatever confession or apology is inside to hopscotch them past this Desire Exchange bullshit. For fuck's sake, why didn't Arthur hire his security team to find Ryan in the first place? Why make Emily do it?

Because whatever it is, whatever went wrong between them, it's bad. Real bad. Bad enough that Ryan will vanish into the wind if he gets word his father's trying to contact him. And this is the man's last chance to get within a stone's throw of his only child.

"Dylan…no offense, man, but didn't you do all kinds of fucked up shit in the Middle East? I figured this would just be a beach vacation for you."

"Put him on the phone, man. And I'll owe you. Big."

"You're not my type."

"I'm not gonna make him run crying to Arthur. There's…just. There's just some stuff I need to know."

Dupuy's breath turns into a whistle between his front teeth. "*Fuck*, man. Hold on."

"Is she alright?" Jonathan asks ten minutes later. Ten minutes, Marcus assumes, is how long it took Leonard Miller to buy ridiculous overpriced shoes with Arthur's money.

"She's fine."

"Are you sure?"

"I need to ask you something."

"Okay…"

"If I wait for her, are you going to make problems for me?"

There's a shocked silence from Jonathan. Marcus hears foot traffic and canned music. It sounds like they're in some outdoor shopping center. Maybe he's standing in one place, trying to get his bearings back.

"*Wait* for her? What do you…I don't…"

"If I tell her no matter what I have to watch her do, no matter *who* I have to watch her do it with, that I'll be right here, waiting, ready to start *something* with her when all of this over, are you gonna get in my way?"

"So you're asking for my blessing? Is that it?"

"No. I'm asking if you're gonna keep your hands off her when this thing is over."

"When she's one of the richest women in the country, you mean."

"Don't even. Not for a minute."

"Don't what?"

"I'm not sitting here going out of my *mind* over the smell of her perfume because I'm some gold digger. She's…"

"What? She's what?"

"If I wrote songs, I'd have written five about her already."

"But you don't write songs."

"Can't sing."

"You don't need to be able to sing to write a song."

"Look, I just don't fucking write songs, alright. It's a figure of speech."

"So this is hard for you? Having feelings for someone?"

"Who's it easy for? You? Do you have some great relationship history I'm not aware of?"

"There's a lot about me you aren't aware of."

"Which brings me back to my original question…"

"Look, if this place turns out to be some weird sex club and it's a choice between letting some sleaze put his hands all over her or me stepping in, playing the part so we don't lose our access to Ryan, you're gonna wish it was me, Marcus."

"I'm talking about *after* The Desire Exchange, not when you're…*in* it. None of that will count."

"Why wait, friend? Go for it. You've got her now. She's all yours. Make your mark."

"I don't share."

"Lord. Straight people. Ruining sex one phone call at a time."

"We're not talking about sex here."

"We're not?"

"I want more than that from her. That's what we're talking about. We're talking about her head, her mind, and your ability to mess with it if you touch her in the right place."

"She's not a child, Marcus."

"No, but you are."

"Excuse me?"

"You use your body to get what you want, but you don't know what you really want so it's all body, all the time with you. And shoes. You like shoes apparently."

"You're doling out a lot of insight for someone who doesn't know me very well."

"I knew someone just like you and—"

"That's not possible for you to say because you don't know *me*. So just stop right there before you compare me to some ex-girlfriend, or your sister who likes to shop and fuck a lot, or the one gay guy who used to train at your gym."

"I guess you're right. I don't know you very well. Maybe that's why I'm afraid of you."

"Afraid of me? Seriously?"

"I can hear you in her voice. I can see the power you have over her."

"I'm her best friend, Marcus. I've been her best friend since we were children. That's never going away. No matter what happens. I'm never just going to toss her to the wind. She's too…"

"…amazing," Marcus finishes for him.

"That's a good start, yeah. Look. Whatever happened between us this past week, she put the kibosh on it two nights ago, before we left. We even spent the night together in the same bed, fully clothed. G-rated from start to finish, okay? So relax."

"She put the kibosh on it but you didn't. You're still leaving it open and she knows that and I can tell she knows that and she's not going to be done with you unless you're done."

"Has she said any of this?"

"No, I can tell. Part of her isn't here. It's with *you.*"

"It's not with me, Marcus. That's just the way she is."

"I asked her if she thought she could change you and she wouldn't answer."

"Because she overthinks everything. That's the way she…"

"What?"

"I shouldn't be telling you this…" he mutters, then there's a long silence, and Marcus can imagine Dupuy staring Jonathan up and down from a safe distance, trying to determine if Marcus broke his promise by upsetting the guy too much. "Her father was a good man, but he was a cop and cops bring their shit home no matter how hard they try not to. Don't get me wrong. He wasn't abusive or a drunk or anything like that. But, he made her so *afraid* of everything. In their house, being smart meant being scared all the time. And I was the joker. I brought the fun. That was my role. But it's not like I could change the way they were. But, for Christ's sake, she was valedictorian of our high school class and she's been working in a restaurant now…for how long?"

"She quit a few days ago," Marcus adds.

"Right, but if this whole thing with Arthur hadn't happened, she'd be working there for another ten years. I mean, it wasn't a surprise for me. I was a party boy who slept around a lot. But Emily wrote papers in college her professors wanted to publish, but she wouldn't let them. Because her dad was a good man who taught her how to defend herself in a dark alley and how to show up and honor her commitments, but he scared her out of *risking* anything.

"She's capable of such amazing things. Everyone around her knows it. *Everyone.* But whenever there's an opportunity, whenever there's a new man, she thinks it to *death* and by the time she's done thinking, it's gone. Or he's gone. And to be honest, it's starting to look like a strategy, if you ask me. Hell, maybe that's why Arthur's leaving her everything. Maybe he hopes his money will take away all the fear her dad left her with.

"But my point, Marcus, is that the part of her that's not there with you has never been there with me either. She's too busy trying to figure out what she *should* want, and it makes her forget what she does want. I can't touch that part of her. And I sure as hell didn't touch it during our one *whole* night together, all right? But if you *can*...if you're the man she wants, Marcus. If you're the man she can finally try for, then I will move mountains to get out of your way. But, I swear to God, if you ever treat her like anything less than the queen that she is, I will be the hell on your earth."

There's a scraping sound against the phone before Marcus can say anything else, and then Frank Dupuy says, "Well, that sounded really peaceful."

"We're cool."

"Kid seems pretty riled up."

"He's an emotional guy."

"He wasn't until you called."

"We're cool, Dupuy. Relax."

"If we have to keep shoe shopping over this...I swear to God."

It takes Marcus a few seconds to realize Dupuy just hung up on him.

14

Marcus isn't sure who he's talking to. It's either Tyler or Chase. Both of them are guardhouse guys back at Magnolia Gate. Both of them were Recon Marines and both have those twangy East Texas accents that make them impossible to tell apart on the phone.

But it doesn't matter who the voice in his ear belongs to right now. What matters are the man's assurances; no one went near the beach house during Marcus's absence. And what matters even more than that, apparently, is that Marcus finds the perfect height for his cushy desk chair. For some reason, he can't stop playing with the adjustment no matter how hard he tries to focus on the guard's words. He figures it's his body's reflexive way of keeping him from passing out face down on the table in front of him.

Thank God he's allowed to keep the trailer's cooling going after he leaves; otherwise the tiny bulletproof box would be a sauna by now. Four CPU towers and twenty-seven flat screen monitors make for a lot of heat in a small space. That's why the tech guys ordered him to always run the ductless AC at seventy degrees, tops. He doubts, however, Arthur's computer geniuses factored in the body heat he gives off watching several different angles of Emily's every slinky move, so he's been running it at sixty-eight just to be safe.

The displays are color and HD, some of the best money can buy, and they're organized into three banks of nine—one bank for upstairs, one for downstairs, and one for all the exterior views on the house, including the walkway to the beach. Each bank is at a slight angle with one next to it, like the components of a church altarpiece. The setup is designed to ensure sudden motion in one bank of screens will show up in the corner of his eye even when he's studying another bank. But the way he's watching bright sunlight pool in Emily's luscious cleavage as she moves through the kitchen, it's doubtful he'd notice a murderous, marauding clown waving a bloody knife in front of one of the other cameras.

Emily is shelving groceries, groceries she insisted they stop to buy on their way back from The Shore Club, despite Marcus's insistence that a woman as rich as Lily Conran would never be seen out in public buying her own groceries.

Also, wasn't the house fully stocked when they arrived? Wasn't there anything in the cabinets she could snack on?

Not Wheat Thins and sliced salami, apparently.

God forbid anyone should have to go a day without Wheat Thins and sliced salami.

"Not even any birds," the voice on the other end of the line says.

"Birds?"

"You know, like on the roof? We didn't even see any birds land on the roof. Hey, you tired, man? You sound like you could use a—"

"What about the beach? Anyone take a conspicuous stroll?"

"Yeah, no, I had the feeds from the roof cameras up and it got everything from the edge of the pool deck to the sand. I mean, I guess someone could have been pressed up against the dunes the whole time. But how'd they find a hiding spot without walking through my view first? I'm telling you, nobody took a nibble at the place all day. Looks like y'all are gonna have a quiet night."

"Maybe. Or these people don't do recon."

"Which means they're not very organized. Less for you to worry about, I guess."

Except for this whole falling for the woman who's about to inherit my employer's estate. Maybe if I could stop staring at the way the sun is kissing the nape of her neck through those giant plate glass windows.

"Let's not jump to any conclusions about how this crew operates. Not yet anyway."

"Marcus, you sound tired. We can keep the feeds up here for a while so you can get some rest."

It's a tempting offer. But just thinking it's a tempting offer makes him feel like a wuss.

He should have waited to bathe, that's for sure. He thought the sputtering shower with its occasional shotgun blasts of air-pressure driven spray would wake him up a little, but the feel of even lukewarm water against his skin had the same effect as downing a pint of chamomile tea.

"No, I'm good. Thanks, though."

"You sure?"

"Yeah. I'm sure."

"Thanks, Tyler."

"It's Chase"

"Sorry. You guys sound alike."

"Hey. Don't mess with Texas!"

To save himself further embarrassment, he ends the call.

Then it's just him and the screens, and Emily standing on her toes to put a jar of Nutella in one of the top cabinets.

It takes him a second to realize his right eye has closed.

He grabs the mouse for the central computer, starts clicking on the microphone icons next to the directory listing for each camera feed.

The trailer fills with a clamorous mess. By itself, each sound is relatively pleasant, but thrown together the gentle roar of the surf, the clatter and slam of Emily opening and closing cabinet doors and the caws of two seagulls fighting on the house's back deck make for enough of a racquet to keep him awake and alert.

For about five minutes.

Maybe if she'd pressed down three times on that special ring he gave her the night they met, some kind of alarm would've shocked Marcus out of his stupor. But there's no rousing the guy now.

She feels like someone in a Pink Panther cartoon, perched outside the trailer door, just inside one of the looming shadows cast by the skeletal, unfinished mansion a few yards away. But after calling out his name over and again inside the house and getting no response through the earpiece, she had to be sure he was down for the count. She's sure now. He left the door open by about half an inch before he passed out and now she can hear him snoring like her grandfather in a Nicholas Sparks movie.

She shuts the door gently. The lock makes a small click when it catches, but that's all. She jogs back toward the house, making a beeline for the gleaming Aston Martin parked in the driveway. Thank

God she ditched the sundress she wore that morning. Her previously unworn silk blouse and chinos are the perfect outfit for this fleet-footed escape; it's too bad the pants are too tight for her to fit a cash-fat envelope in any of the pockets. She has to clutch it in one hand as she runs, then as soon as she's behind the wheel of the Aston Martin, she shoves the envelope inside the glove compartment as if all of the bills inside are about to take wing.

It's a lot of cash. No, it's a ridiculous amount of cash. No, it's an absurd, ludicrous, Arthur Benoit-sized amount of cash. And it was waiting for her in the nightstand drawer, just as Arthur promised. Still, she can't believe it. Did Jonathan get the same envelope? God help every shoe store in Atlanta if so.

Or maybe Jonathan and ten thousand dollars cash *is* God's plan for helping every shoe store in Atlanta.

There's no way she could spend that amount of money in the next few days. Not without feeling like some ridiculous, selfish brat.

She'll spend some of it, for sure. Just not on herself.

After a few minutes on the highway, there's no sign of Marcus's Navigator. Lily's cell phone is silent and dark where it rests in the cup holder. She thought about putting the top up to be less conspicuous, but is there any way to make a golden Aston Martin inconspicuous? Besides, she likes having her hair blow all over the place like someone in a car commercial.

There was no mapping her destination before she left. Given how deeply the house is wired, Marcus would probably be able to pull up any web search she performed on that giant computer in the master bedroom, and that would ruin everything, for sure.

But she's got a general idea of where she's headed and that's all she needs. The last time she visited this part of the Florida coast, the stakes were lower, but her stress level was about equal.

It was her last weekend getaway with Charles, the Xbox lover who would roll off of her as soon as he'd come, and then make all sorts of vague inferences that she might have a sexual compulsion when she had the temerity to ask if he might be able to, you know, help her finish too. Charles, the same guy who ran for the hills when she finally gave in to pressure and told him about her most secret sexual fantasy.

Maybe if the fantasy had involved another *woman*...

She wasn't with Charles now, thank God.

They're tangled on the lounger together. The sand is whiter than it should be, the sky a shade halfway between day and night, a deep pink that matches Emily's flushed skin as she parts her thighs and guides his head to the succulent triangle between. Her juices slather his lips and chin.

And then some seagull decides to ruin the moment with its cawing.

"Stupid seagull," Marcus whispers into Emily's heaving pussy.

Then he wakes up face down in his own drool.

Shit.

He sits up so fast he sends the chair rolling backward into the wall with a loud crash.

Fuck fuck fuck. Where is she? Goddammit!

With a single mouse click, he maximizes each interior camera angle on the center bank of monitors. Sun gleams across marble floors. Barely touched furniture looks ready for its Architectural Digest photo shoot. The beds are still made. One after the other, each feed shows an empty house. The beach is mostly empty too, save for a single family of four, their two kids playing right at the surf's edge, close to where he stood watch over Emily that morning.

A few seconds of fumbling with his headset and then he's stupidly calling Emily's name to the empty house, hearing the wacky reverb of his own voice coming back to him through the camera's microphones. He's on his feet now, holstering his 9 mm SIG even though it feels like he's closing the barn door after the horse got out.

Then he sees the driveway.

The Aston Martin is gone.

Images of Emily being gagged and abducted by a team of masked sex freaks start to fade. As the panic and sense of failure drain from him, they're replaced by a much darker emotion, one that's much harder to control.

Jealousy.

Jonathan. She's trying to call Jonathan.

He pops open his laptop and clicks on the app for the tracking device Arthur's advance team planted on the Aston Martin's undercarriage.

Twenty minutes later, he spots her Aston Martin exactly where the tracking device said it would be, parked outside some kind of high-end art gallery just off the coastal highway. The surrounding mini-mall is made up of designer clothing boutiques and stores that sell things like tea and soap for the same prices kidneys fetch on the black market.

The gallery sits at the juncture of the mall's two long, sandstone-colored wings. He figures the place has to have a name, but whatever's emblazoned on the sign looks more like a child's scrawl than letters of the alphabet; the most he can make of it is a B and an A. In the massive cathedral window over the entrance hangs something that looks to Marcus like a giant squid that's been bronzed and caked in gold dust. It's someone's idea of art, and while it's pretty enough, it only makes him wonder how much of a nightmare it would be to move into his apartment. Because the closer he gets to it, the more he realizes it's about the size of his apartment.

He's parked the Navigator far from the gallery's front windows. He's casing the place, he tells himself. Dropping back so he can make sure Emily didn't pick up a tail after slipping his grasp. But that's bull and he knows it.

He wants to surprise her. He wants to *catch* her. And that's wrong, because she doesn't belong to him, might never belong to him. And if she really did slip off to call Jonathan, he can deal with it like a professional and not some jilted lover; even if he did just wake from a delicious dream of tasting her for the first time only to find the drapes fluttering ghost-like in her sudden absence.

There's no entry chime when he steps across the threshold to the gallery. It's not like they need one for security. Marcus can't imagine a shoplifter sneaking off with a giant glass coffee table supported by a massive piece of blond driftwood. Now that he's inside, he realizes the place is more of a furniture store than a gallery. Still, there are plenty of paintings on display throughout the rows of modern, nautical-inspired sculptures, and each one sports a jaw-dropping price tag.

He can hear Emily's voice coming from the back of the store. It sounds like she's talking to a clerk, another woman. And from the casual tone of their conversation, it doesn't sound like they're being secretive. But when he spots her through a sudden break in the labyrinth of shelves, Marcus ducks into the nearest hiding place, then starts creeping down the aisle in the direction of the register until he can make out what she's saying.

I have literally killed terrorists. Literally. And now, I'm hiding in a Florida gift shop, eavesdropping on a woman who makes me weak in the knees. It reminds him of something his father used to say. *You wanna be in the military, son? Then learn your history. Biggest war the Greeks ever fought was over a woman!*

He's close enough to make out their chatter.

"...it's not the nicest place between here and Destin, but it's pretty nice," the clerk is saying while she wraps something in crinkling tissue paper.

"It was alright, I guess. For just a weekend. I mean, it wasn't my favorite trip to begin with so..."

"So I take it you and the guy you were with are..."

"Yeah, that didn't work out," Emily answers.

"Sorry," the clerk says.

"I'm not."

"Oh, okay."

"Let's just say he wasn't the one," Emily says too cheerfully.

Is this Emily or Lily talking? Marcus wonders.

"I hear yah," the clerk answers. "But honestly, is there any such thing?"

"As what?"

"Oh, you know. The *one*."

"I'm starting to think there might be..." Emily says distantly.

Marcus tries to will his heart to slow down, but it's no use.

"Really?" the clerk asks. Marcus can hear her smile in her tone.

"Yeah, I just...if there is such a thing as the one, I think they crash into you when you're least expecting it. And it's not always clear in that moment, you know, that they're the right one for you, but then they do something totally unexpected that changes the way you see them and you're like, well, maybe. Maybe if there is such a thing as *the one*...it could be them, you know?"

Like one minute he's your gay best friend, and the next he's...he's... Marcus doesn't realize how tightly he's gripping the shelf next to his head until a bolt of pain shoots up his forearm.

"That's lovely," the clerk says. "So is that who you're getting this for? The guy who crashed into you?"

"Yep."

"Well, it's a beautiful piece. So romantic. I hope he likes it."

"Me too. You take cash?"

"Uhm...wow. For that price? Yeah, sure. I guess."

None of the degradations he went through during SEAL training can hold a candle to the humiliation he feels now.

He stalks back to the store's entrance, trying not to curse under his breath.

He's a goddamn idiot, is what he is, thinking he could be anything other than her hired gun. She wanted him last night, at four in the morning. But she doesn't want him today and she won't want him tomorrow, and she sure as hell won't want him when she becomes one of the richest women in the country.

Sure, maybe she'll eventually ask him to ride her in the guardhouse late at night, but only after her new hubby Jonathan gives into temptation and starts dipping into the dude pond again. Because one thing's clear for sure—Jonathan Claiborne is going to be Mr. Emily Blaine. Not some spec-ops has-been whose war wounds will probably get the best of him as he enters old age.

"*Marcus!*"

He's positioned himself outside the entrance, as if he's just tracked her down, as if he hasn't heard her say words that have cut him to his soul. Under her right arm she's holding something the size of a small surfboard; it's been bundled in a mix of butcher paper and tissue paper. He steps back inside the store, closing the distance between them even though he knows the proximity alone might show her how deeply he's feeling her rejection.

"What are you doing, Emily?" He shouldn't have spoken because now she's heard the frog in his throat. He sounds a lot angrier than a bodyguard who's been successfully evaded thanks to his stupid unwillingness to take a fucking nap.

"Don't you mean *Miss Conran?*" she whispers.

"What are you doing, Miss Conran?"

"Well…it was supposed to be a surprise…"

"A surprise?" he asks, his voice a rasp.

"Yeah. Arthur left me some cash in an envelope. A *ridiculous* amount of cash in an envelope so I thought…"

An envelope full of cash just like the one Jonathan went shoe shopping with. She'd had it the whole the time but she was keeping it a secret because she was going to spend it on a surprise.

His head is spinning now. He tries to remember the exact words she'd told the clerk. Something about how *the one* crashes into you at first and then…

"Here," Emily says, jerking one shoulder in his direction. "Take it. Since the surprise is ruined anyway… Also, I'm about to drop it. It's *really* frickin' heavy."

Marcus rushes to her and takes whatever the hell this surprise is out from under her right arm. Emily guides him to the nearest shelf, rests the top edge of the piece against it, then she begins to carefully peel back the wrapping.

It's a painting, a painting on the side of a large piece of driftwood that's been polished and varnished and turned into a kind of canvas. The colors are all bright pastels, not exactly the type he'd hang in his apartment, but he couldn't care less about the colors or the wood they're painted on. What he cares about is the couple at the center of the frame, the two black silhouettes standing at the edge of the surf line on a beach just like the one where he watched over her that morning. The surf shoots up around them, but it doesn't look like they're about to be consumed by the waves. Rather, it looks as if the couple's embrace has the power to split the surf in two. He can't breathe and he can't speak, because it feels like Emily somehow conjured a painting of the two of them from early that morning, only she moved herself off of the beach lounger and into his arms.

And it's for him, this gift, this surprise. Not Jonathan, him.

Her breath tickles the inside of his ear as they both look down at his present.

"I was in here a few months ago," she whispers. "The whole trip was kind of a last-ditch effort with this guy I was seeing, and I saw this and thought, 'Gosh, I wish that could be the two of us...'"

"You and the guy you were seeing, you mean?"

"Yeah."

So it wasn't a cover. The story she told the clerk was true...

"But you didn't feel that way about him?" Marcus asks. It feels like he's breathing through a straw.

"No."

He pushes the painting back so that it's resting fully on the shelf. It feels like it takes all the courage he has in the world, but he turns and looks into her eyes.

But you feel that way about me...

Her eyes are so wide it's as if she's taking in every inch of him. And it's taking all of his strength not to lift his hand to the side of her face, to bring their lips together. But the longer he doesn't ask the question, the harder the struggle gets. If he pressed his body to hers right now, would there be enough of an answer in the flex of her muscles, in her willingness to accept his embrace?

No. That's how he went down the last time, by listening to a woman's body and not her words. That's how he ended up hearing things that hadn't been said. That's how he ended up mistaking his cock for his heart and getting used and thrown away by someone who was counting on him to confuse the two.

Her lips haven't moved, but her eyes haven't left his either. Over the sounds of his own heavy, hungry breaths, he hears Jonathan's words. *Whenever there's an opportunity, whenever there's a new man, she thinks it to death and by the time she's done thinking, it's gone. Or he's gone.*

"And then they do something unexpected and suddenly you see them in a different way," Marcus whispers.

"Oh my... That's what I just— Were you *eavesdropping?*"

"I thought you were talking about Jonathan."

"Well, I wasn't," she says, a trace of offense in her voice, but her eyes search his face hungrily and her chest is rising and falling visibly. "I wasn't talking about Jonathan."

"You were talking about me, this morning. On the beach."

Her cheeks are crimson and she's biting her lower lip the way he usually does when he's nervous. He's never seen her do that before. Maybe it's something she's picked up from him, and maybe she picked it up by studying him as intently as he's been studying her.

"Anyway," she says too quickly. "I figured since you're so big on waiting, this would tide you over."

"Tide me over, huh? Is that...an *ocean* joke."

"Very funny, you big..." And her eyes flutter closed before she can finish the sentence. She draws a deep breath, as if what she wants to call him has sent her into a trance, a trance that causes her lips to part and her breath to come in a long sigh, a trance in which she's thinking about him the way he was just dreaming of her a half hour before.

He can hear his pulse in his ears, and to his mind's eye, he's already got one arm around her waist. Then she catches sight of something behind him and fear makes her body go rigid.

Marcus spins, follows her frightened gaze to the Aston Martin outside.

After a few seconds, he sees it too, something large and white clamped under the car's windshield wiper. If it were just a sheet of paper, it would be rustling in the wind. But whatever it is, it's heavier and shinier.

"Go," Marcus whispers. "I'll watch..."

He steps back into the shelves, scanning their surroundings. No lurkers visible in the nearby pine trees, no cars idling suspiciously anywhere in the parking lot.

Emily lifts the windshield wiper.

Marcus hikes the hem of his T-shirt up a few inches and poises his hand next to the SIG's holster.

Now that she's holding it in both hands, he can see what it is; a huge, shiny white envelope that folds out from the center into four leaves, the kind used for graduation and wedding invitations.

Emily reads it, her expression fixed, and then she looks in both directions before stepping back inside the store.

When she hands it to Marcus, it's trembling in her grip.

The outside bears Lily's initials and nothing more.

Inside, in cursive so elegant he can barely read it, are the words.

Tonight, after sundown, your desire will be tested.

- JDE

15

The note had the same effect as a shotgun barrel shoved between their bodies, and with each hour since she pulled away from Marcus inside of Blake Gallery, her body temperature seems to have dropped another degree. Now she's shivering in front of the balmy beach scene visible through the great room's soaring plate glass windows, her only warmth a sense memory; Marcus gripping her trembling hand after he removed The Desire Exchange's ornate offering from her fingers. But the memory is sure to fade after a while, and then what will she have to comfort herself with until sundown?

The light from the westward-leaning sun silhouettes waves stronger than the ones that were rolling to shore that morning when she woke to the sight of him standing watch, when she realized the hours during which he'd guarded her sleeping form constituted one of the most selfless, generous things a man had ever done for her. Watching over her was his job description, for sure, but not from so close, and not when he was scheduled to sleep. And then there was the blanket and the pillow, and the gentle graze of his fingers along her cheek.

She'd never been one of those people to claim chivalry was dead. But she hadn't realized until that morning how much chivalry could set her heart to simmer. Most of her relationship history had been defined by a series of what Jonathan had called the *Oh, goods.*

Oh, good, he's not late. Oh, good, he didn't show up drunk. Oh, good, he isn't still involved with his ex.

With Marcus, the *Oh, goods,* seemed monumental.

Oh, good, there's a man of focus and dedication behind that swagger. Oh, good, he's gorgeous but doesn't skate through life on his looks...

The slanting sunlight gives definition to every fold in every dune and every footprint in the sand. Finally, she realizes she's looking for theirs. It's a silly endeavor, but not impossible. The beach didn't see that much foot traffic that day, and maybe, after a few hours, it would be possible for her to mark the twin-trails they made that morning as he followed her toward the walkway. But it's a silly distraction from the unsaid words burning a hole in her throat.

She pulls the earpiece from her pants pocket and slides it into her ear.

"Marcus?"

"Yeah."

"I can't do this."

He's stricken silent. Were her words too ambiguous? Does he think she can't *do* whatever's growing between them, that she's taking back the gift she just gave him and throwing away their moment of restrained, electrified passion inside of Blake Gallery.

"I want to speak to Arthur," she says quickly.

"Emily..."

"If it's not Ryan who shows up tonight, I'll just give whoever it is the letter and then I'm done. The rest can be in God's hands. Because, seriously, I just can't..."

"That's pretty dangerous at this point, babe."

"Why is it dangerous?"

Babe. He called me babe. What would it be like to hear him whisper it against my neck as he—

"Because it gives Ryan a chance to vanish into the wind."

"Even if he knows his father's dying?"

"He might not care," Marcus answers.

"Well, then what's going to make him care when I say it to his face?"

"It ups the odds in our favor a little but..."

"A little?"

"Emily, this is...this is about getting deeper into whatever this place is. Even if you get all the way inside and the letter *doesn't* get to Ryan, it won't matter."

"Why?"

"Because we'll have gathered all kinds of intell along the way just by being there. Locations, associates, his recent history. That's more than any private detective Arthur's ever hired. Arthur could use all of that on a second go around, and he might be able make contact in the time he has left even if we don't."

"I thought you didn't want me to do this," she whispers.

"God, Emily, I *don't* want you to do this. I really, really don't want you to do this. But you made your promise to Arthur before you ever met me. And I couldn't live with myself if I asked you to go back on it just because I'm a jealous, possessive bastard who's moving too fast."

"You're not moving too fast," she says.

"Really?"

"You wouldn't come to me last night. I'd say that's pretty slow."

"I'm the one who woke you up at four in the morning, remember?"

"Well, that's true, I guess."

"It *is* true," he says.

Emily starts for the kitchen. Suddenly, Marcus is filling her ear with his best sports announcer's voice. "Ladies and gentlemen, after several hours of staring out the front windows and wishing she had fingernails to chew, Miss Conran finally relents and heads to the kitchen for a small snack. The odds-on favorite for tonight's tasty treat? The *very* Wheat Thins and salami she was spotted buying in a grocery store *just* this afternoon. What a multimillionaire heiress was doing buying her own groceries in a Winn-Dixie is still a matter for tabloid speculation… Oh, oh, oh. Wait just a minute! In a stunning upset, ladies and gents, she pulls out a jar of Nutella and slides some bread in the toaster, both sure signs that she's experiencing some *serious* nerves in anticipation of tonight's just announced visit from *The Desire Exchaaaaaange…*"

She wants to tell him to shut up, but she's laughing too hard.

When he runs out of breath for his little routine, a silence falls until the toaster pops.

"Charles," Emily says.

"Huh?"

"The last guy I was with. I mean, *really* with, not like—"

"Not like one-night-with-your-gay-friend with."

"Yes. Thank you for that…specificity, Marcus. The last guy I was boyfriends with. His name was Charles."

"Okay…"

"I thought it was only fair, you know, since you told me about the last woman you were with."

"But I didn't tell you her name," Marcus says.

"Okay. What's her name?"

"Natalya."

"Was she Russian?"

"No. Just pretentious."

"Ugh."

"I'm kidding," he responds with a throaty laugh. "Of course she was Russian."

"But she was pretentious too, I take it."

"Oh, like you wouldn't believe."

"And a criminal too, apparently."

"Yep."

"Was her father a criminal?"

"I don't work for criminals, Miss Blaine."

"I wouldn't blame you if you did."

"Seriously?"

"You're in private security now, not law enforcement. A job's a job as long as you don't…"

"Kill people?"

"Commit crimes."

"I'd rather not be an accessory to any either."

"Probably a healthy boundary. I was just…you know, trying to be accepting of the field you're in."

"Natalya's father was one of the first guys to privatize Russia's electrical industry after the Soviet Union fell."

"A Russian oligarch. I've heard of them. So he had some cash?"

"Yeah, and you're gaining on him, Miss Blaine."

"So why did his daughter need to embezzle from him? A guy that rich, his kids are usually set for life."

"Unless you're Ryan Benoit."

"True, but you're deflecting…"

"Her father knew what she was and he put her in a cage. She used me to get out of it. So…Charles?"

"Hardly as dramatic."

"Still…."

"He had a cute smile," she says, and then she shoves a piece of Nutella-covered toast in her mouth.

"Seriously?"

"Yes," she says, in between chews. "Just adorable. And dimples."

"Okay. So...what happened? He lost his dimples?"

"Let's just say his dimples lost their effect."

"So after the cute wore off, the guy was a douche."

"I'm not sure I'd be that harsh."

"Well, I'll be. He's my competition. I'm gonna track him down and vanquish him to the hills."

"*Vanquish him to the hills?*" she asks through Nutella-laced laughs. "What does that even *mean?*"

"I don't know. It's probably something I heard on *Game of Thrones.*"

"Okay," Emily says, clearing her throat. "Well, trust me. The guy's not your competition. By a long shot."

"Really?"

"Yeah, really."

"How would you know?" Marcus asks.

"You mean because we haven't slept together?"

"Kinda. Yeah."

"Let's just say you wouldn't have to be amazing in the sack to be miles ahead of Charles. In *everything.*"

"Wow...I'm not sure if I should be flattered or if Charles is just...completely pathetic."

"Go with both."

"Fine by me."

"So why did it end?" Marcus asks.

"Better question is why did it last as long as it did."

"Sure, but there had to be some kind of death blow."

Nutella, spoon, toast, mouth. Nutella, spoon, toast, mouth.

"Guess we're not going there..." Marcus says quietly.

"He asked me a question he didn't want the answer to."

"Ouch. Burn. So was it...do you love me?"

"No."

I can't, she thinks. *I can't go back to this place. With Charles, it didn't matter. But with Marcus...*

"Want to talk about something else?"

And Emily thinks, *No, I don't want to talk about something else. I'm not putting this part away now so you can discover it later and decide you don't like the smell of it, of me. I'm not waiting to be Emily Blaine anymore.*

"He asked me to share my most secret sexual fantasy."

"So you guys could act it out?"

"No. I mean, I don't think so. Maybe. We never got that far."

"I see. Did he return the favor?"

"He'd already volunteered his by the time he asked for mine."

"Kind of an *I'll show mine if you show me yours* type of thing."

"Something like that. Yeah."

She's shelved the Nutella and now she's rinsing the spoon in the sink. Her heartbeat has turned into a patter, and her shortness of breath is causing a light tingling in her arms.

"So what was his?" Marcus asks.

Clever guy, Marcus. Take the indirect route and come in from behind.

"Girl Scouts deliver some cookies…it goes from there."

"Tell me he wasn't really into little girls."

"*No!* It was all about the costume and the fantasy. And you know, the pig tails."

Don't ask me if I ever dressed as one for him. Please don't ask me if I ever…

"I see…"

Her cheeks burn. She rinses her hands under the sink because it gives her an excuse to keep her head bowed and hopefully shield her face from at least one or two of the surrounding cameras.

"And what was yours, Emily?" Marcus asks.

She wants to half-ass this, to give the quick, relatively safe one-line description. But wasn't she just about to burst into a Gloria Gaynor song about her personhood and how she wasn't going to wait to be her real self anymore?

Marcus says, "Sorry. Maybe that's too—"

"Right after we started college, Jonathan and I would go out to the gay clubs in the Quarter and anyway, he started dating this go-go boy, this really hot go-go boy…and anyway, one night they danced up on either side of me and made this little sandwich out of me on the dance floor and I just …"

"You just what, Emily?"

Is there the slightest hint of judgment in his tone? She can't tell.

"Ever since then I fantasize about what it would be like to be with two guys at the same time. If I'm masturbating in the shower, it's usually the one thing I need to think about to…you know, have a moment. It's about being the *center* of something…like that."

Okay. Maybe the shower line was too much information but…

How long has this silence actually gone on? Is it her frayed nerves making it seem like it's already dragged on for twenty minutes?

Is this it? Is this the moment when she experiences, once again, the real price of honesty, only in this instance, it dooms all possibilities of anything with Marcus in the future?

"Mine's a mother and a daughter at the same time," Marcus says.

For a second, she thinks he's making fun of her, but he doesn't laugh, and he doesn't rush to qualify it in any way and there was a shaky edge of embarrassment in his tone. *Not embarrassment,* she realizes. *Vulnerability.*

"Really?" she asks.

"Yeah, and in the fantasy, the mother and I have already been together so she's instructing the daughter on how best to…tend to my needs."

"Really?"

"Yeah, see, so yours is kinda tame compared to mine."

"Yeah, I mean, I guess…there's no incest in mine."

"There's isn't any in mine either. *I'm* the focus."

"I see."

"Are you?" he asks.

"What do you mean?"

"I mean, in your fantasy do the guys…touch each other."

"Sometimes. Depending on what mood I'm in."

"And does…"

"What, Marcus?"

"Does one of the guys have to be Jonathan?"

Her heart is hammering. She feels like she's standing on the edge of a cliff.

"No," she answers.

And to her astonishment, she realizes it's the truth.

"Thank you," she whispers before she can stop herself.

"For what?"

"I just…the last man I ever talked to about this, he was so busy freaking out that he never got around to asking me what you just did. But now, because you asked, I know the answer."

"You know that it doesn't have to be Jonathan."

"Yeah…"

A silence falls. She pads into the living room and eases down into one of the giant, cushy white sofas. She feels like she's sinking into a cloud.

"You want to know what's even hotter than the idea of a mother and a daughter working me over at the same time?" Marcus says, his low, smooth voice as arousing as a gentle breath inside her ear.

"What?"

"The fact that you just shared your fantasy with me, especially given how badly it went for you the last time."

"Thank you."

"They're just fantasies, Emily. No one should judge us for our fantasies. No one who cares about you anyway."

"You don't..."

Cushioned by the massive sofa as she stares up through plate glass at passing clouds now streaked with bands of night darkness, Emily feels both the terror and the joy of being weightless and untethered. Who knew she would feel this sense of relief? Did Jonathan have a better sense than her of how deeply the rejection from Charles had wounded her? Had her rush to dismiss and demean her ex ever since been part of her determination to conceal that wound?

"I don't what, Miss Blaine?" he asks her gently.

"I..."

"Come on, babe," he whispers. "We're this far in. There's no turning back now."

"You don't think we have to act them out to be..."

"To be what?"

"I don't know. Free?"

"No. I think the only thing that matters is that we find someone to share them with."

"Like this?" she asks.

"Yes. Just like this."

She feels a drowsy smile take hold of her face.

"I always crash after I eat sugar," she whispers.

"Uh huh."

"I'm serious. Sugar makes me sleepy."

"So does relief, I bet."

"That too," she says, giggling in spite of herself.

"You're cute when you laugh, Emily Blaine."

"Thank you, Marcus Dylan."

"No thanks necessary."

"Marcus..." she says.

"Yes, babe."

"I like it when you watch over me."

"Get some rest, beautiful. I'll be watching over you the whole time."

"Promise?" she asks, hearing her own voice from a foggy distance.

"Yes, Emily. I promise."

Sleep claims her, deep and dreamless, until she hears the clear, unmistakable call of a single handbell from just outside the house.

And then Marcus's voice in her ear.

"Emily, wake up. They're here."

16

She feels as if she's only been asleep for minutes, but it must have been at least an hour given how dark it is outside. The dunes have been reduced to just those fat pools of white sand captured by the two streetlights that line the wooden walkway to the beach, and the waves beyond look like vague bands of froth moving through a sea of ink.

"Don't talk. There's four that I can see. They're watching the house. Look, I know you're sleepy, but I need you to focus, okay? Because in about a minute, you're not going to be able to talk to me again until this over. Yawn and run your hands through your hair to let me—"

She does both.

"Okay. Good. The ring. If they make you take it off for any reason, your distress call's three taps, either with your foot or the side of your fist. Three taps. But only if you want me to bust in there with all the firepower I've got and shut the whole thing down. Tap the coffee table three times right now if you read me."

She follows his instruction.

"Alright, we're good to go. And Emily—"

Blackout is too simple a word to describe what happens next. It's as if the electricity is drained from every light source in the house by some invisible, sucking force. The darkness isn't as frightening as the burst of static in her ear. It cuts Marcus off mid-sentence, bringing sudden silence along with impenetrable black.

If they're watching her now, it's through night-vision goggles. She spins toward the plate glass windows. The power's gone out at the neighboring houses as well; like the dunes, they've been reduced to slight tonal shifts in a sea of dark.

A candle flickers to life in the center of the room. Several feet away, just on the other side of the glass coffee table, a shadow brings a gloved finger to his lips in the small flame's strengthening glow. All she can see of the man are his generous lips and strong jaw. His eyes are hidden behind some sort of mask and a hooded, tailored robe conceals the rest of his imposing figure. The mask's eyeholes are filled with some kind of reflective black glass.

Ryan? She almost says his name aloud. But her heart is racing and the breath that reaches her lungs feels both electrified and stale. But after a second or two of peering at him through the dark, she's sure the man is not Ryan. This man has an olive complexion, an angular face, and no real resemblance to any of Ryan's age progression photographs.

He points down at the coffee, where he's placed a message for her right inside the candle's halo. The paper is some kind of expensive cardstock. Its edges are frayed and the words engraved on it are lined with some type of reflective ink that catches the flame's steady flicker.

GOOD EVENING, LILY. PLEASE FOLLOW THE FLAMES

Flames. Plural.

Another candle flickers to life several feet behind her visitor. Its glow reveals another robed, masked figure and the figure's prim little cupid's bow of a mouth. Emily assumes this ghostly visitor must be a woman. The process repeats itself halfway up the stairs: another candle, another eye mask, another tense, set mouth, and then, at the top of the stairs, yet another. Then, in what appears to be a well-rehearsed sequence, all four figures turn their backs to her and begin a silent procession up the carpeted stairs.

There's a slight burst of static in her ear. Suddenly, Marcus is back. "—your hand through your hair if you can hear me. Dammit! *Emily*, if you can hear me—"

She runs one hand through her hair.

"Okay, good," he whispers. "We're back. We're back in business." But he doesn't sound confident or calm.

Fresh shadows divide the living room. The lights over the beach walkway have come back on, and a glance over her shoulder confirms they're back on at the neighboring houses too. The minor electrical disturbance that heralded the arrival of these silent, robed visitors has passed. But inside Lily Conran's beach house, there is only candlelight to guide them.

Candles that came to life by themselves, without the scratch of a match or the telltale click of a lighter. What kind of magic trick is that?

When she reaches the door to the master suite, she discovers all four figures have gathered inside of the bathroom. Standing rigid as monks, they've formed an inverted V in front of the glass-walled shower that sits in the center of a tiled bathroom half the size of her apartment. There's something inside the shower, but she can't quite make it out in the darkness. It looks like some sort of cube they've somehow hung six feet off the shower floor.

"I'm here, Emily," Marcus says quietly. But he sounds distracted, as if he's working as hard as she is to try to interpret the scene before her. "I'm here, babe," he whispers.

As soon as she starts to search for Ryan's features among her four visitors, her silent messenger steps forward. The candle he holds in his left hand is fat, purple, and balanced impossibly, it seems, in his open palm. In his right hand he lifts another sheet of paper on which is printed a new direction in the same elegant script as the previous one.

PLEASE DISROBE

"I'm here, Emily. You're safe..."

Can he read the message too? Is he giving her permission to keep going?

Even as she debates this question, her hands fumble with her belt buckle. She tugs her blouse from her chinos. Her fingers are shaking and slick with sweat, her breaths so short she's afraid she's wheezing. For the first time, she can see they're all holding their candles in exactly the same way, balanced in their open palms. Are they illusionists? Circus performers?

We're sorry to tell you, Arthur, but in your case, it looks like your son actually did run off and join the circus!

She expects some sort of reaction from the figures before her when she unhooks her bra, but their robes don't even rustle; she might as well be undressing in front of statues. The half-light helps her feel less vulnerable and afraid, but she has a sense that vulnerable and afraid are exactly how they'd like her to feel. Because this is a test, she reminds herself. A test of what exactly she's not quite sure, but she figures they're not just here to determine how quickly and easily she can get naked in front of strangers.

Once she's completely nude, her clothes piled neatly on the counter next to her, the three figures behind her silent messenger all take several precise steps to the left, clearing an even broader path between her and the shower and its strange new addition.

Her messenger lifts a finger on his right hand. One request slides away, the paper scraping lightly across the tiles before it comes to rest at her feet. This simple gesture has revealed another request.

STEP INTO THE SHOWER

Every step she takes toward the shower seems to drive the breath from her lungs. She isn't sure if she's really cold or if fear has set her bones to trembling. As soon as she's inside the shower's four glass walls, something grazes her shoulder. She cries out and jumps to the side before she sees a pull-chain swinging in the air next to her head. Even more frightening than the chain's sudden touch is the realization that she's turned her back on her visitors.

They've fanned out now, facing her, but also blocking the only exits. The silent messenger is still in pole position, his companions now behind him. The candlelight dances in the strange black glass that fills the eyeholes of their masks. The eyeholes, she can now see, are generous and tapered like a cat's, and the bridges over the noses are encrusted with strips of tiny, clustered jewels.

Once again, her silent messenger lifts a single finger on his right hand. Once again, a new request is revealed.

PLEASE GRIP THE HANDLES. DO NOT RELEASE THEM UNTIL GRANTED PERMISSION

Handles?

For the first time, she looks directly overhead. The cube is transparent, probably Lucite, and full of some kind of swirling, amber liquid. A single steel bar runs through the top, its ends secured to opposite walls with suction cups. Attached to the underside of the cube is what looks like two bicycle handlebars swaddled in black velvet.

Even though it makes her feel more exposed than being naked does, she lifts her hands into the air above her head until her fingers find their grip on each handle. The cool air teases her armpits, causing a sensation somewhere between being tickled and caressed. The instruction, the demand that she not release the handles until they say so, suggests that they're not going to tie her up, and this slows her heartbeat some. Once she's secure in her two-handed grip, each figure turns and places their candle on the nearest available surface. Now the bathroom flickers with diffuse candlelight that makes it seem as if it's been staged for a surprise romantic evening by one lover for another.

When her silent messenger takes a long step forward, his three companions each drop to one knee behind him. Their heads are bowed like Olympic runners getting on their marks, but the pose turns their robes into draping shrouds, their presence suddenly more spectral, impossible, magical.

"I'm here, Emily," Marcus whispers. "I'm here. You're safe."

Her silent messenger dips a hand into the folds of his robe. She can't make out what he's holding in it until his gripping fingers are inches from her mouth.

A peach.

He lifts a finger on his right hand, revealing a new request.

TAKE THE OFFERING IN YOUR MOUTH. DO NOT CONSUME IT. DO NOT RELEASE IT UNTIL GIVEN PERMISSION.

Don't let go of the handles. Don't bite through the peach. Simple enough.
He cups her chin gently with gloved fingers. Her lips part, first to take a much needed breath, then further, so that he can place one side of the peach snugly in her mouth. Fear has run her mouth dry, which is a good thing, or else the peach might have slipped to the floor upon contact with her yawning mouth.

Another lift of his finger and a new message appears.

ARE YOU READY TO SURRENDER, LILY?

Her mind fills with every dark possibility roiling beneath the surface of the scene before her. The hooded figures are poised for some terrible act of violence, she's sure. The amber fluid swirling through the chamber overhead is some horrible poison, or worse, gasoline. She has been raised to think this way. Not just by her father, but by the world itself. Raised to believe this kind of vulnerability will cost you your life, especially if you're a woman. All things being equal, the darkest possibility was always the most probable. But it's not always true. And she prays it won't be true now.

"Emily…"

Yes, Marcus. I'm here. Even though I can't speak to you, I'm here and if you said the word, if you told me to stop, I would. For you, I would. For the promise of the two of us becoming that little painting someday, I would stop this right now. But I'm here because you told me not to bail. Even though I would have bailed for you, you big beautiful bastard.

The question hovers several feet from her face, as insistent as a demand barked in anger.

"You're safe," Marcus whispers.

She tries to find the man's eyes through the darkness, finds instead that strange, impenetrable glass flickering with the reflection of her face bathed in candlelight.

Gently, so as not to jostle the peach from her mouth, she nods.

The silent messenger closes one gloved hand around the pull-chain. He gives it a single, determined yank, and everything that follows seems to happen in one dizzying, impossible instant.

Two threads of amber-colored fluid pour down onto her chest from the Lucite cube overhead, painting her breasts with something sticky and thick.

The three figures crouched on the floor spring to life, lunging across the floor like jungle cats, their robes falling away behind them, revealing flashes of muscle and shiny leather outfits that only cover their genitals, and in the case of the two women, their breasts.

Her silent messenger drops his robe, revealing plates of olive-skinned muscle. All four mouths take to her body at once, and only as they suck it from her nipples and lick it from the undersides of her breasts and trace its wet, oozing path down her thighs with flickering tongues, does Emily realize what it is that's pouring down on her from the cube overhead—honey.

Grip. Don't bite. Grip. Don't bite.

Her hand aches from the exertion of holding fast to the handlebars, and at first the assault of pleasure overwhelms her senses, and in the resulting shock, she has no trouble holding the peach in her yawning mouth. But then two sets of lips begin to suck threads of honey from her pussy, while another mouth sucks at her right breast with the desperation of someone satisfying a long buried craving. And suddenly it feels as if a second skeleton has been electrified beneath her flesh, a skeleton composed entirely of raw, humming nerves that when fully stimulated, as they are now, become solid, scorching, radiant bones unto themselves.

After several minutes of being devoured, it starts to feel as if she's floating up off the floor. But maybe that's because one of the women working her over has lifted Emily's right leg and draped it over her shoulder so she can run her tongue along the sole of Emily's foot before sucking honey from her toes. Meanwhile, her male partner licks up the inside of Emily's opposite thigh, then cups her mound in both gloved hands, kneading its outer walls, studying the pressure against her folds with a cocked head, his lips parted with evident hunger. And then there's her silent messenger and the other woman, who are catching every fresh current of honey sliding across the top of her breasts just as it reaches her nipples.

Grip. Don't bite. Grip. Don't bite...

Behind the peach, her groans are choked, agonized things that catch in her throat. To a blind bystander, they would sound like agony. But no one here is blind. Everyone here can see, and they can all see her. She is their sole focus. The sense of being the center of such raw, animalistic hunger sets off a delicious war within her body, a war between the parts of her struggling desperately to hold on to the handlebars overhead and keep the peach tugged snugly in her mouth, and those parts of her that have been rendered skinless by the feral ministrations of her slobbering, slurping visitors. The only aspect of this experience that lessens the raw physical pleasure of it are the flashes of their glassed-over, anonymous eyes visible through their masks. They leave her hungering for faces, not necessarily their faces. But *real* faces, not suggestions of them.

Marcus's face...

If the peach weren't in her mouth, she would mouth his name clearly and decisively, so there would be no missing it through the cameras. She would do something to alert him that even amidst this storm of unexpected, incapacitating pleasure, it is his face she sees, his mouth she wants suckling at her breasts, her thighs, her heaving, honey-slicked folds.

Marcus...

Her lips start to form his name. When the peach almost slips from her mouth, panic surges in her chest. She tightens her grip on the handlebars overhead, tilts her head back to maintain the peach's precarious balance. Her silent messenger pulls himself from her breast; he runs his gloved hands up her body, driving small tides of honey ahead of his leather-sheathed fingers.

She's close. She's terribly, irreversibly close, and apparently this man can sense it. He's running his hands over her racing heart, tracing the underside of her breasts, gently kneading her nipples in between thumb and forefinger. His slow, sensuous motions make for a delicious counterpoint to the frenzied mouths working on her down below.

"God, you're beautiful…."

Where did this whisper in her ear come from? Did she imagine it? Did it come from the masked man tracing paths of pleasure across her skin with his gloved fingers?

When she realizes it was Marcus's voice, that it was Marcus who just spoke them with a tone of hypnotized abandon divorced from jealousy and possessiveness, if only for a fleeting moment, then her orgasm rocks through her, and another war beneath her flesh begins, a desperate struggle to obey their only two instructions even as it feels like her body is flying apart beneath their fingers, lips, and tongues.

Maybe it's cheating to throw her head back like this, or maybe it's exactly what they expected, but it certainly keeps the peach lodged firmly in her mouth as the rest of her body bucks and writhes.

The fight also prolongs the orgasm, until she seems to have lost all sense of herself, and her entire being seems to have coalesced around the resonant memory of Marcus's whispered words. Her silent messenger has cupped one arm under the small of her back. He's staring down at her now, his only trace of an expression the proud, satisfied smile on his slick, glistening lips. He brings his mouth to hers and gently removes the peach with his teeth.

She sucks in a desperate, pained breath; feels both of her feet come to a firm rest on the icy floor. All four of them are standing before her. One after the other they bend forward and take a small bite from the peach their leader holds firmly in his mouth, until there's only one small chunk left, and her messenger swallows it in one easy gulp. Once this ritual is complete, they turn to face her and then sink to all fours, as if she is a temple goddess and they have just completed paying tribute.

The black woman standing in the bathroom doorway is unmasked, and while her outfit covers most of her body, it's the same style and material as those worn by the four prostrate pleasure-givers taking up the expanse of tile between them; a shiny leather that looks like it's been poured onto her ample figure, a lustrous cape tailored snugly at the waist to give the bottom half the effect of being a long skirt. Her hair is a thick brown halo even in the flickering candlelight. Under her right arm, she carries a large leather-bound book.

"Congratulations, Miss Conran," the woman says. "You've passed."

17

"And if I hadn't?" Emily asks in between gasps.

Despite being ravished, her naked body is still slathered with honey trails, and it will remain so until she can take to it with steaming hot water and a pile of loofahs.

"We would have offered you some additional exercises designed to unlock the combination of stamina and willingness essential to a rewarding visit to The Exchange. But in your case, they won't be necessary. Stamina and willingness are two things you seem to possess in spades, Miss Conran. Congratulations. You'll join us tomorrow night."

"Where?"

"First, a bit of business to conclude," the woman says, stepping forward into the candlelight bathroom with the crisp but casual air of a real estate agent presenting closing documents. On cue, Emily's silent messenger rises onto all fours. The woman places the leather-bound notebook on the man's bare, rock-hard back and opens the book to an empty page somewhere in the middle.

"What's your name?" Emily asks.

"You will learn my name in The Exchange, along with many other things, mostly about yourself." There's a trace of impatience in the woman's voice. There's also a trace of a Southern accent that sounds as if it's been worn away over the years by a kind of cultured timelessness that outside of these crazy circumstances would sound absurd.

"I don't usually sign the guest book until I get to the party," Emily says, trying for her best *I'm too rich to be bossed around* voice.

"This is far more than a guest book," the woman responds. Then she removes a small hourglass from a leather satchel that's been camouflaged against her robe.

"Once I set the timer, you will have ten minutes to provide us with your fantasy."

"My *fantasy?* Just…one?"

"Yes, Miss Conran. You know the one. The one you're afraid to speak aloud even in this room where you have already revealed the most tender and intimate parts of yourself to us. *That* fantasy. Share it with the page exactly as it unfolds for you in the hours before sleep, when it's just you, the bedroom, and your racing heart. Don't outline, but leave nothing out once you begin to write. And please, fear no judgment or retribution. Seek clarity, honesty, and desire as you bring pen to page. It's your fantasy, Miss Conran, but we are the ones who will teach you how to trust it."

The pen the woman places gently in Emily's right hand is a Mont Blanc with a black body and gold trim. It's shaking in her grip.

"Shall we begin?" the woman asks.

No, Emily thinks. *We shall not, lady. You don't get this part of me too. Who the hell do you people think you*—Emily steadies her hand, reminds herself of the role she's playing, reminds herself these people have to come to her in the night because they believe this is what she wants. And if she holds out on this part of the process, she's not betraying them, she's betraying Arthur. But she's astonished to learn that this is the limit of what she can offer this undercover operation to fantasyland. Just a few days prior, she could have confessed it to them easily, seen the whole ritual as a wonderful release from the shame Charles inspired in her when he walked out on her. But something has changed since then.

You can have the taste of me, the feel of me, but you can't have this. And it's not because I'm ashamed of it. It's because it belongs to Marcus now, to both of us. It's our first shared secret, and I'm not giving that away to anyone.

"Are you ready to begin writing, Miss Conran?" the woman asks.

Emily closes her eyes. Maybe it gives the effect that she's summoning courage. But that's not what she's doing. She's groping for some fragmented memory of the last stupid porn movie Charles made her watch before they broke up, some memory beyond the awful acting and the bad lighting and the stupid music and the fake stage grunts coming from the obviously bored performers. Finally, she remembers the setup and the scene. It's as obvious as she hoped it would be, but it has a flash of taboo that will make it seem like something she'd want to keep a secret.

"Yes," Emily whispers.

The woman sets the hourglass down on the nearest counter with a loud *thunk*.

Emily starts writing.

Despite the man's rigid pose, his muscular back doesn't make for the most even surface, and she can't reach out to steady the edge of the notebook for fear of smearing its pages with honey. But all of that seems to be by design; they don't want her to pause and reflect, to spend time crafting her sentences. She's supposed to let her innermost sexual fantasy spill out onto the page unfiltered, unexamined, so that's the style she adopts as she rehashes some tired porn cliché about a woman, a doctor's office, and a lecherous internist with wandering, invasive hands. She adopts the female patient's point-of-view, describing everything in terms of *and then he's*. And then he's touching the inside of my thighs, and then he's telling me he'll need me to take my robe off so he can see closer. *And then he's, and then he's, and then he's...*

None of what she describes arouses her in the slightest. But that's the idea, and maybe that's why the words flow so easily, because each new, inauthentic sentence makes her feel safer, more comfortable, and more removed from the mind-altering series of events that have just taken place inside this beautiful but strange bathroom that doesn't actually belong to her.

She writes until the hourglass runs out.

"And we're done," the woman says quietly. She slides the leather-bound notebook out from under Emily's still traveling pen before closing it with a dramatic thud and tucking it into her satchel. There's a warm, satisfied smile on her face. Emily would place the woman in her early thirties at the oldest, but the candlelight could be playing tricks on her. The flickering candles are surely to blame for the small flecks of gold that appear to dance in the woman's irises.

Emily is so stricken by her visitor's beautiful eyes she's barely noticed that her four ravishers are stealing away across the tiled floor in a series of whisper-quiet contortions. They somehow manage to collect their robes around them as they go. But they rise to their feet only once they cross the threshold into the bedroom, at which point they don their robes without so much as a pause.

Maybe they are *circus performers*, she thinks.

The woman has removed another envelope from her satchel and is holding it in the air between them. When Emily tugs it from her grip, the woman smiles and follows her charges through the bedroom and then, out of sight.

"I'll tell you when they're gone," Marcus whispers into her ear. "Just stay right there."

His voice is as clipped and neutral as that of an air traffic controller.

She tears open the envelope and parts another four leaves just like the ones she had to pry back that afternoon to read their announcement. While the script is the same as the earlier requests, the message is far more clinical.

8:00 PM
30.313616689930676
-91.60560250282288

Map coordinates. Or GPS coordinates. She's not sure if there's even a difference. She places the card on the counter, right next to where the hourglass stood as she fibbed her way through the night's final exercise. She's shivering. Surely enough time has passed for their visitors to clear the house, at least.

"Are they gone?" she whispers.

"I think so," Marcus answers.

"What do you mean you *think* so?"

"They're not in the house anymore, but I can't... I'm going to check the perimeter myself. This doesn't make any sense. Stay where you are."

She's too cold to stay exactly where she is. Too cold and too sticky and too naked and too drained and too something else she's having trouble putting a name to. And then all of the lights come back on, a reverse of the same lazy process in which they each appeared to be drained of life. The strange event lacks the sudden cacophony of clicks, pops, and whirs that usually accompanies power coming back on after a blackout. That's when she sees they left the four purple candles behind; that's when she sees the flames flicker out in the same instant.

The AC. It must be. The AC came back on at the same time and blew them out.

Even though she knows Marcus has left his surveillance trailer, she can't stand being exposed to this sudden burst of harsh, overhead lighting. He told her the earpiece was waterproof, but she doesn't want to test it, especially after that little disruption downstairs. She sets it on the counter next to one of the candles. Inside the shower, the drained Lucite cube still hangs overhead, but it blocks only two of the shower's four showerheads. Hands shaking, she turns one on and lets the steaming water pour down her body, even though it does almost nothing to shift the second skin of honey coating her naked flesh. Despite the sudden rush of hot water, she's still shivering, bone-deep tremors that seem driven by so many emotions at once she's having trouble naming a single one.

What good is it? she thinks. *What good is all that pleasure if at the end of it you're wrapped in a blanket of loneliness and cold?*

She tells herself it's to send the hot water sluicing through the honey all over her back, but when she sinks to her knees underneath the spray, the prayerful pose allows her to take her first deep breaths since her shattering orgasm. She's still sucking air hungrily when she hears confident, hurried footsteps.

Marcus. It has to be.

But as soon as his sneakers squeak on the bathroom tiles, a silence falls.

What does she expect him to say? *Excellent form!*

But still, the longer Marcus is silent, the more she wants to attach some sense of shame to what she's done. To what *they* did. To what she allowed them to do. To what he did not stop her from doing.

The touch of his fingers startles her. Bare flesh. No gloves. He shushes her in a long gentle exhalation between pursed lips as he gently kneads her shoulders under the spray. Is he getting wet too? She can't tell. His slow massage is too relaxing, too perfect, for her to do anything to disrupt it.

"You okay?" he asks her.

"Are you?" she asks.

"Stand up," he says.

She complies, and he pulls her gently out of the spray until they're standing in the driest part of the shower stall together. She has trouble looking into his eyes at first, but when she finally risks it, she sees he can't make eye contact yet either. He's too busy wrapping her in a plush bath towel, and then prying his feet out of his sneakers when he realizes they're both hopelessly stuck in honey puddles.

"Alright, now," he says. It sounds like he's trying to prepare her for something, not comfort her, and she's not sure what until he lifts her up with one arm under her back. He carries her out of the bathroom bride-over-threshold style and begins to walk through the house with her. She buries her head against his chest, breathes in his smell for the first time; sandalwood with a strange sweet tang, almost like slightly burnt shortbread cookies.

Even though she's completely swaddled in the bath towel, she still jerks when she hears him sliding a deck door open with his free hand. But when the ocean wind hits her, she boroughs more deeply against his chest and allows him to carry her down the long wooden walkway to the beach. She doesn't monitor their progress, but she can hear the surf getting closer, and when he stops, she assumes they've reached the waterline.

"Put your legs around my waist."

"But..."

To answer her question, he gently removes the towel from her. The sudden flush of salty wind across her naked back inspires her to assume the position more quickly. And then, once her breasts are pressed against his chest, and her exhausted sex sealed to his stomach just above his belt buckle, and once her head is resting comfortably against his broad, muscular shoulder, he walks with her into the surf.

When the surface of the water reaches his waist, he stops, which leaves her more exposed than she'd like to be, but then when the first wave washes over her, coming up as high as her shoulders, she realizes he's positioned himself in relationship to the incoming whitecaps, so that each one douses her, doing more to strip the honey from her skin than a long shower ever could. Instead of standing rigid under the sea's steady assault, Marcus allows himself to rock slightly back and forth in every swell; pliable, patient, determined, silent, his embrace never loosening.

It's a ritual—no, it's more than that—it's a *service* that exists somewhere between the two responses she feared most from him—complete rejection or the sudden, jealous expectation of sex. Instead he has sensed not only her exhaustion, but also the loneliness that closed in around her as soon as the sticky feast was over. More importantly, he has sensed her need to be cleansed; her need to be released from the blank stares of glass eyes that chilled the passions unleashed upon her by those practiced, hungry mouths.

There are so many questions he could be asking her in this moment, so many questions a different man wouldn't think twice about peppering her with, confronting her with, bullying her with.

Did she fake her orgasm? What fantasy did she write down in that leather-bound journal? Was it the same secret she shared with him earlier that day?

But instead, he holds her silently, his embrace creating a quiet, sacred space in which her conflicted feelings can unravel themselves from each other, and her body can become her own again. It's the first time in her life she can remember being this aware of her fundamental need for tenderness and love to accompany passion and pleasure.

After a long while, he turns her around and starts a slow walk back toward the shore.

Once they're standing in water up to his waist, he tells her, "Wait here."

He pulls gently free of her and black jeans and black T-shirt streaming water, he jogs up onto the sand, picks up the bath towel he discarded earlier, and holds it open against the wind. Arms clasped over her bare breasts, she runs into its embrace, allows him to gather it around her body until she's fully cloaked, and then, with one hand pressed gently against her upper back, allows him to steer her toward the walkway back to the house.

Once they reach the sliding door to the kitchen, he stops, and when she turns, they look into each other's eyes for the first time that night. His soaked black T-shirt is plastered to the ridges of muscle beneath, his short cap of hair flattened forward like a helmet. Seawater drips from one corner of his mouth. His eyes appear to be pleading with her, but she's not quite sure what he's saying.

"I can't come in like this," he says. "I have to change."

"Okay."

"The note, the last one she gave you. Can you bring it to me?"

A minute later, she returns to the sliding door to find him standing in exactly the same place. "It's some kind of coordinates, I think."

He nods, as if the information is barely relevant to the riot of thoughts fighting for dominance in his head.

"I'll be back in a minute," he mutters, but he's staring down at the deck boards between them. "I need to change and I need to just check a few things and then I'll...I'll be back." He says these words after he's staring into her eyes again.

"Yes," she says. "Come back...please."

"If they left anything, don't touch it. I'm going to bag it all and send it back to Magnolia Gate."

"Yeah, sure."

He nods, and then he's gone.

As soon as she reaches the bedroom, she hears a strange, loud clatter and scrape from somewhere outside. It sounds like a small piece of debris being driven across asphalt in hurricane force winds. But there isn't a hurricane outside, and when she arrives at the nearest window, she sees what caused it.

Marcus has just torn an aluminum mailbox from the wooden post behind the neighboring house and hurled it down the street. He's bent at the waist like he's just finished a marathon and for a few minutes he grips the back of his head with both hands as if his skull is about to fly apart. She can see the force of the agonized, furious breaths he's taking from the rise and fall of his back. And then, whatever eruption of jealousy he's just allowed himself, the same eruption he managed to keep plugged as he held her against the waves, has passed, as he's trotting back to his surveillance trailer as if he were a local out for an evening jog.

18

If Emily lies down, she'll trigger disorienting flashbacks to an orgasm so powerful it made her forget her name, so she sits on the foot of the bed instead, dressed in a T-shirt and boxers as she waits for Marcus to come back, even though she's convinced, on some level, that he's never coming back. That her orgasm shattered him as well, only beyond repair, and that he's now speeding out of the subdivision in the Navigator, calling Magnolia Gate to arrange for his replacement.

And so, when she hears the door to the deck outside of the kitchen slide open, when she hears his powerful footsteps coming up the stairs, she finds herself choking back something that feels like a sob.

Exhaustion, stress, postcoital confusion. Those are only a few of the excuses she can think up for the rawness she's feeling now. But when he appears in the bedroom door, dressed in something other than the black jeans and black T-shirt that are practically his uniform, she is blinking back tears. Can he see the threat of them on her face? Is he just choosing to ignore it? He holds up the card. "GPS coordinates," he says. "Atchafalaya Basin, just south of the 10. Jonathan was given a different set, due south and on the eastern flank. But it's the same swamp."

"It's a pretty big swamp," she says.

"Yeah, and my bet is wherever you're going tomorrow night,

you're both going by boat."

Is that what she gets now? Is it going to be all business from here on out?

"So he passed apparently," she says.

"With flying colors, I hear."

"Did he get any names?"

"No, and no sign of Ryan either apparently. Doesn't matter, though. I got some shots of Miss Fantasy and sent them back to Magnolia Gate. They'll use face-matching software on them and we should know something about her by tomorrow."

"Jesus. Tell me you didn't record that, Marcus."

"Of course I didn't!" he snaps, visibly offended. "I used one of the cameras to take still images of her face, and only her face. I would never..." He stops short, maybe to keep himself from describing what's just happened in terms that might embarrass her.

"We'll have to get moving first thing in the morning. The good news is we're going close to our base of operations so we can put everything in place pretty quickly. Dupuy and I will follow either by car or by boat. If things get really gnarly, we'll have a four-man security team as close to your final destination as we can get it."

"Who's on this team?"

"Guys from a private security outfit I used to work for. Not Arthur's regulars. They're very skilled. Let's just leave it at that."

"We're not talking about a plan to kidnap Ryan here, are we?"

"No. This is to protect you and Jonathan."

"But...trained killers. Is that really necessary?"

"*I'm* a trained killer, Emily."

"Coulda fooled me," she whispers.

"I'll take that as a compliment."

"It is. It is a compliment, Marcus."

Her gentle tone catches his attention as effectively as if she'd closed the distance between them and gripped his chin in one hand.

"Thank you," he whispers, and there's a tremor in his voice, a tremor that sounds like it could turn into a low growl if he let himself release the angry beast within, the same beast that just tore down the neighbor's mailbox.

"Look," he says, trying to get a businesslike tone back into his voice. "These people managed to shut off power to the whole subdivision and I'm still not exactly sure how they got in or out of the house. There's probably an explanation for both, but the fact is, they're pretty damn skilled at what they do so I want to make sure we have plenty of manpower to counteract their little magic tricks if something goes wrong out there tomorrow night."

"Sounds good," she whispers.

"So I think I'm going to hang out downstairs for a while and—"

"I would have stopped, Marcus. If you'd asked me to, I would have stopped the whole thing."

He nods, purses his lips, rolls his head from side to side as if he's trying to casually work a crick out of his neck. But she can tell he's measuring his next words in exactly the way she just gave herself permission not to. "I promised you I won't stand in the way of you keeping your promise to Arthur. That's how it's gonna be. For another twenty-four hours, at least."

"Still…"

"I'm a patient man, Emily Blaine."

"Tonight would have required a lot more than patience out of me if our roles had been reversed."

"Who says it didn't?"

"Fair enough."

"You didn't cheat on me," he says quietly, but it sounds like he's trying to convince himself as well. "That's not what happened. So get that off your back, okay?"

"Okay," she whispers.

"Do you need anything? Water? Something stronger, maybe?"

"I need you to tell me something."

"Shoot."

"That thing you said to me, while it was happening. Do you remember what you said?"

"I told you that you were beautiful."

"Yeah. That. Did you say it just to make me feel better about what was going on?"

"No."

"Why'd you say it then?"

"Because you're beautiful."

A flush sweeps through her body from head to toe.

"Is it my turn to ask a question?" he asks.

"Shoot."

"Did you enjoy it?"

"At first, it was overwhelming, and then it was…pure pleasure. And then…I heard your voice in my ear and…"

"And then?" His voice is tight as a bowstring.

"I came."

He's been trying for a casual pose, arms crossed over his chest as he leans one shoulder against the doorframe. But now it's his crossed arms that betray his sudden, desperate inhalation. His muffled groan has the threat of a bellow quavering in the center of it. She can feel his desire as if it were a spectral presence leaping out from his oh-so-patient body, pressing her to the bed, claiming her for his own in the wake of having to witness her ravishment by such sleek, wild, and anonymous competition. But he steadies himself, an act that causes his thick neck to flush red and his nostrils to flare and his eyes to burn.

"Good to know," he whispers.

"I thought you'd think so."

"Yeah. Thanks for sharing."

"You going to go take things out on another mailbox?"

"I think I got it all out the first time. But I am going to hang out downstairs for a while. Just to, you know, make sure everything's secure."

"Secure. Right."

"You sure you don't want a drink?"

"I'm sure."

He nods and turns toward the landing.

"Marcus?"

He stops, but he doesn't turn around.

"I admire your patience," she says. "But I don't require it."

"Maybe not," he says without turning. "But you deserve it, Emily Blaine."

And then he's gone.

But the comfort of hearing him moving around downstairs, checking locks, opening drawers, maybe fixing himself a drink as strong as the one he offered her, has her drifting off to sleep within minutes. She wakes a little while later to the sounds of Marcus bagging all the evidence in the master bathroom. Then a soft click tells her he's hit the wall switch that kills all the lights in the master suite.

As silence falls, sleep threatens to take her again.

But he hasn't left the room.

She hears him carefully stacking the evidence he's just collected on the desk next to the computer, followed by the hard *thunk* of his holstered gun coming to rest on the nightstand. Then he's sinking down onto the bed next to her, his movements careful and hesitant but deliberate. One powerful arm curves over her stomach just as his breath begins to tickle the back of her neck. Is he taking in the smell of her for the first time, the same way she subtly took in the smell of him while he carried her to the beach?

She snuggles back into his spooning embrace.

In a gentle whisper, he says, "Sweet dreams, Emily Blaine."

"You too, Marcus Dylan."

And then, carried into sleep by his powerful arms, she starts to think his patience might not be such a bad thing after all.

19

The room isn't the worst she's ever seen. The curtains and bedspread both came up clean when she subjected them to swipes of her index finger. But what makes this little roadside motel a good choice for a staging area is its location, not its décor. It's a twenty-minute drive to the rendezvous point, and for some reason, that strikes her as the perfect amount of time; just enough to get centered, not so much that she'll be able to work herself into a panic before she gets there.

The three potential outfits she took from Lily's closet are spread out across one of the double beds; a pleated belt chiffon dress the color of swamp water, a silk blouse paired with designer jeans, and a red sequined cocktail dress. Even though she's been studying these items for almost an hour, only now is she realizing what a ridiculous exercise this is. You can't pick an outfit when you don't know the occasion, and while the emissaries of The Desire Exchange who visited her last night took plenty of information from her, they offered little in return.

A sharp knock startles her. The burst of laughter that answers her startled cry is so unexpectedly familiar, Emily literally jumps the foot of the bed in her rush to answer the door. Jonathan gives her his thousand-watt smile, takes her in his arms and forces her backward across the doorframe as he tightens his embrace. *"Surprise!"*

His chest-shaking laughter is an instant balm on her nerves. Their brief time apart seems to have invigorated him, given them both a chance to reboot. His Leonard Miller costume consists of a pressed white dress shirt under a leather motorcycle jacket and skin-tight designer jeans that hug his every muscle below the waist. "I thought we weren't supposed to see each other," she gasps into his chest.

"You're not," Marcus says, stepping into the room. He carries a closed laptop computer in one hand. Frank Dupuy is right on his tail.

"Hey, listen! For once, I was actually following the rules," Jonathan says. "My man Dupuy's the one who brought me here."

"Yeah," Dupuy says. "I did it to save the shoe stores of Atlanta."

"I knew you were going to spend that money on shoes," Emily says.

"I was playing the part of a conspicuous consumer!" Jonathan wails.

"For you that's not a part, Jonathan," Emily says.

"I am going to ignore this bullying and revel in the fact that my dear, good friend, who is *only* a friend, by the way"—he narrows his eyes in Marcus's direction as he says this, leaving Emily to wonder if the two men just discussed this topic outside—"is certainly a sight for sore eyes. Sore eyes, I might add, that were covered in honey the night before by some full-on Cirque du Soleil weirdness, I am telling you! What was going *on* with those people anyway? I mean, don't get me wrong. I get up to some freaky shit when the sun goes down, but usually I don't have to shower for a whole day after it. I still smell like Burt rubbed his bees all over me."

"Too bad you didn't have anyone to help you clean up," Marcus says, and then he gives her a quick wink.

"Well, well, well," Jonathan says with a raised eyebrow. "What happened to waiting?"

"What happened to keeping your mouth shut?" Marcus asks.

"I'm sorry?" Jonathan says. "There was a moment when I agreed to keep my mouth shut? That doesn't sound like me."

"So I take it I've been a topic of conversation between you two," Emily says.

"Oh, indeed," Jonathan says then he leans in as if they're sharing a conspiratorial whisper, even though he doesn't lower his voice in the slightest. "He called to ask for my blessing—"

"I did *not* ask for your—"

"— I said he could have it as long as he treated you like a queen. That's what I was supposed to say, right?"

"Something like that," Emily whispers.

Dupuy says, "Chatterbox here's got a rendezvous point that's about an hour south. If we're going to do this, I need to get him in position soon. One of his *upright* positions."

"He doesn't like me," Jonathan whispers to Emily.

"I never said I didn't—" Dupuy tries, but it's no use.

"See, he's gay but he's a bear and I'm not, and bears apparently think they're, like, the manliest gays of all. *So* even though I spend every moment of my free time at the gym, in Frank's world, I'm just this annoying sissy ballerina who keeps doing pirouettes across his crawfish boil."

"He's lying," Dupuy says to her. "I hate crawfish."

"I'm sorry," Emily says, having heard only every other word of Jonathan's stand-up routine. "*If* we're going to do this? What does that mean?"

Marcus answers her by opening the laptop. He holds up the computer in both hands so all three of them can see the night-vision angle from one of the beach house's exterior cameras that currently fills the screen. At first, she assumes it's a live shot until she remembers there's still sunlight lancing the live oak branches above the parking lot outside. The view includes the beach house's driveway, and the driveway of the house next door. Only when she sees the numbers ticking by on the counter at the bottom of the screen does she realize the video is already playing.

"Remember how I said I couldn't see them leave?" Marcus asks.

"I remember..."

"Well, here's one of 'em, coming up at two minutes, thirty-five seconds."

Sure enough, just as he predicted, her silent messenger, fully robed, descends the staircase from the kitchen door to the driveway. Once he steps outside the bright halo cast by the security light over the driveway, he jumps into the air and...

Emily can feel the air in the motel room stop moving as all three of them have the exact same reaction.

"What the hell?" Jonathan whispers.

She's still trying to make sense of what they've just seen when Marcus reaches around the side of the computer and taps a key. The clip replays. Robed, hooded, and moving swiftly, her silent messenger descends the wooden steps to the driveway, passes outside of the security light's halo, bends his right leg, jumps up into the air and then somehow vanishes against the patch of night sky visible between both houses.

"It's a trick," Emily finally says. "They're circus performers or something. Illusionists. I don't know…"

"If it's a trick, that means they knew we were watching," Dupuy says.

"Which means tonight could be a trap," Marcus adds.

"That weird thing with the power," Jonathan says. Hearing him reference the same strange phenomena she witnessed the night before sends a shiver through Emily. "Did we ever figure that out? Maybe they were hacking into the system. Maybe they just cut the footage out so it looks like the guy vanishes into thin air."

"*Also* a sign that tonight could be a trap," Marcus says quietly.

"Did you pick up anything like this?" Jonathan asks, turning to his minder.

"No," Dupuy answers. "But you were in a townhouse. I didn't have as many exterior angles."

"Which means what?" Jonathan asks.

"Which means I didn't see them leave at all," Dupuy answers. "Unless they went off the roof."

"Which would mean they could fly," Jonathan asks, suppressing a laugh when he notes the somber mood that's settled over the motel room. "Oh, come on! You're not telling us you think these people can…*fly*, are you?"

Marcus sets the laptop down atop the chunky circa 1999 television. Emily can sense the struggle within him, the struggle to be impartial even as he burns with a desire to put a stop to this whole thing.

"We are presenting you with evidence that cannot be easily explained," Marcus says. "Evidence that suggests there might be more risks to tonight's operation than previously thought."

"It's just a magic trick," Jonathan says. "It's like the candles."

"The candles that lit without matches or any kind of flame?" Emily asks. "Those candles?"

"They had a switch on the bottom or something," Jonathan says. "I don't know."

"They don't have a switch on the bottom," Marcus says.

"How do you know?"

"Because they left them behind and I bagged all of them, and they don't have a switch or a battery or any kind of internal compartment. There's nothing electronic about them at all. And you want to know something else?"

"Not really," Jonathan says quietly. "You're kind of freaking me out."

"I couldn't light them," Marcus says, only he's staring into Emily's eyes now. "No matter what I did, no matter how hard I tried, I couldn't get one of them to light. And I couldn't get them to light because—"

"They don't have wicks," Emily finishes for him. He nods and no one says anything for several long minutes filled by the hum and rattle of the AC unit.

"You're not saying we hallucinated those flames, are you?" Jonathan asks.

"Couldn't have," Dupuy chimes in. "We could see them clear as day on our monitors."

"I want to see one," Emily says. "Right now."

"I dropped them at Magnolia Gate when we went through New Orleans on the way here," Marcus says "They can't make them light either."

"Look," Dupuy says, his tone a stark contrast to the heaviness in Marcus's voice, a sign that the two men have been at odds over this issue for a while now. "I'm sure if we had the time, we could find an easy explanation for all of this, but everything about this has been so damn *rushed.* I just don't think we can—"

"It's rushed because Arthur's dying," Emily says. "I want to speak to him. Right now."

"You can't," Marcus says.

"What do you mean *I can't?*"

"I mean he's been intubated." He misreads her silence as a lack of familiarity with the term. "It means he's sedated and he's got a tube down—"

"I know what intubated means," Emily snaps.

"He's got pneumonia," Dupuy says, probably to take some of the heat off of Marcus. "They rushed him to Ochsner about twelve hours after Jonathan and Dupuy went to Atlanta and we went to Florida."

Her rage is so sudden and powerful, her throat feels straw-sized, but she manages to get a few words through it. "And you've known this for how long?" she asks Marcus.

"Ten minutes, Emily."

Dupuy says, "Apparently, Arthur ordered everyone not to tell us anything. He said he didn't want us being interrupted. Staff at Magnolia Gate finally caved this afternoon. And not to, uh, rub it in, here, but if Arthur doesn't want us to know he's in the hospital then…"

"That he doesn't think he has much time left," Marcus says.

"So Arthur hasn't seen *any* of this?" Emily asks.

Marcus and Dupuy both shake their heads.

"What about the picture? The woman who brought the book. You said they were going to use face-matching software on it."

"No hits yet," Marcus answers.

"You had a woman?" Jonathan asks. "I had a man. What about him?"

"No hits yet on him either," Marcus answers.

Emily sinks down onto the foot of the bed, hears her sudden weight shift the outfits on the bedspread behind her. If Jonathan weren't afraid of making Marcus jealous, he'd probably have his arms around her by now, but instead he lays a comforting hand on her shoulder.

"What do you think we should do, Marcus?" she finally asks.

He clears his throat and swallows, shuts his eyes briefly as if he's trying to get his balance back after a dizzy spell. It reminds her of the transformation he underwent the night before when she told him it was the sound of his voice that had ultimately sent an orgasm tearing through her in that candlelit bathroom. She prepares herself for military doublespeak, but when he looks into her eyes, there's an unguarded vulnerability there that makes her want to swim in them.

"Don't ask me what I want you to do, Emily. Everyone in this room knows what I want you to do…what I *don't* want you to do. But I'm putting that aside, for now, as best I can, and I'm looking at this whole thing with the clearest eyes I've got. And all I can see is one of two things happening tonight. One, we walk into a trap. Or two, we're all about to find out that the universe operates off a different set of laws than we thought."

"Oh, come on, man," Dupuy says. "These people can't *fly*, and those candles? They're some kind of chemical compound we haven't figured out yet. Guys, seriously! Let's just all take a deep breath and allow for the possibility here that this is just a bunch of circus performers who started some kind of stupid sex club in the swamp, and *we*, on the other hand, are four really tired, weirded-out people who could use a lot of sleep."

"So your vote is that we do it, Frank?" Emily asks.

"There's not a vote here, Emily," Dupuy answers. "This is your call."

"That's what I was afraid of," she whispers.

Jonathan sinks down onto the bed next to her, strokes her back gently. After the silence becomes unbearable for them all, he says, "Penny for your thoughts, Miss Blaine."

"Y'all don't want to hear what I'm thinking right now," she says.

"Try us," Marcus responds.

"Fine," she says. "I'm thinking that I can't stand the thought of you, any of you, even you, Frank—"

"It's nice to be included," Dupuy answers.

"I can't stand the thought of you thinking I want to do this just to get Arthur's money."

"Well, I wouldn't blame you," Jonathan says. "It's a lot of goddamn money."

"Be serious, Jonathan," Marcus says.

"I'm being very serious, *Marcus*. We're talking about *fund eighteen scholarships money*. We're talking about *building schools all over New Orleans* money. Arthur's an amazing businessman, but he's no Emily."

"Is that a compliment?" she asks.

"Yes," he says, eyes ablaze with conviction. "Yes, it is. I know you love the man, Em, but he's been a citizen of Magnolia Gate, not New Orleans. And if you had his money you would change the city for the better. I know you would."

"I may be the odd man out here," Dupuy says. "But I know Arthur well enough to know he'd still leave you his money even if you didn't find his son."

"Yeah, but she wouldn't be able to accept it," Jonathan says.

"And that's exactly what Arthur is counting on," Marcus adds.

Another long silence falls. Emily is surprised to hear herself break it.

"He was going to take me out of school," she says.

"Who?" Jonathan asks. "Arthur?"

"No, my father. After he got hounded out of the department, he was going to have to take me out of school. He was broke. The cops he ratted on, they made trouble for him all over town. He couldn't get a job doing anything he was qualified for. He didn't want to just throw me in some random public school in the middle of the year, so the best-case scenario was wait and see if I could get into a magnet. His brother had a farm in Hammond. He was even talking us going there and maybe home schooling me. But, the point is, I was thirteen years old and he was going to have to take me out of school. And then he met Arthur and...I got to stay in school."

"I didn't know you guys were that close to the line," Jonathan says.

"We didn't *want* you to know. We didn't want anyone to know."

This revelation has brought the room to a halt, she can tell.

After a while, Jonathan gets to his feet.

"Alright,' he says brusquely. "Time for the nuclear option."

"The *what?*" Marcus asks.

"Just everyone be quiet until I tell you to speak," Jonathan says. "We have a phone call to make."

20

After a minute of canned-sounding rings, George Dugas answers, his voice tinny-sounding through the speaker on Leonard Miller's brand new, barely used phablet. "Well, Mr. Miller. Did we pass our test?"

"Good evening, George," Jonathan says. "How are you?"

"Uh oh. You don't sound so good. Oh, no. Tell me you didn't fail! A man of your talents? I can't believe it. Now Little Miss Sunshine, on the other hand. I wouldn't be surprised if a little eleventh-hour uptightness caused her to—"

"We both passed," Jonathan says. "But thank you for your concern."

"Okay, then. To what do I owe the pleasure of this call?"

"We have some more questions."

"Well, that's a shame because I don't have many more answers for you. I feel I've been quite generous so far."

"And you're sure you've told us everything we need to know about these people?"

Dugas practically chokes with laughter. "I've told you everything *I* need to tell you about these people, you silly boy. How's that?" His tone drips such condescension, Emily wouldn't be surprised to see it pooling on top of the dresser where the phone sits. "Am I on the clock right now, Jonathan? Because I might not have answered if I'd known. I'm a wealthy man, but I'm not liquid enough to afford the inconvenience of you in the long run."

"No, you're not on the clock, George."

Emily searches Jonathan's face for signs that these insults have wounded him. But there's no evidence of it. Still, Jonathan has never been one to wear his heart on his sleeve. He covers his emotional wounds in humor and sarcasm, only to have them erupt in unexpected crying jags or furious tantrums.

"But I am on speakerphone, apparently," George says. "So who else am I speaking with?"

"Well, there's me and then there's Emily, and then there's two of the guys who are going to hunt you down and break every bone in your body if it turns out you sent us into a dangerous situation without warning us."

Marcus and Dupuy exchange a look, as if they're each assessing whether the other is capable of carrying out the threat Jonathan just made. From their mutual shrug, Emily figures both men believe themselves to be up to the task.

"Oh, my," Dugas says. "I must say I remember being far more relaxed the day after my honey test."

"Is that what it's called?"

"It's my little nickname for it. But apparently, more than one is required to fully soothe the frayed nerve endings of a whore."

"Oh, trust me, George. I'm very relaxed. You want to know why? I have excellent people around me now."

Marcus pulls his SIG from its holster, then cocks and releases it right above the phone. Apparently he's angrier at Dugas for calling Jonathan a whore than Jonathan is.

The answer from the other end is a long, stilted silence.

"Still there, George?"

"This is a remarkably hostile phone call given all I've done for you."

"We can discuss unpaid debts later, once we've contacted Ryan Benoit and we're all home safely and in one piece."

"What do you want, Jonathan?"

"There are some things about these people that don't make sense."

"Like what?"

"We have surveillance footage of one of them vanishing into thin air, it looks like, and those candles they left behind. Did you get one?"

"That's only the beginning. Trust me."

It's such a far cry from the response they were all expecting, Jonathan takes a moment to swallow and look around the room.

"Well, I don't trust you, George. You're a client, not my uncle. So tell us what to expect."

"I can't tell you what to expect because I don't know what's in your hearts, either of you. And that's the only thing you'll have to fear while you're there. My advice to you both? Make peace with the fantasy you wrote down in that book of theirs because you're about to experience it in *all* of its dimensions. Now if you'll excuse me—"

"That's not good enough," Marcus says.

"And who might this be?" Dugas asks.

"The guy you're gonna see when you least expect it if something bad happens to either of these two."

"Well, why don't I make this easier on everyone then?" Dugas says. "Why don't I call my friends at The Exchange and tell them they're being deceived? Then I'll spare you all the dangers of living out your fantasies, and I'll also extricate myself from what in retrospect appears to have been a misguided act of charity on my part. What do you say? Sound like a plan?"

"Sure," Jonathan says. "It's a great plan. And I'll just send NOLA.com that video footage I have of you riding me like a Shetland pony around your pool house. What do you say?" In the shocked silence that follows, Jonathan turns to all of them and says, "Yes, folks, and just in case you're wondering, it's not a figure of speech, he really did dress me up like a Shetland pony and ride me around his pool house. Oh, it was a fine time, yessiree bob, and I bet it'll go over huge with that construction project you've got going in Dallas. It's a megachurch, right? Those guys *love* Shetland ponies."

"I must say I underestimated you, Jonathan," Dugas says, and he sounds so winded and hurt Emily almost feels sorry for the man.

"The hell you did," Jonathan mutters. "You saw a kindred spirit."

"Maybe there's more truth there than I thought."

"What *are* they, George?" Jonathan asks.

The silence stretches on for so long, Emily starts to wonder if they've been hung up on.

"I don't know," George finally answers. "And I don't want to know. I only know what they do and what they do is magical. And if you surrender and go with it, you will come out the other side a changed person, a *better* person. Maybe a person with enough self-awareness to know that this phone call was to punish *me* for the fact that you chose to sell your body to the highest bidder, Jonathan Claiborne. Goodnight, all. Enjoy The Desire Exchange!"

Once it becomes clear Dugas terminated the call, Jonathan crosses to the phone and clicks END. Then he returns to the foot of the bed, takes a seat next to Emily. The four of them spend the next few minutes in such a deep, reflective silence; it starts to sound as if their breaths are almost in synch.

"Did you really make a tape of him..." Emily starts, but she can't finish the sentence.

"No," Jonathan says. "But he did really dress me up like a Shetland pony and ride me around his pool house"

"That was a dangerous threat, Jonathan," Marcus says. "Especially if you've got nothing to back it up with."

"Good thing I have you guys to protect me," Jonathan offers with a weak smile.

"And now he's got an incentive to blow your covers," Marcus continues.

"Which he's not gonna do because then he'll have to explain why he referred us. And also, why is he the only person in New Orleans who's met our alter egos? And also, how come no one else can remember us attending those parties where we supposedly had our pictures taken with him? Please. He's in this as deep as we are and he knows it."

"Then why did he agree to help in the first place?" Marcus asks.

"He's telling the truth," Emily answers, startling all three men. "He had some kind of spiritual experience there and like all of the converted, he wants to share the message. When we started talking about it the first time, we barely had to force anything out of him. He was offering to set us up with references and recommendations...like some church member trying to get people to join their congregation."

Jonathan says, "I had an appointment with him the next night. I didn't expect him to pay, given what he'd agreed to do for us. I didn't even *ask* him to pay. But he did anyway."

"Fine," Marcus says. "But he doesn't know what they are. I mean, that's what he said. 'What are they?' That's what Jonathan asked him, and George didn't say. 'Are you crazy? They're people, they're magicians, they're acrobats.' He didn't say *any* of those things. We asked him what these people *actually are* and he said, 'I don't know.' Are we gonna stop a minute to consider what that means?"

"No," Emily says, rising to her feet. "We're not. Arthur is lying in

Ochsner Hospital with a breathing tube down his throat and this may be our last shot at finding his son before he's gone. Lord knows we've all got plenty of reasons not to do this and if we stay here all night we could think of them all. But the only thing that's going to get this done is getting it *done*. And so help me God, if I have to go back to Arthur's hospital room and tell him I blew this because I was afraid of some screwy camera footage and some weird candles..."

Marcus nods, but he drops his gaze from hers for a minute or two, as if the cheap carpet between their feet will give him the strength to continue. Jonathan seems stricken by her assertiveness, but there's also an admiring look in his eyes.

"Well, alright then, Miss Blaine," Marcus finally says. "I'll be behind you every step of the way"

"Do y'all want some time alone?" Jonathan asks.

Dupuy clears his throat and chucks Jonathan on the shoulder. "They can have all the time they want right now. Come on, buster. We need to move if we're going to get you in position."

Jonathan stands, takes Emily by the shoulders and plants a long kiss on her forehead. "See you on the other side, Miss Blaine."

"You said that last time and we're not on the other side yet."

"Yeah, well, we're closer, right?" Jonathan turns to face Marcus, and then gives him a stiff salute. "Special Ops."

"Mr. Shetland," Marcus answers.

Jonathan cackles and drops his saluting arm to his side.

"I'd say take good care of her but tonight, I hope you'll be watching out for both of us," Jonathan says, and it's clear the sudden sincerity has disarmed the former Navy SEAL standing a few feet away from him.

"You can count on it," Marcus answers.

From three feet behind Jonathan, Dupuy says, "Apparently he has more faith in your abilities than mine, Dylan."

"That's correct," Jonathan says. He claps Dupuy on one shoulder and pushes past the guy out the door.

The older man turns to face Emily and Marcus, shaking his head in dismay. "Love this gig," he whispers. "*Love* it!"

21

"So! What college did you attend, Miss Conran?"

"University of Mississippi, Class of 2004."

There's a blush of sunlight on the western horizon, but the cypress-flanked highway is already blanketed in night shadows. In another few minutes, the GPS will route her onto a rutted swamp road that makes up the final leg of her route. The map they studied back at the motel suggested she'll have to walk for another few minutes after she parks the car. That final, lonely stroll through swamp darkness is the part of this evening she's dreading the most, for now, at least.

The Navigator is so far behind her she can only glimpse a flash of its headlights every now and then, but Marcus's voice comes through the earpiece clear as a bell. The microphone and tracking device taped to her scalp don't itch, but they're bringing out her OCD. Every few minutes or so, she gives into temptation and checks the rearview mirror to make sure they're not visible through her hair.

"I see, and did you attend a lot of Tomahawks games while you were at Miss U?"

"While I was at *Ole Miss*, I attended many *Rebels* games because that's actually the name of their football team."

"Good catch, Miss Conran."

"Seriously? Come on, Special Ops. Nobody in their right mind would nickname a college Miss U," Emily says. "Shoot me some tough ones."

"As soon as you stop calling me Special Ops."

"Why? I thought that was your new nickname."

"Only for people who want to annoy me. Come up with your own. I want you to have your own. For me, I mean."

"Okay. So like Stud Muffin?"

"Close."

"Gorgeous."

"Warm."

"Knight in Shining Armor."

"*Barf.* Too old school."

"Man of my dreams," she offers.

"Really?"

"We'll see. I mean, it's just a nickname, and most of the time nicknames are the opposite of what people really are, right? You know, like, how mob guys will call some enormous guy Tiny."

"Let's get back to your pop quiz before you charm the pants off me."

"Okay. Try some hard ones this time."

"Alright, well, since you were obviously a football fan during your time at Miss State—"

"Ole Miss."

"How'd you celebrate when your team trounced LSU in November of oh-three to secure its first ever SEC West title?"

"Well, given that the stellar defense exhibited by LSU prevented Ole Miss from securing its first ever SEC title that day, I'd have to say we didn't do much celebrating but we did drown our troubles at The Library."

"You went to study drunk after your team lost?"

"Nope. The Library also happens to be the name of one of the most popular sports bars in Hattiesburg."

"Oxford," Marcus says.

"What?"

"Ole Miss and The Library are both in Oxford, Mississippi. Not Hattiesburg."

"Oh, lord. Why couldn't he have had her go to Tulane? I went to Tulane. I can answer *anything* about Tulane. And LSU! I dated three guys who went to LSU. I could tell you anything about LSU too. But no, Lily Conran had to go to the one Southern university where I never got wasted."

"I wouldn't sweat it. I don't think there's going to be much football talk where you're going anyway."

The GPS flashes a warning, and a second later, the blink-and-you-might-miss-it dirt road appears through the dense canopy of trees. She slows to make the turn and suddenly the Aston Martin's penetrating headlights illuminate a narrow tunnel of low hanging-branches and uneven, oyster shell roadway. The knowledge that Marcus is no longer following her bathes the pit of her stomach in something icy; he's turned off just shy of this isolated road where he'll board some kind of special motorboat with a whisper-quiet engine that's been tied up about five hundred yards from the rendezvous point.

Zebotec, she remembers. *That's what the boat's called.* Lithium-ion batteries power them, and there are three more on the Atchafalaya tonight; one carries Frank Dupuy, and the other two carry the four members of the strike team she doesn't want to talk about because just the idea that they're out there somewhere scares her to death.

According to the car's GPS, she's practically at the water's edge. But Marcus gave her a handheld GPS monitor so she can pinpoint the rendezvous point exactly; it's map is far more detailed, and it tells her she's got some walking to do. She steps out of the car.

"Alright, so there won't be any football talk. But what do you think is going to happen where I'm going?" she asks

"Based on what Dugas said, I'm guessing it'll have something to do with whatever fantasy you wrote in their notebook last night."

"So, like, a fantasy room or something? Are those a thing in sex clubs?"

"I don't know. I've never been to a sex club."

"Really?"

"Yes, *really?* What? I seem like I've been to a lot of sex clubs?"

"I don't know what you soldiers get up to overseas."

"Most of it ain't sexy, I'll tell you that much."

"Alright, well, a fantasy room I can deal with, I guess."

"Really? Why's that?"

"Because I didn't tell them my real fantasy."

"The one you told me, you mean?"

"Yeah. That one. That's ours now."

He's silent.

"That belongs to us," she adds.

"I see…"

"So," Emily finally says. "If I could see you right now, would I see you smiling?"

"A little. Yeah."

"Okay. Good."

"Yeah. It is good. I like having a secret with you, Emily Blaine."

"You have *a lot* of secrets with me right now, Marcus Dylan."

"Yeah, but the rest of them involve other people. Not this one."

"I guess you're right. Want to know another secret? I *hate* the swamp!"

"Have I told you that if anything happens to you I'll be there in five minutes, tops?"

"Tell me again."

"If anything happens to you, I'll be there in three minutes. Tops."

"Okay. Now tell me where you're going to take me out to dinner when all of this is over?"

"Just dinner, huh? Am I going to get to hold your hand too?"

Thank God she decided to wear the jeans and the blouse. She can't imagine braving the trail ahead in some shiny cocktail dress. The leather jacket she's wearing has a zippered pocket on the inside flap and that's where she's placed Arthur's letter. From the Aston Martin's trunk she removes a Maglite and starts sweeping the ground at her feet for snakes.

"7:45," Marcus says. "Let's do a little refresher. When I ask you a yes or no question, yes will be..."

She sniffs once through both nostrils.

"Great. And no?"

She sniffs twice through both nostrils.

"If you ID Ryan?"

"Two quick coughs."

"If you want me to extract you?"

"Four quick coughs."

"If you want the strike team?"

"I'm not going to want the strike team."

"Let me rephrase that. If either you or Jonathan are in grave and immediate danger and require the use of the strike team."

"Marcus..."

"How 'bout we work on getting over our fear of the strike team in the ten minutes before your pickup. What do you say?"

"If I want the strike team, I say the words, *That's enough.*"

"Excellent. Thank you."

"You're welcome. But I'm not going to want the strike team."

"Yeah, I got the message. Fingers crossed we won't have to use the strike team."

"And I am *not* walking down this road to the water until it's time."

"I can see that... Hey, Emily."

"Yes, Knight in Shining Armor."

"I know it's probably sounding pretty repetitious at this point, but whatever you have to do tonight to get that letter to Ryan, I still want to take you out to dinner later and, you know, maybe hold your hand and stuff."

"And stuff?" Emily asks.

"Yeah. Stuff."

"Stuff could be fun."

"With me, it usually is. I'm really good at stuff."

She's trying to think up a witty, flirty response to this line when the Maglite's beam falls across a wooden post marking the entrance to the trail ahead.

"There's something up here," she mutters, dropping her voice when she sees some sort of shiny gift has been hung from a nail in the top of the post.

"What is it?"

"A handbell."

"Like the one they rang last night?"

"I didn't see that one so I won't know if they're the same unless I ring it."

"Alright, well, it's three minutes to eight. I say ring it. But after you do, I, uh, guess that's the end of you being able to talk. To me, anyway."

"Yeah," she says.

There's a small catch attached to the tip of the bell's handle. She slides it gently off the nail, careful not to ring the bell by accident before she's good and ready.

"One more time, quick review," Marcus says.

"Okay."

"Yes."

She sniffs once through both nostrils.

"No."

She sniffs twice.

"If you spot Ryan?"

She coughs twice.

"Extraction?"

She coughs four times.

"Strike team?"

"That's enough."

"Okay. And as soon as you're inside I'm going to ask you for a headcount. If it's a double digit figure, do taps for each digit separated by five seconds."

"Got it."

"Alright. You are green to proceed, Miss Conran."

"See you on the other side, Hot Stuff."

"Emily?"

"Yeah?"

"I'm not sure if I said this already, but I love that painting you gave me."

"Thank you. I wanted you to love it."

"Well, I do. Now ring that bell, Miss Conran."

She does. The chime is clear, resonant, and soothing. As it echoes out across the dark swamp, two strings of swaying paper lanterns come gradually to life before her. With rounded purple shades swaying gently in the breeze, they line the trail down to the water's edge, and in their sudden spreading light, Emily can see the walk before her is far from being the tangled, predator-concealing mess she feared it would be. Rather, it's as manicured as a garden path, and the small dock at the end looks freshly painted and in perfect condition.

She's halfway to the dock when she hears a boat's engine groaning across the water.

"Incoming," Marcus whispers.

By the time the vessel is within sight, she's struck a surefooted stance on the dock, the handbell in her right hand, Arthur's letter burning a hole in her jacket pocket. The boat has a single running light on the bow, so for several minutes after she hears its engine, the vessel is just a burst of noise and one tiny pinprick of light advancing toward her out of the blackness.

Once it's within the halo of soft light given off by the lanterns behind her, she can see its shiny varnished wooden body, its small wheelhouse tucked up against the bow, and the flapping canopy covering the small open area in back. The boat carries four shadows, and one of them is leaning halfway out of the wheelhouse on the side opposite the pilot. She recognizes his mask, his familiar full lips and strong jawline. It's her silent messenger from the night before, the same man who may or may not have vanished into thin air while on camera. Only tonight, he's missing his robe. Along with the other three members of his team, he's dressed in skin-tight black jeans with black leather side-stripes, his muscular olive-skinned chest exposed and shaved smooth just as it was when he helped to ravish her.

It's an odd reversal of their power dynamic from the night before, when she was naked and they were partially dressed. One side of the boat swings toward the dock, and once he's within reach, her silent messenger falls to one knee on the edge of the boat and extends one gloved hand toward her. The sudden move startles her so much she backs up a few steps. The handbell emits a weak ring.

"Was that bell a distress call?" Marcus asks.

She sniffs twice through both nostrils.

"Cool."

The boat is idling with one side flush against the dock. Her silent messenger turns his extended hand up and spreads his fingers; he's asking for the bell. When she hands it off to him, he passes it to the masked woman behind him and returns his right hand to its original, inviting position.

Emily manages a smile, places her hand in his, and allows him to pull her onto the boat. She has to duck slightly to avoid hitting her head on the canopy, and as soon as her feet come to rest on the rocking deck, three of the team members take a step back, and in the deep shadows, it takes her a minute to see they're each holding up something in their hands, something they want her to see. One woman holds a piece of fabric between two fists—a blindfold, Emily realizes. The other holds a long strap, the use of which is beyond Emily's ability to comprehend in this moment. Meanwhile, her silent messenger has reached into his pants pocket and removed two dangling wrist ties, one in each hand.

"You there?"

She sniffs once.

"Are they restraining you?"

She sniffs once.

Her silent messenger grips both of her wrists, gently raises her arms skyward, turning her around bit by bit as he works. By the time he's fastened her wrists to two metal loops above her head, she's facing the rear of the boat, and just before the blindfold is wrapped around her eyes, she realizes what the long strap is for; they've wrapped it around her waist and are now securing it to the canopy supports on either side of her. It's designed to keep her upright and comfortable during the journey ahead, given that she won't able to use her hands to support herself.

"Have they blindfolded you?"

She sniffs once.

"Are you in pain?"

She sniffs twice.

"Good. Your tracking device is up. We're good to go."

The deck rattles beneath her feet as the boat's motor throttles back to life. Two sets of hands hold her gently in place as the boat takes off, and then, once whomever they belong to is confident she has her balance, the hands retreat, leaving her in total darkness made deafening by the sudden wind ripping across the deck.

22

On the screen the advance team mounted next to the boat's wheel, Marcus watches a flashing blue dot travel south into the Atchafalaya Basin. It marks Emily's position and gives him something to monitor her journey with besides the rush of wind coming through the earpiece. Heading toward her, on a direct collision course it seems, is an orange blip marking Jonathan's northward progress across the dark swamp. A good ways behind him, Dupuy's marker flashes green.

In another few minutes, Emily's ride will pass several hundred yards from where the strike team sits dark and silent, hidden somewhere in the cypresses. Marcus ordered them to a central location an hour ago. He figured that was the best way to ensure they'd be able to make decent time to the final destination once it was established.

Watching the steady progression of these dots across a shiny, new computer screen convinces Marcus, for a moment at least, that maybe, just maybe, this whole thing will go off without a hitch.

But then he remembers a guy vanishing into the night sky, then he remembers turning those candles over and over again in his hands as he searched desperately for a way to make them light, and suddenly his hands grip the wheel so tightly he's sure his knuckles are whitening, even if he can't make out his fingers in the shadows.

While the boat's battery-powered engine is whisper quiet, he's forced to travel dark. Running lights could give away his position, for sure, and despite Arthur's vast resources, they couldn't locate a GPS monitor that would also provide detailed radar information about the shallow, obstruction-filled swamp. The resulting compromise has left him with three different screens to consult; a night-vision camera attached to the bow that feeds a detailed surface view to a TV. set just ahead of the wheel, the GPS monitor, which sits to the left of the wheel, its brightness lowered to the point where it won't give away his location, and then a radar display that makes clear how little room for play the swamp offers if any of them need to accelerate. The setup would drive him bonkers if he weren't forced to drive at a speed a drunken day-tripper would consider sluggish.

The electrical engines that power the Zebotecs the team is using may be silent, but they also require a charge after several hours, which means they're all under orders to conserve energy in the event that this whole thing goes to shit and they all have to throttle it at the same time. He'll also have to shut all of the monitors down as soon as he's got The Desire Exchange within sight to avoid drawing too much electricity away from the engine.

Emily passes the strike team's location, well within earshot of them, Marcus is sure. But he's relieved to see the two red dots remain in position. They're following Marcus's order not to move until he texts them the coordinates of their final destination.

He's been so focused on Emily's progress he hasn't noticed that Jonathan's marker has come to a complete stop. Dupuy follows suit.

Marcus slows, watching as Emily's flashing blue dot starts to slow down as well. In his earpiece, the deafening rush of the wind starts to fade, replaced by the sound of hurried footfalls on the boat's deck, until, eventually, the blue dot representing the woman he'd do just about anything for comes to a complete stop, just a fingertip away from Jonathan's marker.

"Bingo," Marcus whispers.

There's an answering sniff from Emily, probably to confirm the boat is coming to a stop.

"Still blindfolded?"

Yes.

"We've got your position. Jonathan just got there. I'm going to hold back on the questions now. Don't want your new friends to think you've got a sinus infection."

Yes.

He's too far away to see their actual location, but that's the idea.

Slide in slowly and quietly once they've had time to go inside. If there is an inside. *There has to be an inside,* he thinks. No way are they going to conduct their business out here in the great wide open, with the snakes and the gators and who knows what else darting through the trees overhead. *You still don't know what their business is, dude.*

He grabs his phone, texts the coordinates to the other team members. Dupuy follows up with a text as well; same coordinates almost exactly. Now, all four boats are set to begin a slow crawl into position, stopping only once they've each established a reasonably good visual on whatever this place is.

The boat's propeller reduced to a weak sputter, Marcus manages his first deep breath in a while. Then he sees an e-mail sitting in the inbox on his phone.

The subject line makes his heart jump: ARE YOU MESSING WITH US? He straightens, scrolls down, and breathes a sigh of relief when he sees the sender is the security team on duty at Magnolia Gate.

Facial recognition guys got a hit on your fine black lady. Is this a joke? Srsly, what the hell's next dude?

Below this text, one of the still images he captured last night of Emily's beautiful visitor has been framed next to a scan of an old missing persons flyer featuring a black-and-white portrait photograph of what appears to be the same woman. The *exact* same woman, he realizes. The only real difference between the two images is the woman's hair; in the older portrait, the woman's proud Afro has been subdued into a single mahogany wave. With a two-fingered swipe, he zooms in so he can read the text printed above the woman's photo.

LAST SEEN – APRIL 4, 1959

It's a joke. It has to be. Or maybe it's a prop from a movie or a play, which means the woman's an actress, and wouldn't that make sense. Maybe they're *all* actors. But in a rush to look at the photos, he scrolled past the text in the e-mail the security team forwarded, an explanation of the method from the contracting firm they hired to conduct the face match, official-sounding sentences about how this hit came from an archive dedicated to crimes and disappearances among the New Orleans black community the local newspapers of the time refused to report. The date has been verified.

The woman's name is Lilliane Williams and she went missing on April 4, 1959.

And she hasn't aged a day since.

Can u see it? I've got a visual.

Dupuy's text message shocks him out of his daze. He grabs the wheel. Something big and bright has gone inferno on the night-vision screen. But he doesn't need the camera anymore, because he's got eyes on the light source ahead.

A massive purple tent appears through the trees. It glows with a warm, flickering interior illumination, and as he floats nearer to it, Marcus spots at least two identical, covered walkways jutting out from the main tent like the spokes on a bicycle wheel. Both walkways are completely covered in the same kind of semitransparent purple fabric that makes up the rest of the tent. Two boats, just like the one that picked up Emily, are tied to the floating platforms at the end of each walkway. There's enough space underneath the tent's floor for small boats to pass underneath, but the shadows under this platform are so deep, he can't tell what's lurking under there, if anything.

As he nears it, there's no ignoring the sheer impossibility of the entire structure, the way it's top is strung precisely through an uneven network of giant trees. Despite the fact it appears temporary, there's no way anyone could have built this place without major construction equipment and the barges needed to transport all of it. And no way in hell anyone could get a barge out here, not with all the surrounding obstructions.

Marcus cuts the engine.

Dupuy and the strike team have all done the same.

On the GPS monitor, their four boats now form a radius of blinking lights around the location of this giant, impossible-to-build tent.

Another text from Dupuy comes through.

What the hell man?

Marcus texts back, **My thoughts exactly.**

23

They haven't removed her blindfold, but Emily can tell they're walking her through some kind of enclosure. Two of her companions flank her, each one resting a hand gently on her shoulder. Up ahead are more footfalls; she figures they belong to the other two team members who brought her here. Then, suddenly, she hears the sound of curtains being pulled across rods.

The blindfold is gently removed.

She blinks, finds herself alone inside what at first appears to be a luxurious padded cell. Purple candles burn on two wall sconces. Once she gets her bearings, Emily realizes it's not a cell so much as a curtained off section of the walkway. Her escorts are divided up on both sides of her now; two of them stand outside of each curtain, blocking her in.

The floor looks likes several layers of cheap plywood, much of it studded with knotholes that allow her to see swamp water swirling below, a stark contrast to the lush purple draperies hanging on either side of her and the tufted purple fabric covering the low ceiling overhead. A robe and mask, just likes the ones they wore the night before, hang from a silver hook, and on a tiny antique wooden desk next to them, she finds a sheet of frayed cardstock. The paper type looks familiar, but the message printed on it is lengthier and more substantial than any of the commands they presented to her in the bathroom last night.

She sniffs loudly to get Marcus's attention.

"I'm here," Marcus says.

"Alright, now," Emily says quietly, "let's see what we have here." And then, as if she were simply reading aloud to herself, she continues. "Welcome, Miss Conran. We hope you enjoy your visit with us. Tonight we give you the gift of freedom. Tonight we will free you from the words and the labels you use to keep your true desires at bay. We will free you from the crushing need to control how you desire, how you love, and how others perceive you. We shall, in turn, guide your every step, and in return, we ask for nothing from you but compliance, silence, and willingness, a willingness to see your own truth, as we shall reveal it to you through pleasure and fantasy. Please undress completely before putting on the mask and robe."

She checks the shadows on the other side of both curtains. If they thought her little performance sounded like something other than a woman reading quietly to herself, there's no indication of it from their movements.

"The letter..." Marcus whispers, reading her mind.

She curses herself for not having seen this, for not having predicted that whatever ceremony she was about to walk in to would be as wordless, regimented, and choreographed as the test they subjected her to the night before. And she can't leave Arthur's letter here in this little cell. Just the thought of doing so makes her see his withered, bruised hand clutching the pen as he struggles through the painful haze of chemo and radiation to put each word to paper. Nothing about this room is private enough to protect this secret. It's not even a room, really. Once they draw the curtains back, it will be completely exposed to its immediate surroundings.

"You okay?"

Yes.

"Okay. We've all got a visual of the place. You're in some sort of giant tent. There are about five walkways coming off the thing. They each lead to a boat just like the one you came in on. So if you need to make a run for it, just head for one of those walkways, hit the water, and we'll have you in thirty seconds. Dupuy just gave Jonathan the same message."

Yes.

She knew a moment of decision would arrive at some point this evening; she just didn't expect it to come this early. She doesn't disrobe, not all the way, not like they asked her to. Instead, she leaves her panties on and slides Arthur's letter through the sideband, making sure the envelope is flush against her skin. There's no ignoring the eventual consequence of this choice. As soon as she's required to take off the robe, the letter, complete with Arthur's handwriting across the envelope, will be exposed where it sits against her right hip. The jig will be up. And that's fine, because, goddammit, that's as far as she's willing to go. She will not allow herself to be subjected to another frenzied burst of pleasure divorced from all intimacy. She's not willing to make love to masks again, not while a man like Marcus sends promises of contentment surging through her body with every word he whispers into her right ear.

One curtain is suddenly pulled back, and her silent messenger extends a gloved hand toward her. There is something less intimidating about his presence now that she is masked as well, and when she takes his hand, she does so with confidence, as if the barrier between them has collapsed, temporarily at least, and they are now compatriots who shall together solve the mysteries of the night.

The other three members of her group have fallen back now. Her silent messenger lifts her hand slightly above their shoulders. When they step through a draped opening into the giant tent, part of her is expecting him to spin her out into the first steps of some elaborate waltz. But instead, he guides her to a nearby podium three steps off the floor. On its flat desk surface, two purple candles burn, and when she sees the slender, flickering flames have no wicks at their center, she sucks in a frightened breath.

"Hey, you good?" Marcus asks.

Yes.

"You inside?"

Yes.

"You have the letter?"

Yes, and yes, you're the reason I took the letter with me, babe. Part of the reason, anyway. Because I know as soon as they see it on my body, we're done, and that'll cut down on the chance of more strangers touching and tasting me while I dream of your eyes, your lips, the feel of your muscular arms protecting me from the cleansing surf.

Four other podiums just like her own form a circle around the perimeter of the tent, facing inward where a round dais sits in the center of the entire space. Atop the dais is a throne-like chair made of dark, intricately carved wood. As her eyes adjust to the dim, wavering candlelight, she can see the throne's spine, legs, and struts are all

190 / Christopher Rice

carved into billowing columns of flame, flame the color of obsidian. There are three other shadows standing at podiums identical to hers. Like her, they are robed and masked. Two of them are Jonathan's height, but out of those two, one has a long mane of dark hair spilling out from the sides of her hood. The other is Jonathan, she's sure of it. The sight of him slows her heart rate, allows her to rest her hands flat on the podium before her as opposed to clenching both sides as if she fears being blasted into outer space.

Thank God, he's here, she thinks. *When he volunteered to come, I thought he was being insane, but now? But if I'd had any idea what this place would really be...*

Another robed figure, surrounded by a team of four masked minders, enters the tent. The woman's frightened gasps have a steady rhythm to them. She's not just gasping. She's on the verge of hyperventilating. That, and the way her minders stick closely to her side, as if they're preparing for her knees to buckle, suggest the woman is giving in to the same kind of panic attack Emily feels on the verge of herself. But the masked, shirtless figures surrounding the woman support her and gently guide her up onto her podium. They stroke her back with their gloved hands, and though they are as wordless as the figures that brought Emily here, the physical treatment they grant their frightened guest is delicate, tender. Comforting.

It comforts Emily, at least. Their newest visitor still looks like she's about to collapse.

A handbell chimes. The beautiful black woman who visited Emily the night before steps out from two flaps in the side of the tent, revealing a cluster of shadows gathered in the private room behind her. The plunging neckline of her black leather dress exposes one half of each breast, just shy of each nipple, and is lined with diamond-colored jewels that shimmer in the candlelight. The same jewels line the lower flaps of her dress, which shift around legs turned muscular from supporting her ample upper body.

Leather? Emily thinks. *In the swamp? And she's not sweating?*

She makes a beeline for their still frightened, still gasping recent addition, reaches out and gently runs her fingers across the woman's chin as she walks past her. "Fear is a survival instinct that spills far outside the borders of nature's purpose for it. Fear assaults us in a million different ways, every second of our waking lives. It disguises itself as reason, maturity, and even *common sense,* as if there is such a thing. You are here tonight because you have decided there are some fears, fears about *yourself,* that you can no longer abide, and so, with your consent, we shall strip those fears of their costumes and their disguises so they can be exposed for what they truly are."

She takes one step up onto the dais at the center of the room. It begins to slowly revolve beneath her. "My name is Lilliane. Welcome to The Desire Exchange."

As if on cue, the flaps covering the private room part and a young man emerges carrying a silver tray loaded with five silver goblets. A compact woman holding a decanter so large it looks like it could accommodate several bottles of wine follows him closely. Masked and shirtless, the man circulates the room, stepping in front of each podium only as long as it takes to set a silver goblet down on each one. Even masked, the guy has some resemblances to Ryan, to be sure, the same dirty blond hair with a slight curl to it. But he's way too young. Maybe ten years ago this masked man and Ryan Benoit could have been mistaken for brothers, but not today...except that mouth looks a lot like—he's placed Emily's goblet and departed before she can get a good look at his chin and jawline, and now the goblet is being filled by a young woman who moves with just as much speed and a refusal to look Emily in the eye that's just as strong.

I swear to God, if we went to all this trouble over a case of mistaken identity, she thinks, and then the booming authority in Lilliane's voice jerks her away from her thoughts.

"Based on your experience with us so far," the woman continues, "some of you may have already decided we are magicians or illusionists. To you we suggest this: if an illusion changes the course of your life for the better, are you still willing to dismiss it as dream and vapor? Obviously you are all free to believe everything you're about to witness tonight isn't real, but you are also free to take it into your hearts as if it was. The choice will be yours. We are not here to convince you we possess special gifts. We are here for one reason, and one reason only. To teach you a single lesson."

She surveys each one of them in turn, walking in a slow circle counter to the lazy spin of the dais. "Trust the fantasy that guides you to your heart."

Lilliane allows these words to settle over them, and, Emily notices, she's also checking to make sure each goblet has been filled.

"Any sign of him?" Marcus asks.

No.

"The libation we have just provided you with is perfectly healthy and safe, but it will also open your mind to everything you're about to witness."

"Oh, Jesus," Marcus mutters. "Can you fake it?"

Emily scans the room. It looks as if every other visitor has also been assigned a four-person team as well, probably the same team that administered their test. Those teams have assembled in the shadows behind each podium, and when she risks a glance over her shoulder, she finds her four minders standing exactly where she thought they'd be, between her and the walkway through which they entered moments before.

Are they watching her every move, or are they just there to catch her if she passes out? The reflective black glass filling the eyeholes of their masks sends a shiver through her limbs, an unwanted flashback to the pleasure unleashed by their raw assault on her flesh the night before.

No.

"Ugh...okay, then. If you start to feel sick or like you're gonna pass out, I want an extraction order. Immediately. Got it?"

Yes.

"Please," Lilliane says. "Drink!"

Across the tent, Jonathan hesitates before taking his first sip. But he still takes it, and that gives her permission to try one as well. She expects bitterness, or at least the familiar bite of something alcoholic, but the bland sweetness of the dark liquid is such a shock, she begins to gulp it rapidly before she pauses to consider that its innocuous flavor could be part of its seductive recipe.

She sets the goblet down on her podium, shocked to see it's still half full. Lilliane surveys the room, her heels clicking against the wooden dais underfoot as she continues her slow counter-walk to its lazy spin.

Every second Emily doesn't bring the goblet back to her lips feels like an eternity. She expects one of her minders to appear beside her and force its stem back into her hand. But they don't approach, and Lilliane's eyes pass over her podium without stopping to examine how much of the dark liquid Emily has consumed.

Okay, good, Emily thinks. *They're not forcing us to down it all right off the bat. That's a sign it's not poison or some crazy drug.*

"Does it taste weird?" Marcus asks.

No.

"Good," he whispers. "Emily, that woman. The one from your test. Is she the one speaking?"

Yes.

"Does she look the same?"

Yes...and what the hell kind of question is that, Marcus? But they haven't worked out a signal for the later so she grips the edges of the podium instead of whispering it.

"Alright," Marcus whispers. "You ready to give me a headcount."

Yes.

"Are there five visitors?"

Yes.

"Don't include them. Just The Desire Exchange folks. Okay. Wait ten seconds and give me the count. If it's double digits, leave a five second space in between each number."

Yes.

She begins her headcount.

Two people emerged from the private room—the guy who could be Ryan Benoit's younger brother and the woman who used the decanter to fill each goblet. Throw in five four-person teams, plus Lilliane, and that made twenty-three people total.

She taps her podium twice, counts off five seconds, and then taps her podium three times.

"Twenty-three?" Marcus asks.

Yes.

"Alexandra Vance!" Lilliane cries. The guy who could be Ryan's younger brother hands Lilliane the leather-bound notebook in which Emily lied her heart out.

The woman on the verge of a nervous breakdown wretches at the sound of her name, clutching the flaps of her robe. One of her minders steps forward and places a hand gently against the small of her back. Emily assumes he's just offering comfort until he grips the woman's elbow and guides her off the podium.

Leather-bound notebook open against one supporting arm, Lilliane begins to read as the trembling woman is walked to the carved, obsidian-colored throne. "The boys from down the street are home from college for a vacation. I've seen them all week long, coming home late. Lounging by their parent's swimming pools with no shirts on. I'm in the garage one day cleaning up the mess my ex-husband left behind when I find a box of sex toys and bondage equipment he left behind, none of which we ever used on me when we were married."

Alexandra's minders push down gently on both of her shoulders until she's seated, then they stand on either side of the throne as Lilliane continues to read, circling the dais as if she wants to sprinkle all four of the other guests with a little of Alexandra's most private fantasy. Even though the scene before her has the trappings of a trial or a judgment, there is no recrimination or disdain in Lilliane's tone as she continues to read. "I'm sitting there, crying my eyes out over my ex-husband's betrayal, when I hear a knock on the door, and there they are. The boys from down the street. They are shirtless and muscular. They are smiling at me until they see my tears. And then they're coming toward me because they see what's in the box, and it's almost like they care more about my ex-husband's sex toys than they do about me or my pain.

"I stand there watching them as they start taking out whips and chains and all sorts of bondage stuff, and then they grab me and tie my wrists to the light fixture over my head and I am helpless to stop them as they use everything in the box on me over and over and over again."

Lilliane closes the book, standing a few paces from where Alexandra sits, trying to catch her breath.

"Is this your fantasy, Miss Vance?"

"Yes," the woman gasps. "Yes…it is."

As she approaches the dais, Lilliane studies the terrified woman with an expression somewhere between thoughtful and stern. "Describe your fear to me, Alexandra," she says in a softer, less commanding tone. "Use any words or images you'd like. But describe it to me, if you can."

"Like…it's like someone's sitting on my chest and I can't…Can't breathe."

"I understand," Lilliane says. "Now, please, consider for a minute, that you are actually choosing not to breathe. That a part of you is literally trying to prevent you from taking your next breath. Because if you don't breathe, if oxygen ceases to enter your lungs, then you won't *be*. And if you cease to exist, your fear will end. This strategy of your body, of your mind, may seem like it's designed to protect you, Alexandra, but really it's designed to punish you. And you do not deserve to be punished. Not in the slightest. So please, listen to my voice, dig deep, and *decide* to breathe."

If Alexandra's chest is any indication, Lilliane's words have had a positive effect; it appears still now where only seconds before it was heaving. "Your body's instincts and reflexes will try to end your fear by ending your life," Lilliane says, and it's clear she's addressing all of them again. "We, on the other hand, remove your fear from you so that you may live your life the way it's meant to be lived."

She turns to the young woman who filled each goblet and gives her a slight nod. When she steps up onto the dais, the two minders depart, and suddenly Decanter Girl is gently sliding the flaps of Alexandra's robe apart. She reaches up and removes Alexandra's mask, revealing the woman's tear-filled eyes. She gently caresses the side of Alexandra's face. She whispers something only Alexandra can hear.

As she continues to gently caress one of Alexandra's furiously blushing cheeks, the young woman reaches up with her other hand and removes her own mask. And that's when the drug starts to take effect, or at least Emily hopes it's the drug; how else can she explain the tendrils of gold luminescence that have emerged from the young woman's eyes, lips, and nostrils, the same ones that are now floating up into the air above her head, the same ones that pulse with intensity when the young woman brings her lips almost to Alexandra's and takes in a sudden, sharp breath? How else can Emily explain the cobra's hood of glittering gold that is now coalescing in the air high above the dais, twisting and becoming more solid, as if it were a living thing unto itself?

"Oh my God," Emily whispers.

"Emily? Are they hurting her?"

"Oh my fucking God."

"*Emily!*"

Emily is about to answer when she hears Lilliane say something. But just then, the twisting, rising cloud of gold high above the dais seems to collapse in on itself, and for a split second, Emily assumes it's over. And then a silent, glittering shockwave of blinding light flies toward her, and it's only in that instant that she makes out what Lilliane just said almost too quietly for anyone to hear.

"Prepare for radiance."

The last time Marcus witnessed a burst of light like the one that fills the tent he was at 30,000 feet, flying over a line of thunderstorms in a passenger jet. He's thrown one arm up to shield his eyes from what he's sure will be a line of tent-fragments and other shrapnel. But when he blinks and opens them again, the tent is still very much intact. Its flaps billow slightly, but that's all, and the only sound that accompanies this blinding series of flashes is a burst of static in his ear just like the one from the night before when Emily's strange visitors first arrived at Lily Conran's beach house.

He's poised on the tip of his boat, hand on his gun holster, the other pressing his earpiece deeper into his ear.

"Emily!"

There's no response; there's no sound coming through the earpiece at all.

Dupuy sends a text to the thread they opened earlier that includes the strike team: **What the hell's this light show?**

Marcus texts back. **Get audio confirm from Jonathan. Emily dark.**

K

The light show inside the tent settles into a regular, silent rhythm, but the brilliance of it is staggering. Thirty seconds go by according to the clock on his smart phone, but it feels like he's been forced to wait an hour when the next text from Dupuy arrives. It reads: **No confirmation. Same as house entries. Some kind of interference. Only longer.**

Bring yr boat 2 my post. Strike team take Frank's current position.

The strike team confirms in their typical long-winded manner: **Got it.**

Good idea? Dupuy texts.

Can't hear her Frank.

Could clear up. Move in now might blow cover.

I CAN'T HEAR HER

There's another pause that feels longer than it is. Then, finally, Dupuy says: **Moving in. Go with God, buddy.**

There's about three hundred feet between his tied off boat and the end of one of the giant tent's walkways. If there was any sound accompanying this crazy blaze of light inside the tent, he wouldn't think twice about driving the boat in closer, but from this close, just the noise of the propeller cutting water might be enough to alert them to his approach, so he dives headfirst into the water instead.

24

It has the fearsome brilliance of a miniature thermonuclear explosion, but it comes without sound, and at the very moment when Emily braces for some sort of terrible impact that could tear her apart, she finds herself griping the sides of the podium as a wave of light washes right through her, blinding her briefly but leaving her unharmed.

Some kind of digital projector, it has to be. It's using some crazy computer program. What's the difference between magic and computers these days anyway?

The dais is gone. The throne is gone. It's as if some hole has been torn in the fabric of time and space itself, and now she's staring through a glittering membrane into another dimension, a dimension inhabited solely by a cluttered garage like the one Alexandra Vance mentioned in her written confession. Alexandra dangles from the solid block of the light fixture attached to the track for the garage door, her wrists wrapped in a coil of rope that's been looped over the fixture's plastic casing. But the garage door and most of the surrounding walls are invisible, cut off in various places by the glittering membrane that seems to encompass a living, breathing piece of Alexandra's very soul.

The entire scene is slowly revolving, so its borders must have a substance that's being supported by the dais, the dais she no longer sees, but that is rotating from the motion of this… Every name she tries to come up with to describe what she's watching now seems inadequate. Dream? Visual? Movie? What? What can she possibly call this?

Can't be real. It's not real. The drugs. Some kind of film projector. And where the hell is Decanter Girl? All that crazy gold light came pouring out of her orifices and then—poof! This!

While Decanter Girl is nowhere to be seen, Emily can see glimpses of the other four podiums, standing just outside the border of this display like her own. Her fellow guests are paper-thin silhouettes.

Meanwhile, two shirtless, muscular college-aged boys are materializing on either side of Alexandra's dangling body. A lean blond takes shape behind Alexandra as he forces a ball gag into her mouth, securing the strap behind her head with his other hand; he sucks hungrily on her neck the whole time. The other, a dark-skinned linebacker type, is placing nipple clamps on Alexandra's breasts, giving them light tugs as he checks their security with a leering grin. Both men are gorgeous and bristling with a kind of youthful, swaggering menace that makes them irresistible and dangerous, their absurdly huge cocks beet-red and dripping pre-cum. This isn't a flashback. It's a projection of Alexandra's mind, of Alexandra's lust, only for some reason Emily is seeing all of it play out before her.

They're all seeing it, everyone in the tent, she's sure. That's why the podiums are positioned around the room the way they are. But are they seeing exactly the same thing? Could the drugs and the reading they just listened to have combined in each one of their minds to produce a different hallucination based on the same story?

The dark-skinned linebacker type sees something in the cardboard box he likes, falls to his knees next to it, and pulls out an oily looking cat-o'-nine-tails. He grins like a jack-o'-lantern. Cackling, he shows it to his friend and they both take up a position behind their struggling captive as she jerks her wrists against the rope. They cock the whip, slapping its tails against the concrete floor with a loud whack that makes Alexandra cry out into the ball gag. Then the blond raises it over his shoulder, his pose amateurish and unskilled. He strikes.

The cat-o'-nine-tails wraps around the light fixture. The boy curses. The whip is stuck, its tails threaded around the light fixture's plastic casting, wound through the struts of the garage door opener. He yanks back on it too hard. The plastic casing tears free from the ceiling, followed by the light fixture itself. Alexandra drops to the floor suddenly, a small shower of debris following her. By now the scene has revolved so completely, Emily finds herself staring right at the two young men as they throw their arms over their heads and drop to the floor to shield themselves.

Just as both boys manage to rise up onto all fours, Alexandra stands, freed from her restraints, the whip in her right hand. With her left hand, she yanks the ball gag from her mouth and tosses it to the floor.

"Bad boys," Alexandra says, cracking the whip beside her. To Emily, Alexandra's voice sounds amplified, but also like it's traveling through several feet of water before it reaches her ears. "Bad bad bad bad *bad* boys!"

She cracks the whip across the blond boy and plants one foot in the small of the dark-skinned muscle boy's back, driving him face down to the concrete. From the force of the blow, the blond arches his back like a cat, his open-mouthed groan trembling with pleasure, his cock weeping pre-cum as it bounces against his stomach. She takes her foot off the dark-skinned muscle boy and then, just as the guy tries to right himself, she brings the whip down across his back as well. The painful pleasure renders him submissive as well.

Alexandra drapes the whip over one shoulder, grabs them both by the backs of their necks, and pulls them to their knees until they're facing each other.

"Is that what you boys want?"

"Yes, Momma," they both answer in unison.

She pushes their heads together. At first, they resist the feel of each other's lips, but the harder Alexandra presses on the backs of their heads, the more their kiss becomes a hungry war of tongues; two leering, youthful predators turned submissive and fluid by one sloppy strike with a tool they had no experience with.

Alexandra pulls their heads apart, guides their mouths to her sex. Both of their tongues begin fighting for access to her clit. As the pleasure intensifies, Alexandra's hand travels slowly up her chest to where the whip lies draped over her shoulder, the handle resting just inches above her left breast. Just at the moment where it seems like she might come, she pries the boys from her pussy, sends each one down on all fours again, one after the other, with a single, determined shove on the back of his neck. And then she goes to work with the whip, her own grunts of exertion vibrating with as much pleasure as the boys' ecstatic moans.

The whip flies through the air with increasing, unnatural speed. Each new strike begins to shed threads of the same gold luminescence that snaked out of Decanter Girl's eyes and mouth at the very start of this impossible event. The scene begins losing definition, turning into a blur of flesh-colored clouds and brilliant streaks of gold, an impressionistic riot of fading desire.

And then there's a scream.

The authentic, unguarded scream of a woman in the midst of absolute abandon.

Once again, Alexandra sits on the carved throne. Decanter Girl stands over her, their faces inches apart as Decanter Girl grips both arms of the throne, steadying herself as the raw components of the vision they all just witnessed coalesce into thick snakes of floating gold, snakes that are either emerging from Alexandra's lips and nose, or just now entering them; Emily can't tell which.

Emily almost misses the pulses of light that travel up the walls of the tent. They look like tides of bioluminescent plankton. For a few seconds, they congregate at the top of the tent. Then they vanish completely as Alexandra's breathless climax subsides.

The woman's first deep breath tugs at the floating snakes of gold laced through the air surrounding the dais. They jerk toward her and then vanish, as if she's been able to take their entire, twisted lengths into her lungs with just a single breath. In the sudden silence that follows, Emily can hear gasps, even a few sobs, coming from the other guests. Jonathan is bent forward over his podium as if he thinks his vision is failing him, his mask pushed up halfway off his face, his mouth a silent O.

Lilliane walks quietly and confidently toward the center of the tent, as if she were a drama teacher and the two women before her had just performed a brief, amusing scene from a Neil Simon play.

Alexandra blinks, bright-eyed, a satisfied, contented smile forming on her flushed face. Gone is the fear that followed her onto the dais only moments before.

Decanter Girl slides her mask back on and steps off the dais, allowing Lilliane to take her place. If the warmth radiating from Lilliane's expression is a ruse, then Lilliane is an extraordinarily good actress. She takes one of Alexandra's hands.

"The box. Was it real? Did your ex-husband really betray you?"

"Yes," Alexandra answers.

"But everything you found inside it, it aroused you, didn't it?"

Alexandra nods.

"And so, because you were afraid to look deeper, you assumed this meant you had an innate desire to be submissive, when in truth, it's dominance you crave, Alexandra. It's freedom from submission your heart seeks, and it is hard male flesh, tied down, exposed, vulnerable to your power, that most enflames your desires."

"Yes," Alexandra says, her voice brimming with a confidence she's yet to display inside of this strange tent.

To the guests ringing the space, Lilliane continues, "There is no truth without fantasy. But our minds can see only the shape of our fantasies, not their interior. At the first blush of arousal, we seize on the raw materials or shallow visuals that have stirred our loins, and out of fear, or sometimes just laziness, we look no further. We look no deeper. And so the full story of our desire remains shrouded in self-imposed mystery. Not here. Not tonight."

Lilliane tugs gently on Alexandra's hand. The small motion is enough to lift the woman to her feet, and after Lilliane gives her a light kiss on the cheek, Alexandra returns to her podium with confident steps, despite the fact that she is still completely nude.

A silence falls. This time, it's Decanter Girl who delivers the leather-bound notebook to Lilliane. When Lilliane opens the pages for the second time that evening there's a small eruption of sobs from several feet away. "No, no, no," comes the unfamiliar male voice. "I can't. Seriously, I just...please. I just...I *can't*. I'm sorry."

No sooner has the tiny man stepped down off his podium than his team has surrounded him, arms curving swiftly around his back, guiding him out of the tent and down the walkway through which they entered.

Emily studies the expression on Lilliane's face as she watches the other guest leave. Lilliane, if that's even her real name, gives off such a profound sense of quiet loss over this man's sudden departure, Emily can't help but believe the woman feels as if some essential part of her being has been rejected by his abrupt, frightened departure. This, more than anything else, convinces Emily that what she's just witnessed has no logical, earthbound explanation.

"No one will be forced to stay," Lilliane says, but her previously confident voice is now shaky. "No one," she adds in a whisper. Her wounded, wide-eyed stare is still fixed on the man's suddenly empty podium. "Anyone else?" she asks the rest of them with a new hard edge to her tone.

No one says a word. Then she seems to remember herself, a process that requires her to clear her throat several times as she carefully opens the leather-bound notebook against her arm. She's about to call out another name when they're all disturbed by the sound of one of the boats throttling up. Emily figures they've dressed, blindfolded, and strapped their defector in, and now they're returning him to his rendezvous point.

Lilliane pretends to study the pages in front of her, but Emily can tell she's waiting for the boat to depart. Once it starts to fade, she lifts her attention from the book, studies each one of them briefly before calling the next name.

"Lily Conran!"

I lied, Emily tells herself as she steps down off the podium. Her team members move to assist her but she holds up a hand to indicate she doesn't need their support. They follow close behind her anyway. *I lied. So none of this will matter. It might be insane or trippy or hallucinatory. But it won't matter, because it won't really be my fantasy. Not unless they're actually able to stare into my soul. But that can't be what's happening here and who cares because I lied.*

Lilliane reads. "I've heard rumors about the doctor. My friends have told me he's inappropriate, that he doesn't respect boundaries. Maybe he's even a bit of a lech. And he isn't the most handsome of men either. But that's part of what makes him appealing. The fact that he's a little rough, the fact that he's a little dirty. When he tells me to change into a robe, I know it's not necessary. I'm there for headaches. Why does he need to examine me from head to toe for just a headache?"

She's about to take a seat on the throne when every limb in her body feels like it's become solid, and for a few seconds, she can't move. Her escorts are prepared for this, however. They press down gently on her shoulders until her butt meets the cushioned seat, which is still sweaty and damp from Alexandra Vance's transformative visit to this very spot.

"Worse, he doesn't leave the room while I change and I can feel his eyes on me as he pretends to turn his back to me and consult his clipboard. Can feel his eyes on me as if it were his fingers. So once I have the gown on, I sit on the edge of the table and spread my legs slightly. It's my signal. I'm telling him I know what he wants. I'm giving him permission to slide one hand under my robe, caress the inside of my thigh. He keeps talking to me as if it were a basic examination, asking me to cough even as his fingers tickle my pussy. Asking me to breathe in and out as his first finger slips between my folds, fingertip eventually focusing on my clit, circling it. Talking to me like nothing is amiss, like I'm not going moist all over his fingers."

As Lilliane reads, the goblet bringer walks toward her across the floor, his hips swaying with what looks to her like a confident, predatory swagger. He's a bit taller than he looked when she was on her podium. Now that she's up close, she can see how finely etched his slender torso is, can see his abs flexing as he walks, his arms chorded with muscle. Broad shoulders offset his youthful, unblemished pale skin, and then her eyes find the strawberry-colored birthmark above his collarbone and her breath leaves her with such sudden force.

And then he's standing over her, gripping the arms of the chair just as Decanter Girl did with Alexandra Vance only moments before. And then he's removing his mask, and suddenly she is staring up at Ryan Benoit. And somehow, Ryan Benoit is still twenty-one years old, even though Ryan Benoit has not been twenty-one years old for fourteen years.

The sight of him comes as a greater, more thunderous shock than the living fantasy she witnessed moments before. Because no special effects machine, no hologram projector, no blaze of disorienting lights, can shave fourteen years off a man whose face she has spent days studying in detail, not at this close, intimate distance.

Could it be the drug? That's the only possible explanation left; that somehow the drug, which didn't even taste like a strange chemical, has somehow, in just this moment at least, frozen Ryan exactly as he looked in all of those photographs taken prior to his disappearance.

He mistakes her shock for fear of what's to come. He parts the flaps of her robe with one practiced hand. His stare is seductive, welcoming, intoxicating.

And then he sees the letter.

The sight of his own name, written in his father's handwriting, drains all the life from his eyes in an instant.

"Ryan..." she whispers.

He locks eyes with her.

"Who are you?" he says, his voice a low rumble that sounds too deep and too adult for his svelte, youthful body.

Lilliane has stopped reading, stopped walking, is looking at them over one shoulder. She's studying Ryan's sudden paralysis, and then her gaze drops to Emily's panties, to the letter resting under the sideband.

"*Who are you?*" Ryan Benoit growls.

"Your father's dying," Emily whispers.

At the mention of his father, he closes his hands around her throat and lifts her up and out of the chair with stunning, supernatural strength. With the few gasps of air she has left, Emily wheezes, "That's enough!"

Everything that happens next seems to happen in the same terrifying instant.

She hears Jonathan scream her name, her *real* name, as he vaults off his podium.

Lilliane orders Ryan to put her down only to be stunned by Jonathan's piercing cry—*Emily!*—and the revelation that she is not Lily Conran after all.

Jonathan races toward them. She braces for the impact of him, prepares for him to knock them both off the dais and to the floor, a blessing if it gets Ryan's hands off her throat. But just then, Lilliane raises one outstretched palm, fingers tensed, and suddenly Jonathan flies backward across the tent's floor, as if he's been pulled by a string, a string that drags him up into the air. He smacks into the tent's wall, which appears to consume him like a hungry mouth.

"*We're done!*" Lilliane roars, and Emily realizes the words aren't meant for her or the other guests. They're meant for the rest of her team.

"Who are you?" Ryan growls, hands tensing around her throat.

Lilliane shakes her head at his display, lifts both arms skyward, and suddenly the walls of the tent sweep in around them as if the top of the tent itself were being drawn skyward by a giant hand.

Darkness swallows her. Four gunshots tear through the air somewhere nearby. She can hear Marcus shouting orders or threats, she can't tell which. But the tent's skin feels like it's suffocating her now. And she's not alone.

Once again, Ryan's hands have closed around her throat.

25

It isn't a death grip. But if he doesn't intend to choke her to death, he's intent on incapacitating her, at least. Or maybe he just wants to terrify her. Either way, Emily is too stunned by the sight of the night sky appearing high above Ryan Benoit to give the man the reaction he seems to crave, and the resulting rage deforms his beautiful face even more.

It's as if the tent itself is flying away through the treetops, snapping tree branches as it goes, showering leaves and snapped limbs to the wood floor all around them. Suddenly, Ryan's hands leave her throat. He's yanked from her body by someone she can't see. As soon as she can manage a full breath, she reaches for the envelope still tucked into the side band of her panties. When her fingertips find its sweaty edge, relief floods her along with fresh oxygen.

Marcus, soaked from head to toe, has aimed his gun directly at Ryan's face. There's chaos all around them, but these two men are locked in a sudden standoff over her prone, half-naked body. With his free hand, Marcus tosses her robe onto her. She tries pulling it on, but she can't take her eyes off of Ryan, whose stony expression doesn't display a single trace of fear at the sight of a powerful handgun pointed at the bridge of his nose.

"Give me the letter," Ryan says calmly.

"How 'bout you apologize to the lady first?"

"I'm sorry she's a liar who deceived us and I hope she's grateful she's still breathing. How's that? Now give me the letter."

It takes Emily a second to process what happens next. Ryan sweeps one hand up through the air in front of him and suddenly Marcus's handgun is sailing through the air on a trail of glittering gold. It flies through the spot where the tent wall was only moments before and splashes into the swamp.

Marcus lowers his now empty gun hand slowly, never once taking his eyes off the man before him as he processes the guy's unfathomable strength.

"Emily," Marcus says quietly.

"Yes."

"Run."

And then, despite being clearly outmatched, Marcus slugs the guy. Ryan absorbs the punch as if it were a light shove on the shoulder. He blinks, gives them both a shit-eating grin, then his eyes land on Emily's new pose and the swagger leaves him.

Robed and on her feet, Emily grips the center of the letter in both hands. From the precise placement of her tense fingers, there's no mistaking her intention.

"If you hurt him," she says, "if you hurt anyone, I'll tear it to pieces right now and your father will go to the grave without you knowing what's in this letter."

"If I wanted to speak to that son of a bitch, I wouldn't need you to find him."

"We know, Ryan," Marcus says. "That's why we moved him someplace safe, in case this didn't go well. And newsflash. It's not going well."

It's a bald-faced lie, but Marcus tells it with utter conviction.

Now that she's standing, Emily can take in more of their dramatically altered surroundings. The four members of the strike team have Ryan surrounded; the guns they've aimed at him look more like cannons, and their gear and night camouflage make them look like something out of a movie. In the absence of the tent, they're now surrounded by a scabbard of broken tree branches and watery, night darkness. She can see two of the other guests, huddling in what used to be a corner of the tent, the departure of which has left behind tattered pieces of fabric that partially cover the walkways. To her astonishment, she sees the boats are all still there, save for the one in which they ferried away the frightened guest. But Lilliane and her team members are gone, vanished. All twenty-three of them.

Twenty-two of them, she corrects herself. One stayed behind.

"This is not a negotiation," Ryan says. "I could take that letter out of her hands in five seconds."

"And that's when we'd empty every piece of firepower in this room into you so we could find out just how strong you really are."

"I'm pretty fucking strong," Ryan says with a confident smile.

"I didn't say it wouldn't be fun," Marcus responds.

"You're not strong enough to keep your shit together at the sight of your father's handwriting," Emily says.

When he turns his furious gaze on her, she sees a pulse of gold light pass through his eyes. Marcus sees it too, but if it frightens him, he doesn't let it show.

"*Tear it up!*"

Emily doesn't recognize the voice at first. It's Dupuy. He's running toward her and he's coming fast. Like Marcus, he's soaked from head to toe. Ryan takes a step toward her. All four strike team members raise their giant guns, and then suddenly the letter's been ripped from her hands, not by Ryan but by Frank who, to everyone's astonishment, is tearing it into shreds.

"*No!*" Ryan shouts, but the ring of firepower around him holds him in place. He's strong, but not indestructible. Or maybe he's just unwilling to endure whatever healing process a rain of automatic bullets would require of him. He does nothing, even as Dupuy casts several handfuls of the letter off the side of the platform, where they flutter like snowflakes to the black water.

"What are you doing, Frank?" Marcus cries.

Dupuy whirls on his employer's long-lost son. He is not just soaked, but exhausted, breathless, possessed of an anger that gives him brash confidence despite Ryan's evident supernatural abilities.

"Where is he?" Dupuy growls.

"Oh, no," Emily whispers despite herself. She's scanning the room now. Two other robed guests, clutching each other in terror. Only two. And neither one of them is Jonathan. "Oh, no. Oh, no…"

"*Where is Jonathan Claiborne?*" Dupuy shouts.

"I don't know anyone named Jonathan Claiborne," Ryan answers.

"Leonard Miller," Marcus adds.

"You're going to take us to him right now and you better pray nobody lays a hand on him before we get there," Dupuy says.

"Or after," Marcus adds.

"And why would I do that?" Ryan asks.

"Because he's the only one of us who read that damn letter, that's why," Dupuy says. "So if you want to hear your daddy's final message, you're going to have to hear it from the guy your boss just kidnapped." When he sees Marcus and Emily's stares, he adds, "He read it tonight before we came here. He said he didn't want us going in blind in case either of the copies got lost or taken away by somebody besides *this* asshole. And no, he didn't tell me what it said."

"If I wanted to speak to my father, which I *don't*, I could find him without you ass clowns."

"Yeah, well, everyone who works for your dad knows where we are tonight and they know why we're here," Marcus says. "They've got our coordinates and if we don't come home safe and sound, *with* Jonathan, you'll have problems, Ryan. Lots of very big problems."

"*Great.* More bullet sponges crawling all over some plywood platform in the middle of the swamp. Look at the setup. We never use the same location twice. Tell me that's not all you've got, Jarhead."

"I've got a picture of your boss Lilliane Williams that shows she went missing in nineteen fifty-nine," Marcus answers. "Oh, and also, she hasn't aged a day since. Magnolia Gate has it too, and they're waiting on my orders for how to proceed. I'm still thinking it over, to be frank. But if they don't get some orders from me soon, you can bet your pretty behind that picture's gonna get splashed all over the news, which is going to seriously screw with your business model, *Ass Clown.*"

The confidence drains from Ryan in an instant, his sharply defined arms going limp at his sides, his bare, muscular chest heaving with suddenly strained deep breaths.

Dupuy says, "Also, take a look around. I think your coworkers have a different attitude about exposure than you do. Maybe that's why they left you to deal with the fallout of your little tantrum alone."

"I chose to stay," Ryan says. "She gave the order and I chose to stay and deal with it all. Don't presume to understand how we operate. You know *nothing* about who we are!"

"Yeah, okay," Marcus answers. "Well, what you'll be dealing with after tonight are teams of highly trained mercenaries combing the swamps for you *and* your friends, not some random private investigator you can scare off with your magic tricks."

"They're not tricks," Ryan growls, but Emily is now the focus of his attention. "What are you, *Lily Conran?* The sister I never wanted?"

"What are *you*, Ryan Benoit?" she asks him. "A vampire?"

"Vampires aren't real," he says quietly. "I'm real."

But it sounds like he's trying to convince himself with these final two words, and in the silence that settles over the platform, his expression becomes plaintive, and for a while no one says anything. The sadness that resonates from him overwhelms her as totally as the expression that passed over Lilliane's face when her frightened guest departed the proceedings earlier that evening.

"The choice is yours, Ryan," Marcus says. "We've all known your father for years, all of us, and he never mentioned you until a few weeks ago. He's dying. His defenses are down, and there's something he wants you to know. So it's up to you. How do you want to spend the last hours of his life? Finding out what he has to say, or knowing he's hunting you and your friends like dogs?"

"I don't need a deathbed apology from that man," Ryan says quietly.

"Who says it's an apology?" Emily says. "Maybe it's something new, something you've never heard before. That's why you want to know what you're walking into before you go, and that's why you're going to take us to Jonathan so he can tell you what was in the letter. Then you can decide if your own father is worth the trouble."

"Or the pain," Marcus adds.

"I'll take you to *Lilliane*," he finally answers. "On one condition: you lose the soldiers of fortune here. I want them to escort our guests back to their rendezvous points. And I can assure you"—he raises his voice as he turns to address the two mortified, robed, masked people cowering at the far edge of the platform—"your money will be refunded, provided you didn't deceive us as well. And perhaps someone should get Miss Conran her clothes."

"Emily," she says. "My name's Emily Blaine."

"Well, I wish I could say it was nice to meet you."

"Same here."

"Try using your real name next time and see if it goes better."

Marcus beckons to one of the strike team members. Without taking their eyes off Ryan, the two men begin to confer in quiet whispers. For the most part, Marcus is the one whispering, the other guy just nods.

"How did they leave?" Emily asks.

Despite the drama of everything that's proceeded this question, it sends a shockwave of silence through everyone around her; it feels as if they've all steeled themselves against the fact that any answer Ryan gives will force them all to accept the full magnitude of how thoroughly bent their minds are by the events of the evening.

"Did they fly?" Emily asks. "Did they *really* fly out of here?"

"We don't fly. We leap. There's only so far we can go." There's a hunger in his eyes, a need to explain himself that catches her off guard.

"What do you mean?"

He shakes his head as if he's shaking off the cloying sound of her voice. "I'm not about to explain our origins to a team of secret agents who blew their way into a ceremony in which *no one* was going to be harmed."

Marcus says, "You had your hands around her throat, dude."

"This is going to be a specific exchange of information and nothing more. Your friend will tell me what was in my father's letter and…"

"And then you're going to give him back to us," Emily says, "which is a lot more than exchanging information."

"My point is that none of us are going to stand there while you assault us with questions about what we are. We didn't invite you into our world."

"This isn't your world," Emily says, even as she feels Frank Dupuy lay a warning hand on her shoulder. "The swamp doesn't belong to you. The night doesn't *belong* to you. And you're more than happy to show off your talents to rich people who are willing to pay for the service, so spare me the sanctimony and stop acting like we shot our way into your peaceful commune. You could have had your letter *and* had all of us out of your hair in ten minutes if your boss hadn't taken my best friend. So stop calling this is an exchange of information because it's not. This is a *kidnapping*, and what we've agreed to give you is a ransom."

"It's Lilliane's ransom you should be more worried about," Ryan says. "I've agreed to take you to Jonathan, but Lilliane's the one who will have to let him go. And trust me, she has her own mind about these things. Are you done lecturing me, Emily Blaine?"

"I'll be done when I have Jonathan back."

"Okay," Marcus says, breaking his huddle with the strike team's leader. "Our guys will escort your guests back to their pickup points. But wherever we're going, you travel with us the whole way. None of this leaping stuff you guys are so crazy about. Is there enough gas in those boats to get us there?"

Ryan nods, but he's still studying Emily, as if the afterburn of her anger is intoxicating.

"Can someone get this guy a shirt?" Marcus asks.

"I didn't bring a shirt," Ryan says. "Stop wasting time."

"Can someone get this guy a ball gag? And maybe a leash?"

"Now you're talking," Ryan answers. He studies Marcus with undisguised lust. But Marcus is too busy directing the other members of the strike team, who have split up into groups of two men each and are now escorting the terrified guests to two separate boats. After a while, Ryan feels Emily's eyes on him and turns to face her.

"I'm a radiant," he says. "That's what we're called."

"Who calls you that?" But she's remembering Lilliane's words before Alexandra Vance's fantasy exploded out across the space they're now standing on like stranded shipwreck survivors. *Prepare for radiance...*

"It's what we call ourselves," Ryan answers.

Just then, Dupuy arrives with her folded clothes in both hands. Ryan turns the hard ridges of his naked back to her and walks to the edge of the platform as if he's about to meditate on the swamp.

26

After thirty minutes on the water in the same boat Emily was picked up in earlier that night, Ryan Benoit points to the dark horizon and says, "That's it!" But Emily can barely see anything, just deeper, looming shadows, no sign of the restored plantation house Ryan claimed would be waiting for them at the end of their journey.

Ryan reduces the engine to a low, chugging sputter, barely louder than the splashes from the propeller, and then, after another minute or two, Emily can finally make out the outline of large trees forming a dense canopy beneath the star-flecked sky and dim tendrils of orange light she assumes are coming from heavily draped windows. The island isn't just small and isolated; it looks barely inhabited. There's no road visible, no dock, no snaking garden paths marked with lights.

Allowing Ryan to drive not only kept his hands full, it also kept him in one place, both of which seemed to make Dupuy and Marcus feel more confident about the trip in general, even though Ryan is probably capable of doing things to them with his bare hands that would render ordinary weapons insignificant. For the entire ride, Marcus has stood at the back of the open deck just behind the wheel, newly armed with a Beretta M9 he got from one of his strike team members—it was easier than fishing his SIG out of the swamp—his intent stare never leaving Ryan's back. Now he stands up straight, still watching their shirtless, hard-bodied pilot instead of their destination.

Just at the moment when Emily is sure Ryan's about to beach

their vessel on the muddy shore, he pulls into a tiny, unmarked inlet that's virtually camouflaged by the night's rippling darkness. Dense walls of vegetation rise on either side of them, with occasional gaps that allow the plantation house to increase in size as they draw nearer to it. A row of boat docks appears up ahead, well kept, but low and unobtrusive. Ryan pulls into one, kills the engine, and then jerks his head indicating they should all disembark.

"You first," Marcus says.

It's too dark inside the boat for her to see his expression, but she guesses Ryan is rolling his eyes and then some. "You're free to put a bullet in me if you'd like, and after it comes out the other side of me like a flattened quarter, I'll even let you have it back so you can make a necklace out it. If you want, I'll even pretend the whole thing hurts a little. But only if it'll make your nipples hard."

"I thought we weren't allowed to ask questions about what you are," Emily says.

"I'm enhanced," Ryan says. "How's that? After you, Miss Blaine." She complies, if only to avoid further sarcasm. She's as big a fan of snark as the next mouthy smartass, just not when her best friend is being held captive. Dupuy's a few steps ahead of her, but Marcus is waiting for Ryan to go first.

"I'm just trying to be polite," Ryan says.

"We're not here for polite," Marcus says. "We're here to get our friend back. After you."

In a flash, Ryan leaps the small distance from the deck to the dock, all without touching a rail or a step. It wouldn't be that impressive a move if he hadn't given off two bursts of gold dust from both feet, which are now skittering across the boat's floor in twin starbursts. Marcus jumps back from them as if he's afraid they might dissolve his shoes.

"Told you," Ryan says. "Enhanced!"

"Or that drug you gave us hasn't worn off yet," Emily says.

"You mean the sugar water and food coloring?" Ryan says, brushing past her as he starts up the dock. "Yeah, I hear it's all the rage with the kids these days."

Marcus appears next to her and grips her elbow. "And I didn't drink any and I still saw that shit clear as day."

"Just try to think of that one crazy thing you've always believed in that nobody else does," Emily responds. "It'll make all this easier."

"How does believing in the Loch Ness Monster make this

easier?" Dupuy asks.

"The guy looks like he can't be any older than twenty-one, right?" Marcus whispers as the three of them start to follow Ryan. "I'm not imagining that, right?"

"You're not imagining any of this, babe," Emily says.

"Dupuy, you really believe in the Loch Ness Monster, man?" Marcus asks.

"I do *now*," he whispers. "I just hope he's not here, 'cause that would be a lot, you know?"

Up ahead, Ryan walks briskly up a raked gravel path. When he's within a few yards of the house's soaring front door, he flicks both wrists, at nothing, it seems, and two beds of flame erupt inside previously invisible kettle drums flanking the front steps. It's no Magnolia Gate, but it's still a mansion by anyone's standards, even though none of it appears oriented toward the outside world. Aside from the heavily curtained windows, there are no chairs on the front porch, and no garden furniture anywhere on the long expanse of manicured grass leading to the house.

"So the candles," Marcus says. "They only light if one of you guys are around? Is that part of your *enhancement*?"

"Pretty much, yeah."

"He's a radiant," Emily says.

"A what?" Marcus asks.

"She said he's positively radiant," Dupuy answers. "You might want to make sure she's still into you, dude."

"No. I said he's called a *radiant*."

"Oh, that makes perfect sense," Dupuy says. "Thanks for clearing that up. You know, I have a sister who's a radiant? She's great, though. Really lights up a room, and you know her kids just love it when she flies off into the night with a circus tent in one hand."

"Are you serious?" Marcus asks.

"No, I'm not serious, you moron! When do we get to freak out about all of this anyway?"

"When we have Jonathan back," Emily whispers.

"Tent removal is a group effort, if you're curious," Ryan calls back. He mounts the steps to the front porch, then spins on one heel until he's facing them. He sucks in a deep breath through both nostrils, clasps his hands together, and offers them a plastic grin, like an affected tour guide preparing to corral a group of rowdy but intelligent children. Emily finds the guy's sudden bursts of playfulness more unnerving than his outright hostility.

"Okay. Allow me to warn you, Lilliane doesn't receive guests often but when she does, she makes a huge fuss out of it, so you'll have to forgive her. Also, some of the pomp and circumstance is a little old school, with a twist…if you will."

"We will," Emily says, "as long as we get Jonathan back."

Ryan shrugs as if that were a distinct possibility, but not absolutely guaranteed, then he spins on one heel to face the front door. He flicks his wrist and the front door flies open.

Suddenly, all four of them are stepping into what the interior of a plantation house might look like if it were gutted and redesigned by a luxury hotel group based out of Asia. Nothing about the house's layout resembles the temples to the Antebellum South she toured on school trips as a child. Instead of white walls bearing portrait paintings of old, dead white people, the front hallway is big enough to drive a Mack Truck through, and it's covered in dark wood paneling so smooth it almost looks like both walls are covered in two expansive pieces of solid red mahogany that's been stained to look darker. Instead of crown moldings, chrome gutters conceal long runs of recessed lighting, and the high ceiling is covered in tufted purple fabric similar to the kind that made up the flying tent. Both glittering chandeliers overhead resemble clouds of icicles. But the centerpiece of the foyer is a grand staircase Jonathan would probably describe as *epic*; two facing staircases descend from the second floor, before meeting in an expansive landing that gives way to an even bigger staircase oriented toward the front door, each descending step longer than the one before.

As they move deeper into the hallway, Emily notices the plush rug underfoot. It would have been easy to mistake its slashes of gold, yellow, and orange as some sort of abstract contemporary design, but the further they walk across it, the more Emily can see it's an impressionistic rendering of a candle's flame. And it looks vaguely familiar, like something she might have seen on the sign for a French Quarter boutique.

On the walls on either side of them, rows of purple candles sit on small chrome shelves arranged in matching pyramids. As Ryan passes the pyramid to their right, one of the candles flickers silently to life, and that's when she sees the initials *R B* on a small plaque just below the candle's shelf. A quick scan tells her that are about twenty-three candles total, one for each radiant.

Ryan stops walking, holds up one hand indicating they should as well.

Just then, the candles start popping to life on either side of them. Emily hears the approach of footsteps.

There's something unnerving about the sound, and she realizes she's hearing twenty people marching in lockstep across hardwood floors. Two groups of radiants appear on either side of the staircase, their storm of footfalls softening as they assemble into formation next to each other on the carpet at the foot of the stairs. They're all masked, but they're wearing skimpier versions of the outfits they had on earlier. Pants have been replaced by leather shorts that look painted on. The women's breasts are exposed. In the unforgiving light of the chandeliers overhead, every inch of exposed skin is smooth, unblemished perfection, and while the body types vary somewhat, even the more full figured among them have a tense muscularity to their movements. But the fact that the body types on display vary at all suggests to Emily that some criteria other than a rigid magazine-approved standard of physical beauty was used to select the people before her.

If they were selected, she thinks. *Maybe it's some strange fate that brought each of them here. Enhanced could mean a lot of different things.*

She's so busy studying the radiants she's missed the fact that Lilliane has descended to the middle landing. She wears the same jewel-fringed, black leather dress, only now she carries a giant whip in one hand that makes the prop in Alexandra Vance's fantasy look like a Tinkertoy.

Lilliane observes them each in turn, without greeting, then she cracks the whip through the air in front of her with a sound so sharp and loud it makes Emily cry out. On cue, all of the masked radiants at the base of the staircase drop to all fours, the crowns of their heads touching as they form two rows of solid, upturned backs. It seems *old school with a twist* was Ryan's preferred way of describing the image of a proud, whip-toting black woman walking across the upturned backs of prostrate white people inside of an old plantation house in the Louisiana swamp.

"Good evening, Miss Conran. Do you feel like telling me your real name?"

"Emily. Emily Blaine."

So Jonathan didn't tell her my name, which means he's either being loyal, or he's unconscious somewhere in this vast house.

Lilliane clears her throat. "Before we begin, a history lesson. It shouldn't surprise you to hear my ancestors were brought across the Atlantic in chains. But for the length of their abominable journey, they were subjected to a far more effective tool of oppression. Nudity. Constant, *forced* nudity. The history books will try to convince you the sole reasoning for this was so any prospective buyer could thoroughly examine them for wounds and other defects. They were salable goods, after all. But how likely were they to rise up in rebellion when their most tender parts were constantly exposed? Ryan, take the lead."

Ryan says, "Why? None of this is my fault."

"It most certainly *is!*" Lilliane's voice is something between a growl and a hiss. "If you wish to question my thinking, allow me to inform you, *young man,* that my major concern this evening is with the ugly impression your loss of control left on those guests who were not involved in Miss Blaine's act of deception. All of you, disrobe. Now!"

With a sigh, Ryan strips out of his leather-lined jeans, holds them up in one hand like proof of kill and then drops them to the rug. Fully naked, he is an exquisitely put together work of art, and Emily tries not to ogle his perfect buns and the hard swells of his quads.

When she sees that Emily, Marcus, or Dupuy haven't so much as unbuttoned their pants, Lilliane gives each of them a long, appraising stare. Underneath her bare feet, two radiants continue to support her weight without so much as a muscle tremor.

"Rest assured, I don't seek to humiliate or degrade any of you. But deception is how you chose to introduce yourselves to us, and so I'm sure you can have no trouble seeing how only total honesty will normalize relations between us. If that's possible."

"Are you actually going to hurt Jonathan if we don't take our clothes off?" Emily asks.

"Oh, no, sweet girl. I'm not going to hurt Jonathan at all. Rather, if you continue to deceive me, I'll give him so much pleasure he'll never want to leave here again."

"If you really want to see us naked," Marcus says, "tear our clothes off yourself. You've got the power."

"I don't want to see you naked," Lilliane says. "I want to see you humbled."

"And then we can see Jonathan?" Emily asks, but she's already sliding out of her leather jacket and unbuttoning her blouse. Lilliane nods.

Marcus whispers, "Seriously? I was hoping the first time you saw the full package was going to be..."

"Special?" Emily asks. "You mean like my honey test?"

"Still..."

"I promise not to look all the way down. How does that sound?"

"Can I go?" Dupuy asks.

"No," Lilliane says. "At the very moment our guests were at their most vulnerable, the three of you injected lies and violence into our ceremony. You all stay until we're done."

"I see," Emily says, unhooking her bra and letting it fall to the floor. "So this is about the other guests, is it?" She unsnaps her jeans and steps out of them, one leg after the other. "The same guests you left stranded in the middle of the swamp?" She slides her panties down both legs and kicks them off her right foot. "I have a hard time believing that, Lilliane."

"Do you?" Lilliane asks, giving Emily's naked body a clinical once-over.

"Yes, I think you left them out there like that because you're afraid of being exposed for what you are."

"And what am I, Emily Blaine?"

"Lonely," Emily says. "I saw it in your face when that guy asked to leave. I saw it in your eyes when you watched him go. That's when I knew it was real, all of it. That there was nothing in that punch, that you weren't using some crazy projector. If it was just a joke or racquet, you wouldn't have looked so hurt. So rejected."

"Well," Lilliane says gruffly. "My fault for requesting honesty. It doesn't always go hand in hand with insight, I see."

"I want to see Jonathan," Emily says. "Now."

"Talk to your friend," Lilliane answers.

At first, Emily thinks she's referring to Marcus, until she realizes she just pointed in the wrong direction, and it's Dupuy who's standing there shirtless, with his hairy chest exposed and his hands folded protectively over his crotch even though he's still wearing jeans. "Dupuy," Marcus says. "Clothes off, man."

And that's when Emily sees that Marcus has disrobed entirely, his hands gently crossed over his crotch. He's got bulk and long, hard planes of muscle where Ryan Benoit has hard pencil-lines of definition, and she's shocked by how aroused she is by the sight of him even in these forced, degrading circumstances. It feels as if all of the brawn on Marcus's body has been electrified by his embarrassment, or his attempt to squash his embarrassment as something he finds unmanly or weak. This conflict tenses his posture and makes her dizzy with desire. But it's only fair, after all, given what he watched her go through the night before.

He's trying his best to stare straight ahead, but his jaw's working as if he's got a tiny piece of gum stuck to his back teeth, and his lips are pursed. "Hi," he whispers as if they're meeting for the first time.

"Hello back," she whispers. "Big boy."

"Not as big as that dude."

She thinks he's referring to Ryan. The guy's letting it all hang out as he leans against the wall with arms crossed over his chest, looking thoroughly bored with the proceedings. But Marcus has jerked his head in the other direction, where Frank Dupuy is still awkwardly kicking his way out of the jeans he's pulled down to his ankles, having just revealed a member for the record books.

"Everyone just shut up," Dupuy growls. "Now."

"Nothing to be embarrassed about," Ryan says.

"Who said I was embarrassed?" Dupuy asks as he turns the color of a tomato.

Emily says, "I'd like to see Jonathan please."

Lilliane drapes her whip over one shoulder and claps her hands twice. A few seconds later, two masked radiants enter carrying a high-backed chair similar to the throne they used in the tent earlier that night. Jonathan is stark naked, his wrists tied to the chair's solid arms, his ankles bound to the chair's chunky legs. His eyes widen when he sees the group assembled before him.

"What's *up*, other naked people?" he croons, sounding drunk or exhausted or in shock, or a combination of all three. "Holy shit, Dupuy. You and I have a date later!"

"As if, kid," the man growls.

"Is he drunk?" Marcus asks.

Lilliane says, "He's still processing the events of the evening."

As soon as the two radiants put Jonathan's chair down on the floor a few feet from where Lilliane stands atop two of her subjects, Jonathan says, "What my new friend Lilliane really means is that I'm still trying to get over the fact she took me in her arms and flew fifty feet into the air, over and over and over again. And I'd just like to say the fact that I didn't throw up then, and that I'm not throwing up *now* just from talking about it, has gotta qualify me for paratrooper school.

I mean, am I right, or am I right?" He gives them a pathetic, dual thumbs-up with his bound hands.

"Seriously," Marcus says. "You haven't drugged him at all?"

"I've been very tempted," Lilliane answers. "Trust me."

"Jonathan, have you been drugged?" Emily asks.

"Yeah. They drugged us all back at the tent."

"There was nothing in it," Emily says. "It was sugar water and food coloring."

"You've got to be fucking kidding me," Jonathan whispers. "Seriously? This shit is for real?"

"Shall we return to business?" Lilliane asks with a sigh.

"Oh, yeah, sure," Marcus says. "Business. Of course. Now that, you know, we're all naked and everything."

"The arrangement you made with Ryan is as follows. Jonathan will share the contents of his father's letter with him, and in exchange we will let Jonathan go so that he can put in his application for paratrooper school."

"Uhm," Jonathan says, "I, uh, kinda lost the letter somewhere over the swamp. See, it's hard to keep things clamped in between your butt cheeks when you're flying through the air and screaming. I don't expect you to understand, Lilliane."

"I do understand, Jonathan," Lilliane says. "I was there the whole time, listening to your screams, remember? The point is, you have actually read this letter of Arthur Benoit's, or so I'm told, and one of the conditions of your release—"

"I'm sorry? *One?*" Marcus asks.

Lilliane holds up a finger meant to silence. It does the trick. "—is that you share the contents of this letter with Ryan. Now."

"Really?" Jonathan asks, then he looks expectantly at Emily. Emily nods, encouraging him to go ahead, but apparently Emily's permission is not enough.

"Seriously?" he asks, and it takes Emily a second to realize he's staring into Ryan's eyes. "You want me to tell you what it said in front of all these people?"

Ryan straightens. "There are only four *people* in this room. The rest of us are something you will never understand."

"Oh, I beg to differ, sweet thing," Jonathan answers. "I could understand you face-first into a pillow all night long."

Emily prepares for another burst of Ryan's hostility. Instead, the young man tongues his upper lip briefly as he sweeps Jonathan's bound, naked body with a lustful stare. "Maybe later," he whispers.

"Suit yourself." Jonathan gives him a wink.

Marcus says, "I thought we were negotiating Jonathan's release here."

Dupuy says, "Check out his wangdoodle. We kinda are."

"Gentlemen," Emily whispers. "Please."

But Emily can't help but glance down at Marcus's cock, still barely concealed by his cupping hands, and still soft, thank God; he's not turned on in the slightest by the electric current of desire that just passed between the two men on either side of them.

"Despite what you may believe," Lilliane says, "this is not why I made everyone disrobe. Jonathan, the letter. Please. What did it say?"

Pity has replaced lust in Jonathan's eyes as he stares at the preternaturally beautiful, completely nude, eternally youthful man standing across the room from him.

"Jonathan," Emily says quietly.

Ryan stands up straight, his arms falling to his sides as if he's bravely preparing himself for whatever blow his father is about to deliver by way of the naked man sitting bound to a chair across the room from him.

"He wants you to know he's sorry even though he doesn't expect you to accept his apology," Jonathan begins. "He wants you to know that it's taken him this long to figure out why he tried to destroy your life."

"He *did* destroy my life," Ryan whispers, lower lip trembling.

"Yes, well," Jonathan continues, "he thought the only reason he did it was because he caught you in bed with his wife. For years, he says, he went on like that, believing his only motive was revenge. And that's why he threw you out and stopped paying your tuition and took away everything you owned. He said he fully expected you to have to sell yourself on the street to survive and he didn't care. At the time, he thought it would be poetic justice, being forced to live off the parts of yourself you used to seduce to his wife. Those were his exact words."

"She seduced *me*," Ryan whispers. "I was *nineteen*."

"Yeah," Jonathan says. "He knows that now. But back then, he blamed you for all of it because he couldn't face the reality of what he'd done."

"You mean throwing my mother away because she wasn't twenty-five anymore?" Ryan asked. "Because she had the nerve to gain ten pounds in the thirty years they'd been married?"

"Basically," Jonathan answers timidly. Emily can tell he's doing his best to remember Arthur's exact words, and it's drained the sarcasm from him, and made his voice sound breathy and distant. "He accepts that, and he says, maybe if he had actually stopped loving your mother, that would have been one thing. But now he can see what really happened. What other people thought of the woman on his arm became more important to him than what was in his heart."

"Of how she *looked*," Ryan growls. "What other people thought of how the woman on his arm *looked* became more important to him. Not her character. Not who she actually was."

Jonathan nods, continuing. "He says you saw even back then what he'd really done, and so you began to live the lesson he had taught you. You began to live as if the only thing of value you had was your body, your sexuality. And when he found you in bed with his new wife, who was closer to your age than his, you came to embody everything he hated about what he had done to your mother and who he had become. So he became determined to stamp you out, as if you'd never been his son at all."

"Stamp me out," Ryan whispers. "These are *his* words? In his *letter*?"

"Yes," Jonathan answers.

"That's how he described having dirty cops plant drugs on me while I was living on the *street*?"

"Yes. But he also paid off the judge to keep it from going to trial. He says he had a change of heart when he realized what was going to happen to a boy as beautiful as you in prison."

"But for a while, he was looking forward to that part, wasn't he?" Ryan asks. "Fitting revenge, isn't it? Me being raped in prison as punishment for sleeping with his *idiot trophy wife* who only turned to me when she realized she meant about as much to him as one of his cars?"

"Easy, Ryan," Lilliane says quietly. "Your father isn't here."

"What else does the letter say?" Ryan asks, trying to maintain his grip on his anger as he wipes away tears with the back of one hand.

"He says he accepts full responsibility for what he did. To your mother, to you, and to your heart. He says that for you, his only son, he has taken this self-awareness into his soul, rather than spend his final hours in peace or denial."

At the very moment when Ryan Benoit looks like he's about to let loose a sob, he roars instead. He throws both arms into the air above his head, fists clenched, and doors slam throughout the vast house, shaking the entire structure to its bones and causing the giant chandelier overhead to rock and sway, its crystals tinkling together like wine glasses being shaken inside of a crate. Then he bolts from the room, running past the staircase and deeper into the first floor, but not before Emily catches a glimpse of his eyes flaming with such gold radiance, his pupils, irises, and sclera have been lost.

"We need to go," Marcus says, and Emily's not sure who he's speaking to.

"We're not finished here," Lilliane says.

"If we'd had any idea what that kid was capable of, no way we would have agreed to bring him that letter. My boss is in danger. You need to let us go."

"You remain loyal to your employer even after hearing about his stellar parenting skills. That's touching, Marcus."

"We've all got sins, lady. I'm sure *your* story has more than a few."

There's a scraping sound against the hardwood floor close to where Ryan was standing moments before. Emily expects the arrival of more radiants, until she sees the actual source. A high-backed chair just like the one Jonathan is tied to is traveling across the floor by itself, thanks, Emily is sure, to Lilliane's powers.

"Using corrupt police officers to frame his teenage son for a crime he didn't commit? Just to punish him for the fact that he was seduced by an older woman? Whatever became of this lovely young wife anyway?"

"He divorced her a year later," Emily says. "Now we know why," she adds in a whisper.

"A whole year? Really?" Lilliane barks with laughter. "How big of Arthur Benoit! Truly, his heart must know no bounds. A whole year while his son lived on the street, paying the price for his father's sham marriage. That, young man, is not *my* story and it never will be. And besides, my story is not the reason any of us are here tonight."

"Yeah, I beg to differ, ma'am, so how 'bout we—"

Marcus flies across the room and lands ass-first in the giant throne-like chair. He's so stunned by the impact, he doesn't have time to get to his feet before the two radiants who carried Jonathan into the room are on him. Marcus gasps for breath, trying to summon anger out of shock, as the two radiants tie his wrists to the chair's arms and his ankles to its legs. When they're done, Jonathan and Marcus are mirror images of one another on opposite sides of

Lilliane's long walkway made of humans.

Maybe human, Emily corrects herself.

"Ryan Benoit has gone to the same place he always goes to when he suffers from a genuine emotion," Lilliane says. "His room. To cry. *Alone.*"

With that, Lilliane steps down off of her radiants and crosses the carpet. Even though Dupuy has rested a comforting hand on her shoulder, Emily's knees begin to shake as the whip-toting woman closes the distance between them.

"Now, Miss Blaine," Lilliane says. "It's time to discuss the final condition of Jonathan's release.

"What do you want?"

"I want to know what else was a lie besides your name, your paper mills, your beautiful Aston Martin," Lilliane whispers.

When she takes Emily's chin in one powerful hand, her grip is anything but gentle.

"Get off her," Dupuy says.

With a flick of her other wrist, Lilliane sends the man tumbling backward over his own feet before he lands ass-first on the carpet with a loud, bone-shaking thud.

"Did you lie to my book, Emily, or are you really a fan of dirty doctors?"

"Tell me what you are and I'll let you do whatever it is...you do."

"Why delay? Are you afraid of what we'll see? Is your heart in conflict? Possibly between these two men?"

"What would you know of anyone's heart? You deal in lust, not love."

"We deal in *desire*, which is both!"

"*What are you?*"

At the sound of Emily's frightened cry, Lilliane softens her grip on Emily's chin.

"We were offered a gift," Lilliane whispers, as if she doesn't want anyone else in the room to overhear this explanation. "All of us. We were offered a very special gift. But we resisted it, and this resistance made us what we are."

"There's something in all of you. Something gold in your eyes. Some type of force that can use fire. I don't understand... Are you possessed? Is that it? Is it some kind of spirit that's in all of you?"

"Spirits, plural," she whispers.

"And if I don't want them in *me*?"

"That's not how it works. We unleash, we don't invade. And you're not afraid of what I might put into you, Emily Blaine." Suddenly, but gently, Lilliane grips the sides of Emily's face with both hands. Glittering snakes of gold pour from her eyes and between her lips, lacing the air between them. "You're afraid of what's already there."

Emily opens her mouth to scream, but in that same moment, a single, slight inhale from Lilliane pulls all the breath from Emily's lungs...

27

....*Darkness encloses her, presses against every inch of her naked skin.*

There's a pulse and throb nearby. It's the dance floor, she's sure. The dance floor she returns to again and again in her mind, that press of male bodies, all that unbridled, uninhibited male sexuality making a mockery of her inhibitions. It's either that, or she's inside the womb again.

Fingers slip against her skin, the feel of them somehow blending with the soft, enclosing blanket of darkness, and then the fingers move across her face.

She's blinking in bright sunlight. She realizes the nearby throb is not the bass beat of some techno track, but pounding surf. And the fingers slipping across her skin now, clearing the sand away from her buried body, belong to Jonathan, who is smiling down at her as he gently pushes grains from her eyes, from the bridge of her nose. He uses several fingertips to gently clear her upper lip.

His other hand works to uncover the rest of her body. Whenever she gasps or sighs, he grins. The sky overhead is cornflower blue. Cloudless and eternal, a stark backdrop to Jonathan's olive skin and jet-black hair.

Now that he's revealed her face, he goes to work on her body with both hands, uncovering more of her legs, her arms, her waist, her breasts. With just one palm, he gently clears a layer of sand from the top of her sex. And then, she feels his arms sliding through the sand beneath her and he lifts her into the air so that the last remaining bits of sand can slide off her body as he walks.

There are no houses along this beach, no walkways crossing the dunes, just an eternal blanket of white and endless pounding sea. And one familiar-looking lounger, which he lays her down on gently, as if he's afraid every bone in her body could break from a sudden impact.

"Jonathan..."

"Shhhhh."

"Jonathan..."

He's working on her again with maddening gentleness, infuriating tenderness. The palms of his hands graze her nipples as he sweeps sand away, but his fingers don't linger. They don't pinch, prod, or probe. It's torture, plain and simple.

"Jonathan...."

"Hush now, Emily Blaine. Tide's coming soon."

The tide? What does that even mean? Why won't he touch her? Why doesn't he devour her? Why won't he taste her?

"Jonathan..."

She's so distracted by her hunger for him, she hasn't noticed he's tying her hands over her head with slender rope he's looped through the lounger's top slates. She doesn't fight. She doesn't resist, figures it's another step closer to satisfaction and release at his skillful hands. Then he ties a length of rope around her waist and underneath the lounger, and then he's straddling her, but he's staring down at her with an almost wistful expression. He grazes the side of her cheek with his fingers. She's trussed up and exposed to him and this is all he wants? This is all he'll do?

Why would he torture her like this? Why go to the trouble of unearthing her, laying her bare before the sun and the surf?

"Jonathan..."

He bends over and gives her the gentlest kiss on her lips. She opens her mouth for more, and he whispers, "Tide's coming, Emily Blaine."

And then he's walking away. Footsteps squeaking over the pounding of the surf and she's staring at his bare, muscular back as he leaves, and she's calling his name, but he's so far away now, so far away she's convinced he can't hear her anymore. But then he turns, and she can see the broad smile on his face, can see him pointing one powerful arm in the direction of the ocean. Is he warning her? How could that be? Why would he tie her up like this and leave her here, vulnerable, and then warn her about the pounding, approaching surf?

Suddenly, a burst of froth picks up the lounger and drives it several feet up the beach, dragging it back in the other direction as it retreats back out to sea. The waves have reached her somehow, or at least their very edges have, and the lounger is being dragged back and forth across the sand.

Terror. This is terror she's feeling. The terror of being abandoned. The terror of being dragged out to sea, alone, and beyond the reach of anything familiar, dragged out to sea to drown. How could he do this to her? How could he sacrifice her to the waves?

A bigger wave crashes down to the sand all around her, and she's struggling with her restraints as the lounger is dragged out to sea by what feels like several yards, at least. She's no longer sure if the lounger is floating or if it's still scraping across the beach. She can feel the surf retreating, feel the next wave gathering terrible, thundering force. Is sure this is going to be the one that submerges her, drowns her.

And then it breaks, and Marcus Dylan crashes down onto her body. Marcus's mouth opens hungrily against her neck. Marcus's hand slides up against her sex, fingers finding entrance, devouring her with unleashed hunger. Naked, his muscular body streaming foam. The next wave drags him halfway off her body, and then the one after drives him against her again, pressing his hard cock up against her entrance. Marcus, the unstoppable force she would have missed had she been able to free herself from the lounger and run for higher ground. Marcus Dylan, a gift of the tides.

And it is Jonathan who brought her to the place where she could remain open and exposed for as long as it took to collide with a passion she's never known before now, a passion that makes the teasing slips of Jonathan's fingers across her skin feel like child's play. It is Jonathan who carried her to the place where Marcus could taste her for the first time.

And it is Jonathan who set her free.

Marcus gathers her breast in a desperate handful, driving his cock against the inside of her thigh, Marcus unties her restraints, and then, the next powerful wave knocks the lounger out from under her. It's sliding away from her in pieces, riding a tide of froth behind her after releasing her to Marcus's embrace. The head of his cock slipping between her folds for the first time, her right leg hooking around his waist, he stands her upright in the surf. His powerful embrace supports her now as she sees that they're standing in the middle of an eternal tide, an endless, interminable sea of whitecaps and white froth. The surf parts around their entwined bodies, charging past them with unstoppable force on either side, unable to submerge them or pry them apart, as he says her name for the first time while buried deep inside her.

And what at first seemed like a terrifying, isolated landscape now belongs only to them, and even louder than the sound of the surf, is the cry of pleasure she unleashes into Marcus's flesh...

...Emily is on her knees, staring up into Lilliane's eyes as the climax that began in her fantasy continues to sweep through her body.

The radiants stand on the lower stairs now, still masked and expressionless. Marcus and Jonathan, still bound to their respective chairs, are both winded and flushed from having watched the spectacle of her fantasy play out in the center of the room between them.

Are those tears in Marcus's eyes? What must it have been like for him to watch himself ravish her in fantasy while being unable to touch her or even relieve himself? Is this why his cock is fully erect, jerking slightly in his lap, even as the sight of Emily returning to her own flesh brings a relieved smile to his face?

She glimpses the tendrils of gold radiating out from her head in their last second of illumination before they appear to be entirely sucked into her lungs by her first full breath.

"Did you not see what you feared you would see?" Lilliane asks.

"No," Emily whispers.

"Do you still think we only deal in lust?"

"No."

"You possess a fascinating mind, Miss Blaine," Lilliane says, gently bringing her hands away from Emily's face, breathing heavily from the exertion of whatever this radiance demanded of her enhanced body. "Most people can't perceive their own fantasies in terms of metaphors and abstractions. But that was most certainly..."

"Beautiful," Marcus says.

There's a part of her that wants to take him right now, right there, in front of all these people. After all, she's already had her soul laid bare to everyone present. And then she remembers the other man from her fantasy, the one sitting across the room from her. He wears a cockeyed grin and he's shaking his head at her with feigned disapproval.

"Just for the record here, folks," he says. "I have absolutely no desire to drown Emily Blaine."

"Once again, you're missing the point," Lilliane says.

"*Once again?* Lady, we just met."

"Someone please bring this man his clothes," Lilliane says. Two radiants depart the bottom step to follow this order.

"No, really," Jonathan says, his grin fading and his gaze finding Emily again. "It was sweet. I want to have ocean sex. It looks fun."

"Really?" Emily asks. "You thought it was sweet?"

"Yeah, of course," he says, a slight catch in his voice. He knows what she's really asking, and for a few seconds, they don't say anything because Marcus's presence across the room is as undeniable as the floor underfoot. He's mourning something, she can see. The loss of some illusion about himself, or who he thought he could turn into just for her.

Or maybe he's remembering the sight of Ryan Benoit, gloriously naked, every inch of muscle a reminder of what truly causes his heart to race, his breath to come up short, his face to redden, his jokes to turn stuttered and silly. If the radiants used their trick on Jonathan now, there's no doubt someone similar to Ryan would make an appearance. A lot of appearances. Or maybe a lot of Ryans.

Still, he's saying good-bye to something, something confirmed by the glimpse he was just given into her soul, and it's not her right, or anyone else's, to take this moment away from him.

"You want to know the best part about being best friends?" he finally asks her.

"The jokes?"

"No breakups!"

"I see..."

And then, Jonathan turns his attention to the other naked man across the room—Marcus, who has watched this entire exchange with the intensity of a hawk.

"And you, mister," Jonathan says, "if you ever decide to switch teams—"

"Shut the fuck up, dude."

"I was just going to say I could roll out one hell of a porn career for you. I know people."

"*Please* bring this man his clothes!" Lilliane shouts.

28

It's dawn by the time they reach Ochsner Hospital, but there's no telling it once they're inside. Closed doors and harsh fluorescent lighting line the long hallway leading to Arthur's private suite. The few nurses that look up as they pass are mostly preoccupied by the rituals of early morning shift change.

Marcus wouldn't let them stop anywhere where they could shower or just change clothes; that's how convinced he is Ryan is going to try to hurt his father. As a result, Emily and Jonathan are now forced to dodge the eye-watering chemtrail his swamp water bath leaves in his wake.

A few paces from Arthur's room, the sight of Ryan standing over his father's comatose body stops Emily in her tracks. Marcus pushes her out of the way with one hand, the other poised near his gun holster. But Ryan isn't strangling the life out of his dad as Marcus feared. Far from it. He's clasping one of the man's withered hands, and when he turns at the sound of their slow, steady approach, he has to work quickly to chase the evidence of sadness from his expression. Finally, he releases his grip on his father and starts walking toward them, giving Emily a terrible glimpse of Arthur, intubated and on his back, the breathing tube jutting out of his mouth like something from a cheap science-fiction movie.

Ryan's civilian clothes consist of designer jeans, some sort of form-fitting white polo shirt with a designer's logo Emily doesn't recognize, and a heather-gray hooded sweater from a different designer with a different logo Emily also doesn't recognize and an apparent fetish for gold zippers. In this bland institutional hallway, Ryan's agelessness is more unnerving than it was in the rarefied confines of Lilliane's mansion. They all take a minute to survey each other before anyone speaks.

"You thought I was going to hurt him, or did you just come to tell him you'd done your job?" Ryan asks.

"Both," Marcus answers.

Ryan nods. He seems drained of his anger, or maybe he's on his best behavior for the nurses.

"Yeah, well, I thought it was strange he didn't have a guard until I saw the guy sleeping in there. He's still sleeping, by the way. I hope I don't get him fired."

"You will," Marcus answers, "but that's not a bad thing."

"I left him a note," Ryan says. "It's on the nightstand. Just so he knows I was here when he wakes up."

"You're not coming back?" Emily asks.

"I'm thinking about it," he says with the strained patience of someone who doesn't like thinking about things.

"Why the change of heart?" Jonathan asks. "You didn't exactly seem in the mood for a visit when we left."

"Lilliane had many things to say about that."

"Oh, yeah?" Jonathan asks. "Like what?"

"She reminded me that I slept with his wife."

"Interesting," Emily says. "After you ran out on us, she spent a lot of time explaining what a bad father she thought Arthur was."

"He *was* a bad father. Let's not get carried away."

"I'm just pointing out that Lilliane seems capable of seeing both sides of every situation. That's all. It's a good idea to have someone like that in your life."

"Well, she's seen more than you'll ever know."

"I'm sure," Emily offers.

"It's sweet that you're concerned, Miss Blaine. But I'm older than I look." He seems to regret the sharpness of his response instantly. "Lilliane asked me to deliver a message."

"We're listening," Marcus says.

"A lot of secrets were shared tonight. She hopes we'll keep them all to ourselves. For everyone's sake."

"Sounds kinda like a threat," Marcus says.

"I'm starting to get the feeling you're the type of guy who thinks most things are a threat," Ryan says.

"Good," Marcus says. "Because that's my job."

"Fair enough. How about a promise then?"

"We promise," Emily says before anyone else can speak up, ignoring the quick, angry look this earns her from Marcus. Jonathan's giving her a pretty hard look too. She returns it, then passes it on to Marcus. "We promise," she repeats, and this time it's an order to the both of them.

"Fine," Jonathan says. "Then we won't have to be the ones to explain to Arthur why his son hasn't aged a day in ten years."

"Longer than ten, but who's counting at this point?" Ryan says. "And hence my...*mixed feelings* about coming back."

"We promise on one condition," Emily adds, catching them all off guard, which was exactly her intention.

"I'm listening," Ryan says quietly.

"You come back when your father's awake," she says.

The silence that falls is agonizing suddenly, maybe because Ryan refuses to look her in the eye as he considers her words. Then he looks over one shoulder at the half open doorway to Arthur's room, as if he wants the sight of his comatose father, humbled by disease and old age, to guide his next words.

"Fine," Ryan says. "I'll come back when he's awake."

"Then your secrets are safe with us," Emily responds.

"Good, but let's make it our last deal for a while," Ryan says.

"Works for me," Marcus says cheerfully.

"So I hear you all enjoyed some radiance before you left," Ryan says.

"That would be me," Emily says.

"Well...was it revealing?"

"Very," she answers.

"Helpful?" Ryan asks.

"I'll say," Marcus answers.

"Well, good, then," Ryan says, and then his stare lands on Jonathan. "And what about you?"

"What about me?" Jonathan asks.

"You didn't take a turn?"

"It wasn't a condition of my release," Jonathan answers.

"But you didn't even ask? Even after you saw how good it could be?"

"Are you offering, Ryan?"

"Not here," Ryan says, closing the distance between them. "Too many fragile hearts. But you know where to find me if you change your mind."

"You're a sexy little beast, but I don't need anyone looking into my *soul* to tell me what I like to do in the bedroom," Jonathan says. "That's not a room in which I've had a lot of problems, if you get my drift."

"Yes I do," Ryan says, "and people like you are the ones who need it the most."

Before Jonathan can react to this challenge, Ryan makes a point of brushing his shoulder with one of his own as he turns to face Emily again, his hand extended. Startled by the gesture, Emily takes his hand and feels him press a small business card into her palm.

"I'm sorry if we weren't able to answer all of your questions," Ryan says. "But we did just meet, after all."

"That's true," she says, and even though it feels like a small betrayal of the two men who have stuck by her throughout this whole strange affair, she pockets the card before either of them can see it.

"Goodnight everyone," Ryan says, then to Jonathan he adds, "See you soon, Jonathan."

Once Ryan's a good distance down the hallway, Jonathan says, "I'm not doing it. I don't care what he says."

"Why not?" Emily asks.

"Sometimes it's better not to know what your heart really wants. Less disappointment that way."

Marcus rolls his eyes. "Fine," he says. "Just sleep with him then."

"Oh, I will, as long as he's got skills in the bedroom other than, you know...altering the fabric of reality and stuff. In the meantime—" Jonathan spins on one heel away from the sight of Ryan's perfect backside and points an accusing finger at Marcus "—*you* need a shower, dude!"

"Amen to that," Emily says.

29

It's exactly the kind of apartment she expected Marcus to have in exactly the kind of building she expected him to live in; a courtyard apartment complex just a few blocks from the Lake Pontchartrain levy. Inside the place is spare and utilitarian, with framed military-themed posters so compact they look like they're about to be swallowed by walls he's painted dark blue. The stack of magazines on the glass coffee table looks like it's been straightened with a ruler, and while not a single item in the entire apartment seems out of place, be it an envelope, coffee mug, or water glass, that might have more to do with the fact that there isn't very much in the apartment to begin with.

She's confident they would have fallen into each other's arms as soon as they walked through the front door if he hadn't smelled like a kettle of fish. Still, ever the gentleman, and despite his exhaustion, he let her shower first.

Now, while he takes his much needed turn under the spray, she sits at his desk, studying the strange business card Ryan Benoit passed her in secret. One thing's for sure: the design on the card, an impressionistic logo depicting some sort of small candle flame, is almost the exact same design she saw printed on the giant rug in Lilliane's giant foyer. *Feu de Coeur*, it reads. And that's it. No phone number, no address. Just a small handwritten message from Ryan on the bottom, a message that makes even less sense than most of what she witnessed the night before.

It's not always in the same place.

She assumes *it* is *Feu de Coeur*, which according to Google means "fire of the heart," and which, also according to Google, has no website or Yelp reviews or any other Internet footprints you'd expect from a business that operated at some point after the Internet was invented. Ryan passed her the card while apologizing for not answering more questions about who he was, about what type of events could have changed him into a creature that didn't age, so Emily has little doubt this is his idea of a clue. But it was a bad one, that's for sure.

Unless that was the point.

As soon as she hears the water cut off, she stuffs the card in her purse and spins the desk chair to face the bathroom. A few minutes later, Marcus appears, resting one raised arm against the doorway and holding the back of his towel together in his other hand. He looks like he's posing for a magazine shoot, or one of those Tumblr pages Jonathan likes to show her on his smart phone.

"How do you like my place?" he asks. "I mean, it's no endless ocean or seven million dollar beach house, but it'll do, right?"

"Drop that towel and I'll tell yah," she says.

"Uh huh. You first."

"Are you kidding? I've been naked for, like, the past forty-eight hours."

"Yeah, but there were always other people there. This time it's just for me."

She'd love to drag this part out, but after the honey test and her time as a robed customer of The Desire Exchange and the protracted naked negotiation with Lilliane, she just doesn't have the patience for a striptease right now. She stands, drops the towel, and flounces down in the desk chair hard enough to send it rolling back into his desk.

Marcus grips the back of his towel as he crosses the room, as if he's waiting for the perfect second to let it drop.

"Seriously," he says, "you like my apartment?"

"It could use a woman's touch, to be honest."

"And how are we defining a woman's touch?"

"Touch a woman and you'll find out."

He sinks to his knees on the floor in front of her, gazing into her eyes, his half-smile fading, caressing her knees with both hands. He lets the towel fall, but he's bent so she can't see his cock or any of the other parts of him she could only catch glimpses of in Lilliane's house the night before.

"You're really taking this patience thing too far," she says. "Although, now that I think about it, it's only been three days. You haven't been that patient."

"Three days of watching your *every* move," he says, hands sliding further up her legs. "So, really. You gotta round up. You know, like dog years or something."

"Ew. Dog years? Different metaphor when I'm naked please."

"Oooo, the English major rears her...*beautiful* head."

"Marcus, why are you stalling? We've waited three whole days for this moment."

"Longer in dog years. Sorry. Alpaca years. Or maybe giraffe years."

Her laughter has sleepless delirium teasing the edges of it.

"I'm nervous, Emily."

"Seriously?"

"Yeah. I saw your fantasy, remember? And I did a *really* good job in that thing. I mean, there was like ocean waves and...I don't even know how I was standing up during all that. What if I don't measure up in real life?"

"You will," she answers.

"How do you know?"

"Because the best part about it is you're not just a fantasy."

He cocks his head to one side and grins, and she can tell it's exactly what he needed to hear, but for some reason he's keeping up the shy-boy routine, even as his hands travel all the way up her thighs, adding pressure to his grip as he goes.

"But you know, there's another thing, though," he says, cupping her mound with both hands, kneading her inner thighs, ignoring her sudden, sharp gasp. "You could make the case that this"—he bends in and gives her a teasing lick—"is"—*lick*—"very"—"inappropriate"—*lick*—"given"—*lick*—"you might be"—*lick, lick, lick, lick*—"my boss someday."

He gazes up into her eyes while he draws three fingers slowly across her clit.

"You get me, Miss Blaine?"

"Yeah, I get you, Marcus. You're looking for a promotion, aren't you?"

"For some reason, I thought we were going to start off sweeter than this."

"We did sweet back in Florida. We did chivalry too, and it was nice. Don't get me wrong. But it's time for phase two."

"Oh, yeah, and what's phase two?" he asks, parting two of his fingers so he can circle the edge of her clit on his next firm pass down her folds.

"Own it," she whispers.

She hooks her ankles behind his neck and drives his mouth against her sex, which is all the permission he needs to unleash seventy-two hours of frustrated lust onto her pussy. After days of watching his tense stare and catching his cautious, sidelong looks, the sight of him devouring her folds, his chin and jaw slathered in her juices, looks so delightfully, intoxicatingly debased, she can only gaze upon it for several seconds at a time for fear the dam holding up her pleasure will break before she's tasted him as well.

Without warning, he slides an arm around her back and lifts her out of the chair while he rises to his feet. When he drops her onto the bed, she lands on all fours with a small bounce. He's next to her in a flash, scooping one arm under her stomach to support her while his other hand travels the crack of her ass as smoothly as if it were gliding through honey. Once his fingers find her sex again, he works her insistently, his mouth finding her neck.

"Own it, huh?" he asks her again.

But he's taken her earlobe in between his teeth, and he's found her clit again with two fingers he's working like a swimmer's kicking legs, and now he's rising onto his knees next to her body so he can drive his fingers deeper into her folds.

"Was I a good bodyguard?" he growls. "Did I take good care of you, Miss Blaine?"

He slaps his throbbing cock against the small of her back with a loud *thwack*. Her answer is in the stuttering groan that feels like it's pouring out of her chest.

"Am I taking good care of you now?" he growls.

"Fuck, yes…"

"I'm sorry, what?" he whispers in her ear. "What'd you say? What was that word you just used?"

"Bastard," she whispers. "I called you a bastard. I called you a gorgeous fucking bastard, Marcus Dylan."

She lifts her mouth to his, their lips inches apart, his fingers still working her.

"Does that mean you want to get fucked?"

"I don't know," she whispers. "I'm not sure you've been patient enough."

Her lips part and she feels his tongue slip inside of her mouth for the first time, and the kiss, their first kiss, is like a magnetizing force that suddenly centers their dirty talk and rough play. They both seem to forget their poses and their dialogue as they rise up off the bedspread into seated positions before wilting into one another. He encircles her back with one arm and slides the other one up between their bodies so he can alternate between preventing her breasts from being painfully crushed against his chest and tweaking and twisting and pinching her sensitive, aching nipples.

Her hand finds his cock while the other grips the back of his neck. Never in her life has it felt like she's drawing strength from someone just by kissing them, by opening to them. Emily wonders for a fleeting instant if Lilliane's radiance has left her more open to pleasure, to intimacy, to a man's hunger for her. But everything about Marcus Dylan is solid, real, here with her. Flexing with her. Bending with her. Tasting her. Searching her with fingers, teeth, and tongue. Learning her.

She slides down his body, takes him in her mouth for the first time, and when she looks up, the expression on his face is full of vulnerability and desire at once; his gasping mouth, his wide-eyed stare that makes him look not just surprised, but thunderstruck by the feel of her lips around his cock, as if, despite all the women he's been with before, there is a miracle implicit in the fact that she can do this to him, that she can make him laugh, that she can fill him with jealousy, that can she turn him into a giddy, sputtering kid with just the right look, and she can also do *this*: unleash tides of pleasure across his cock with her lips, her stroking hand, and her fluttering tongue.

"*Stop stop stop stop stop stop*," he hisses, and when he pushes her off his throbbing, jerking cock, she realizes he's trying desperately not to come. Laughing, she puts her hands out like an umpire declaring a guy safe on home plate, and this makes them both laugh even harder. But they're riveted by the sight of his jerking cock, both of them saying a silent prayer it's not going to fire prematurely.

"Are we good?" she asks after a few seconds.

Eyes locked on hers, he slides backward across the bedspread, reaches out and opens a nightstand drawer without breaking their intent stare. When his hands find the box of condoms, he says, "Now we are."

He tears the box open with his teeth, tries to sheathe himself without breaking eye contact. But she doesn't want him to break eye contact either, so she takes the condom from his hand, opens the wrapper with her teeth and slides it onto him, using the knowledge she's just gathered from several delirious minutes of having him inside of her mouth.

"Still nervous?" she asks him.

"No," he says. "I'm pretty sure I'll be able to make you forget your name, just like I promised."

Straddling him, pressing against his right shoulder with one hand, she guides his cock in, When he feels her part for him, he reaches up and grips the back of her neck.

"Big guy," she whispers.

"Bigger for you," he growls.

"Yeah?"

"Yeah, you make it big. You make it real, real big."

"Don't make me laugh you fucking bastard," she whispers.

"I won't," he whispers, gripping her hips so tight his knuckles whiten, guiding her swaying, grinding motion on top of him. "Can I make you scream instead?"

"Yes," she says. "Yes, you can."

He takes this as license to rise up onto his elbows, and then, after a while of being gripped by her walls as she rides him like a cowgirl, he pushes her gently onto her back, careful to remain inside of her the whole time, until she's spread out on her back, the full strength of him, the full power of him, bearing down on her for the first time, his mouth meeting hers, one hand finding and stroking her clit as he finds a steady rhythm inside of her.

Despite his promise, he whispers her name over and over again, sometimes in her ear, sometimes against the nape of her neck. Sometimes it has the frequency of a desperate chant, as if he's trying to stave off another orgasm that's building too soon, and sometimes it sounds like he's trying to let her know that she's the only one he's ever felt, tasted, the only whose scent he's ever hungrily inhaled. That in this moment, there is only her, the one worth waiting for, if he did only have to wait for about seventy-two hours.

And she loves that, loves that in his passion and hunger, he's forgotten his own Mr. Big Shot promise to make her forget her own name, loves that her name now seems written on his tongue, frozen in his mind. So when the samba beat of shivers starts to travel from her scalp all the way down to her tailbone, when her feet, which she's wrapped around his lower back, start to tremble, warning her that waves of pleasure are poised to radiate throughout her prone body, she says his name right back to him, setting loose the tides of bliss.

30

"I don't normally do that," Marcus says.

They've been walking hand and hand along the crown of the levy for ten minutes. Every now and then a jogger or a bicyclist whizzes past them, but for the most part, they're alone with a sparkling view of the lake's expanse, which is so vast it's impossible for them to see the north shore even on this clear and beautiful day.

"Have sex?" she asks.

"No, fall asleep right after, the way we did."

"Well, we hadn't slept for about a full day. It's not like I blame you."

"Still, I know how important it is to, you know, talk…after sex."

"Because you read it on some website? *Top 10 Things Women Need After Sex?*"

"Oh, okay. So next time it'll be fine if I just roll off you and pass out. Maybe wake up a few hours later and order a pizza or something. Or hey, maybe I'll just leave you half a pizza in the fridge with a note that says, *Thanks for the good time. I'm at the pool hall with the guys.*"

"We needed sleep, Marcus. It's not a big deal." He purses his lips and stares bashfully at the ground in front of them. "You don't have to sell yourself. Not to me."

"I know, I just want you to know that I try. Especially when a woman is amazing."

"Say that last part again."

"The part about the pizza?"

"I actually kinda like pizza," she says.

"Great. I'll remember that for next time."

"Good," she says.

"There's gonna be a next time, right?"

"There better be."

"Good. I mean, I guess you could always go see Lilliane again if I'm busy and do your little ocean thing."

"That's also *your* little ocean thing, too. And you know what?"

"What?"

"Your apartment was a lot better," she whispers, as if it's a secret.

"'Cause no sharks, right?" he asks.

"You know what I mean."

"You're right. I do. Also…"

"Yeah?" she asks.

"That joke I made, I mean… You knew it was just dirty talk, right? A little role-play kinda thing?"

"Wait. Which one?"

"The one about, you know, how you might be my boss soon and I was just angling for a promotion."

"Oh my God. *No.* I didn't take any of that seriously."

"Phew."

"I mean, I'll totally fire you once I inherit, so it's all good."

"*What?*"

She barks with laughter, stops walking, and pulls on his hand to fix him in place. "I'm kidding. For Christ's sake. Oh my God! I'm totally kidding."

"Well, I couldn't tell for a minute."

"Alright, forget I made the joke. Besides, it was in bad taste anyway. Because me inheriting means…"

"Arthur dying."

"Yeah, and it's hard enough trying not to think about what he did to Ryan either."

"Yeah. That was a tough one. But…it's like Ryan said."

"What?"

"He slept with the man's wife," Marcus responds.

"Yeah…the *dirty cops*, though."

"What about 'em?"

"I don't know. I just…couldn't help but wonder how Arthur goes from having cops on his payroll willing to frame his own son for a crime, to hiring my dad, who lost his career trying to get dirty cops out of the N.O.P.D."

"Maybe the two things aren't as related as you think," he offers.

"Maybe," she said, but she doesn't sound convinced, and for a while they stand face to face, their fingers entwined as he stares off toward the setting sun.

"It's Ryan's story, Emily. Not yours. Don't take too much of it on. You'll have enough on your plate soon enough. God knows."

Her cell phone rings in her pants pocket.

"It's Jonathan," she says once she's checked the caller ID.

He pecks her on the cheek and strolls off, probably making an extra effort to give her space in this instance so he can demonstrate how cool he's going to be with their friendship.

As soon as she answers, Jonathan says, "Okay. So basically it's like this. If you don't hear from me in twelve hours, send the cavalry looking for me."

"Woah. What? You do realize I saved you from a kidnapping last night, right?"

"I know, I know. And I appreciate that. But honestly, given what actually went down last night, maybe we can dial back the language we're using to describe it. Just a little."

"Where are you going that I should be so worried about you?"

"Lilliane's house," he offers meekly.

"Why are we friends?"

"Because I'm awesome!"

"I know. You're awesome. But seriously?"

"I can't stop thinking about what Ryan said this morning at the hospital. About how people like me are usually the ones who can benefit from his gift."

"You can't stop thinking about Ryan's ass in those pants."

"Maybe not. But it's a great ass. And those were great pants."

"Then meet him at a motel and enjoy that. Stay away from the other stuff. It seems…intense."

"Uhm. Hypocrisy much? Are *you* sorry you did it?"

"Did what?"

"Let me rephrase that. Are you sorry you let *Lilliane* do it?"

"Not really."

"'Cause you spent the day in newfound marital bliss with your Navy SEAL."

"Let's not get crazy."

"But you did spend the day in bed with him, didn't you?"

"Yes."

"See? I want *my* Navy SEAL!"

"I really don't think that's what The Desire Exchange offers people. I mean, do you honestly think Alexandra Vance went home to find two hot college guys waiting to get whipped in her garage?"

"If there's a God, she did, yes.."

"Still…"

"I want to know, Emily."

"Want to know what?"

"I want to know why I can never fall in love," he says. "I want to know if it's like you said. If it's because of what happened with Remy…killing himself. Or if it's… I don't know, Em. I just want to know if I'm destined to never feel what you're already feeling for Marcus, but won't, you know, actually *admit* to feeling until about four months from now—"

"Easy there, tiger."

"I also want to know if I'm destined to confuse my love for a friend with, you know…something else, like I did with you for three whole days."

"Sounds like a good question."

"Yeah, but do you think they have the answer? Or do you think they'll do that radiance thing on me and I'll just see a bunch of Olympic gymnasts and some whipped cream and still kinda be at square one."

"I can't answer that, Jonathan."

"So answer my other question."

"Which one?"

"Are you glad you did it?"

Several yards away, Marcus is down on his knees, saying hi to an elderly woman's French Bulldog by shaking its paw.

"Yes, I am," Emily says.

"There you go. I'm doing it."

"Alright. But be careful around Ryan, Jonathan. Please."

"Oh, you mean, like, just have sex with him."

"Okay. Or that."

"Well, good, 'cause I'm totally going to have sex with him if he'll let me."

"Maybe right now you could pick someone a little more…"

"More what?"

"Human!"

"He's human. He's just complicated."

"No, Jonathan, people with obsessive compulsive disorder are complicated. Ryan flies through the air and shoots gold dust out of his feet and hands."

"Yeah. That all really happened, didn't it?"

"Yeah. It did."

"I don't know. I guess I'm not having that hard a time with it. I mean, I've always believed in angels. I just never thought they'd be all that fun to hang out with."

"I don't think they're angels, Jonathan."

"Oh, I don't either. I just meant, I've always believed in something weird that might be just around the corner, so I'm not having a very hard time believing in them."

"That's what I told the guys last night on the boat. Try to think of the one crazy thing you've always believed in and that'll keep you from going nuts when you're confronted with something you've never believed in."

"Exactly."

"Alright. But be careful. And call me when you're home safe."

"I will...and Emily?"

"Yeah."

"I love you. And not in the *let's almost destroy our friendship with sex kind of way*. More in the *I don't know where I'd be without you kind of way*."

"I love you too, Jonathan Claiborne. And nothing, *nothing*, could ever destroy our friendship, and don't you forget that."

"Don't make me cry, girlfriend. I want to look my best for Mr. Benoit."

"I'm hanging up now."

She makes good on her promise, and when he sees her slide her phone back into her pocket, Marcus jogs over to her, still laughing over the adorable dog he's been playing with for several minutes.

"Did you see that guy?" Marcus asks.

"He's pretty cute."

"Do you like dogs?"

"No."

"Really? What about cats?"

"I'm not really an animal person."

"Alright, well, see ya later." He makes a show of jogging off, but he only gets a few paces before he turns on his heel toward her and gives her a big grin. "Just kidding."

"I was kidding too. I'm a dog person."

"So what was Jonathan up to?"

"He's going back, apparently."

"Back?"

"To Lilliane's house. They're going to…I don't know, *radiate* him, or whatever they call it."

"Ryan's going to radiate him, and he's going to do it wearing those pants he had on this morning, I bet. Those pants. I mean, I'm as straight as they come but—"

"That's enough. Thanks."

Marcus shrugs and gives her a sheepish smile. "I'm just saying they were great pants, that's all. I'll wear a pair for you if you want."

"Maybe for Mardi Gras."

"So, uhm, do you need to go with him?"

"Oh, no. Jonathan's on his own for this one."

"Good. So we can…" This time the chime comes from Marcus's pants pocket. "Text message," he says, pulling out his phone. "Doctors saw Arthur this morning after we left. They said the pneumonia's cleared and they're going to try bringing him off the ventilator later this week. So…good news. Not *great* news. But you know, it's good."

"Yeah."

"I mean the cancer's still everywhere…" he says, pocketing his phone.

"Right."

He reaches out and takes one of her hands. "Do you have any idea how much your life is going to change when he…?"

She brings his hand to her chest. "My life has already changed, Marcus Dylan."

With a beaming smile that lights up his eyes, he brings his hand to her lips and gives it a gentle kiss. "So," he says. "You want to keep walking?"

"Yeah."

"How far?"

"I'm thinking…as far as we can go."

Sign up for the 1001 Dark Nights Newsletter
and be entered to win a Tiffany Lock necklace.

There's a new contest every quarter!

Go to www.1001DarkNights.com to subscribe.

As a bonus, all subscribers will receive a free
1001 Dark Nights story
The First Night
by Lexi Blake & M.J. Rose

Turn the page for a full list of the
1001 Dark Nights fabulous novellas...

1001 Dark Nights

Welcome to 1001 Dark Nights… a collection of novellas that are breathtakingly sexy and magically romantic. Some are paranormal, some are erotic. Each and every one is compelling and page turning.

Inspired by the exotic tales of The Arabian Nights, 1001 Dark Nights features *New York Times* and *USA Today* bestselling authors.

In the original, Scheherazade desperately attempts to entertain her husband, the King of Persia, with nightly stories so that he will postpone her execution.

In our versions, month after month, each of our fabulous authors puts a unique spin on the premise and creates a tale that a new Scheherazade tells long into the dark, dark night.

WICKED WOLF by Carrie Ann Ryan
A Redwood Pack Novella

WHEN IRISH EYES ARE HAUNTING by Heather Graham
A Krewe of Hunters Novella

EASY WITH YOU by Kristen Proby
A With Me In Seattle Novella

MASTER OF FREEDOM by Cherise Sinclair
A Mountain Masters Novella

CARESS OF PLEASURE by Julie Kenner
A Dark Pleasures Novella

ADORED by Lexi Blake
A Masters and Mercenaries Novella

HADES by Larissa Ione
A Demonica Novella

RAVAGED by Elisabeth Naughton
An Eternal Guardians Novella

DREAM OF YOU by Jennifer L. Armentrout
A Wait For You Novella

STRIPPED DOWN by Lorelei James
A Blacktop Cowboys ® Novella

RAGE/KILLIAN by Alexandra Ivy/Laura Wright
Bayou Heat Novellas

DRAGON KING by Donna Grant
A Dark Kings Novella

PURE WICKED by Shayla Black
A Wicked Lovers Novella

HARD AS STEEL by Laura Kaye
A Hard Ink/Raven Riders Crossover

STROKE OF MIDNIGHT by Lara Adrian
A Midnight Breed Novella

ALL HALLOWS EVE by Heather Graham
A Krewe of Hunters Novella

KISS THE FLAME by Christopher Rice
A Desire Exchange Novella

DARING HER LOVE by Melissa Foster
A Bradens Novella

TEASED by Rebecca Zanetti
A Dark Protectors Novella

THE PROMISE OF SURRENDER by Liliana Hart
A MacKenzie Family Novella

FOREVER WICKED by Shayla Black
A Wicked Lovers Novella

CRIMSON TWILIGHT by Heather Graham
A Krewe of Hunters Novella

CAPTURED IN SURRENDER by Liliana Hart
A MacKenzie Family Novella

SILENT BITE: A SCANGUARDS WEDDING by Tina Folsom
A Scanguards Vampire Novella

DUNGEON GAMES by Lexi Blake
A Masters and Mercenaries Novella

AZAGOTH by Larissa Ione
A Demonica Novella

NEED YOU NOW by Lisa Renee Jones
A Shattered Promises Series Prelude

SHOW ME, BABY by Cherise Sinclair
A Masters of the Shadowlands Novella

ROPED IN by Lorelei James
A Blacktop Cowboys ® Novella

TEMPTED BY MIDNIGHT by Lara Adrian
A Midnight Breed Novella

THE FLAME by Christopher Rice
A Desire Exchange Novella

CARESS OF DARKNESS by Julie Kenner
A Dark Pleasures Novella

Also from Evil Eye Concepts:

TAME ME by J. Kenner
A Stark International Novella

THE SURRENDER GATE By Christopher Rice
A Desire Exchange Novel

Bundles:

BUNDLE ONE
Includes *Forever Wicked* by Shayla Black
Crimson Twilight by Heather Graham
Captured in Surrender by Liliana Hart
Silent Bite by Tina Folsom

About Christopher Rice

New York Times bestselling author Christopher Rice's first foray into erotic romance, THE FLAME, earned accolades from some of the genre's most beloved authors. "Sensual, passionate and intelligent," wrote Lexi Blake, "it's everything an erotic romance should be." J. Kenner called it "absolutely delicious," Cherise Sinclair hailed it as "beautifully lyrical" and Loreli James announced, "I look forward to reading more!" KISS THE FLAME: A Desire Exchange Novella will be available this November from 1,001 DARK NIGHTS. Before his erotic romance debut, Christopher published four New York Times bestselling thrillers before the age of 30, received a Lambda Literary Award and was declared one of People Magazine's Sexiest Men Alive. His supernatural thriller, THE HEAVENS RISE, was nominated for a Bram Stoker Award. Together with his best friend, New York Times bestselling author Eric Shaw Quinn, Christopher co-hosts and executive produces THE DINNER PARTY SHOW WITH CHRISTOPHER RICE & ERIC SHAW QUINN which debuts a new episode every Sunday evening at 8 PM ET/ 5 PM PT at TheDinnerPartyShow.com.

KISS THE FLAME

A Desire Exchange Novella
By Christopher Rice
Coming November 10, 2015

In a standalone novella that combines the worlds of THE FLAME and his novel, THE SURRENDER GATE, New York Times bestselling author Christopher Rice returns you to a mysterious candle shop in the New Orleans French Quarter where the scents of passion provide the courage to embrace your heart's desire.

Are some risks worth taking?

Laney Foley is the first woman from her hard working family to attend college. That's why she can't act on her powerful attraction to one of the gorgeous teaching assistants in her Introduction to Art History course. Getting involved with a man who has control over her final grade is just too risky. But ever since he first laid eyes on her, Michael Brouchard seems to think about little else but the two of them together. And it's become harder for Laney to ignore his intelligence and his charm.

During a walk through the French Quarter, an intoxicating scent that reminds Laney of her not-so-secret admirer draws her into an elegant scented candle shop. The shop's charming and mysterious owner seems to have stepped out of another time, and he offers Laney a gift that could break down the walls of her fear. But will she accept it?

Light this flame at the scene of your greatest passion and all your desires will be yours.

Lilliane Williams is a radiant, a supernatural being with the power to make your deepest sexual fantasy take shape around you with just a gentle press of her lips to yours. But her gifts came at a price. Decades ago, she set foot inside what she thought was an ordinary scented candle shop in the French Quarter. When she resisted the magical gift offered to her inside, Lilliane was endowed with eternal youth and startling supernatural powers, but the ability to experience and receive romantic love was removed from her forever. When Lilliane meets a young woman who seems poised to make the same mistake she did years before, she becomes determined to stop her, but that will mean revealing her own truth to a stranger. Will Lilliane's story provide Laney with the courage she needs to open her heart to the kind of true love only magic can reveal?

On behalf of 1001 Dark Nights,
Liz Berry and M.J. Rose would like to thank ~

Steve Berry
Doug Scofield
Kim Guidroz
Jillian Stein
Dan Slater
Asha Hossain
Chris Graham
Pamela Jamison
Jessica Johns
Richard Blake
BookTrib After Dark
and Simon Lipskar